Allison said, "So, what about your Chicago life? What are you up to here? Are you with anybody now?"

"I thought you'd never ask."

"Hey, honest, I'm not coming on to you."

"Why not?" Sharla asked, smiling.

"What?" Allison drew back dramatically. "Is this you, Meredith? Earth to Meredith, are you there?"

Sharla laughed.

Allison's face became serious. "Now you wouldn't play with me, would you? You wouldn't raise my hopes, then smash me down again?"

"Would I do that?"

Allison took a deep breath. "Would you like to come to my place after dinner?" she asked.

"Yes," Sharla replied.

Sharla could barely believe she was doing what she was doing and what she was about to do. They were in Allison's apartment on Wellington Avenue, drinking wine, listening to music, talking comfortably.

Sharla took the initiative. She touched the back of Allison's hand, then let her fingers wander up to Allison's shoulder. She caressed her neck softly while looking deeply into Allison's greenish pensive eyes.

She proceeded, kissing Allison softly on her lips. Warm lips. Soft, smooth face. It felt fine, very fine. Woman kiss. Allison responded with the feeling that she had always held for Meredith. The kisses and tender touches went on, building gently and gradually. Sharla continued taking the lead. It was her hand that found Allison's breasts and her mouth that took the nipple in, rolling it tenderly between her lips and around her tongue. It was Sharla who moved them to the queen bed in the alcove surrounded by books and candles, and Sharla who began their mutual unrobing. Allison's soft smooth body felt welcomingly inviting next to her own, and Allison reached back to her, taking Sharla in . . .

"Is it mirroring or some deeper psychic process that causes so many double images in women's art? . . . The fear that women describe of looking into the mirror one day and seeing nothing is an allegory of non-identity, which also reveals fear of desertion, of dependence upon an insufficiently integrated self."

Women Artists, Petersen & Wilson

Thanks and appreciation to Barbara Emrys, Tracy Baim, Irene Zahava, and Dan Eierdam for their editorial help

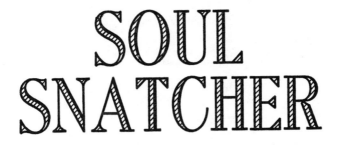

SOUL SNATCHER

SOUL SNATCHER

A NOVEL BY
CAMARIN GRAE

NAIAD PRESS
1988

Printed in the United States of America
First Naiad Press Edition 1988

SOUL SNATCHER was first published in 1985 by Blazon Books

ISBN 0-941483-23-1

WORKS BY CAMARIN GRAE

WINGED DANCER   1983
PAZ   1984
SOUL SNATCHER   1985
THE SECRET IN THE BIRD   1988
EDGEWISE   (FORTHCOMING)

CHAPTER 1

Sharla lit a cigarette, her first in weeks, and looked again at the travel agency receipt. *Return: Flight 346, arriving 7:35 pm, August 2.* The cigarette tasted bitter. Sharla took a deep drag, filling her lungs. Six more days, she thought. Meredith returns. Sharla dies. She stamped the cigarette out. It's as simple as that.

She looked out Meredith's living room window at the green of Lincoln Park, stretching her neck to see the little snatch of Lake Michigan. Last week, she and Allison had taken a romantic evening stroll down there, along the beach, sneaked a kiss behind the boat house; next week, Sharla would be gone, the impossible dream over. Leaning against the windowsill, she closed her eyes and began to recall how much had happened in the three short months since her arrival.

"...making our final descent into Chicago's O'Hare Airport..." The pilot's words jarred Sharla from her thought-free daze, irritating her. She looked down and out from the airplane window, letting her eyes drift without curiosity over the spaghetti streets and rows of tiny houses. Sighing, she leaned back heavily into the seat. There were lines of tension across her attractive, smooth-skinned face and a sad downward turn along the edges of her lips. Sharla didn't feel the way she thought somebody beginning a new life should. There was no sense of anticipation. No excitement.

She made some phone calls at the airport to find a place to stay, then took a cab to the YWCA in Evanston, the first suburb north of Chicago. It was a gloomy, overcast late-April day. Sharla went to her room and slept.

For the first couple of days, though she hardly spoke to anyone, she felt no more alone than usual. She walked along the lake front, lay on her bed, sat in the empty lobby at the Y reading empty words in old magazines and wondered why she was born and if it had been a mistake to run out on Andy.

Until the last minute, Sharla had thought she could go through with the wedding. Andy was a fine, decent man. Everyone said so. They would buy a house, have couples over for dinner, "make love" and have babies and watch TV and she would be settled and secure, maybe even secure enough to write something worthwhile. A fine, stable, reliable man.

But he wears such awful shoes, Sharla thought suddenly. She was in her room, sitting on the saggy bed. She laughed to herself, a tight, self-disparaging laugh. Not liking a man's taste in shoes is hardly a reason to call off a wedding. She lit a cigarette and looked out at the empty alley below, running between the YWCA and the delivery door of Walgreen's. He is a good man. A good person. I do like him. Sharla shook her head. His shoes *are* awful, though, she thought. They're boring, that's what they are. Dull, boring, lifeless, stifling, dead-end shoes.

Sharla felt the tears coming. With angry determination, she blinked them back, and began pacing the length of her tiny room. The light from the 40-watt bulb gave an eerie cast to her high cheek-boned, pale biege face and highlighted the hint of red in her hair. What a cowardly way to end it, she thought, making an about-face at the door. She had written Andy a short apologetic note, packed her bags, dropped the note in a mailbox, and caught a cab to the airport. The first available flight was to Chicago.

Andy probably got the note yesterday, she thought, looking out the window once more. I know he was hurt. And puzzled, I bet. How unfair to him. The tears were threatening again. But I couldn't have stayed in Portland. She shook her head, pulling on the hairs at the back of her neck. I couldn't have told him face to face. She was rocking on the bed. Because if I tried, I would have ended up marrying him.

Sharla shuddered. She added another cigarette butt to the already full tray. I'm sure he's angry. Immediately, her body tightened. Anger frightened Sharla, anyone's anger, but especially her own. Her own too easily became rage. Unconsciously, she pulled more vigorously at the hairs above her neck, her mind flashing to a scene of thrown books and smashed cups and razor thin lines of blood on her wrists.

On the eighth day of her new life, after taking many el rides, wandering vast museums, and walking miles and miles of crowded impersonal streets, Sharla reluctantly bought a Chicago Tribune and began scanning the help-wanted ads. She hated job interviews nearly as much as she hated jobs, but made herself call and set up appointments. After a week of searching, Media One Productions offered her a "position" as a receptionist. She started a few days later. It was a mindless, routine job. Just right for me, she thought, convinced that nothing would ever change. Sharla had no reason to suspect that, soon, everything in her bleak life would change, more radically than even she, who lived so often in fantasy, could have imagined.

The next unpleasant necessity was to find a place to live. Holding the folded newspaper tightly to her body, Sharla made her way up Ashland Avenue in Rogers Park, her shoulders hunched slightly forward in her characteristic way. The proofreader at Media One had told her Rogers Park was a decent area. I suppose I might as well live in a decent area, she thought. At the next intersection, she stopped to check the address in the ad. Someone touched her shoulder.

"Hi, Meredith. What a pleasant surprise!" The woman was beaming.

Sharla jumped, wary, frightened. She hated talking to strangers, any stranger, but especially someone who thought she was someone else; and she hated explaining things. She was about to tell the woman she had made a mistake, but found herself inexplicably captivated by the woman's expression, especially the look in her eyes. Sharla stared, unable to speak. The woman gave her a warm hug.

"I was afraid you might have left town already. I wanted to thank you. I got the job, Meredith!" She grabbed Sharla's hand and shook it vigorously. "It was your talk with Beth that cinched it. She said, 'Pam, Meredith says you're quick and reliable and great with your hands. The job is yours.' Don't you love that 'great with your hands part'?" Pam chuckled.

Sharla kept staring, still feeling the embrace, painfully ill at ease, but also undeniably fascinated.

"Are you OK, Meredith?"

"Oh, yes, I'm... I'm fine," Sharla said softly. "I...but I'm not...I believe you made a..."

"Oh, here comes my bus! I gotta run. I'll talk to you later, OK?" The woman, Pam, was walking as she spoke, backwards, away from Sharla. "When are you leaving anyway?" she yelled. She kept moving toward the bus stop. "I'll call you. Hey, you look different. Send me a postcard. And thanks again." She waved and ran across the street.

Sharla stared after her for a full minute, watching until the bus disappeared. It was a weird feeling to be mistaken for someone else. She adjusted the purse strap on her shoulder and continued walking north on Ashland. But more interesting than that was the way the woman had looked at her. Sharla couldn't get those eyes out of her mind. No one had ever looked at her like that before. The eyes said things, Sharla thought, things she had never seen in eyes looking at her.

The apartment on Albion Street was a three room, $440-a-month dump. Sharla was irritated enough to lodge a meek complaint about the high rent.

The red-nosed manager removed his cigar and shrugged. "This is the 1980's, lady. What can I say?"

She went back to the Y. The scene with the woman on the street, Pam, kept running through her mind. She could see the smile, the big straight teeth with the tiny spark of gold in the back, the make-up-less face, the khaki pants, t-shirt and vest. But it was especially the look in her eyes that Sharla kept seeing. That night she dreamed of her. The two of them were best friends, sitting together at the shore of Lake Michigan, talking warmly together, laughing, enjoying the bright spring day and each other. Sharla felt a wonderful sense of belonging, and of peacefulness.

It continued into the morning. She went to work feeling a little lighter than usual, but it didn't last. Sitting at her desk, the sense of her own insignificance and emptiness took over again. Most of the people at the office ignored her, except the blond, balding copywriter with no eyelashes. He flirted each time he passed her desk and Sharla supposed she should be friendly since she'd have to begin meeting people eventually, but instead she looked away.

She answered the phone and typed and stiffly received the visitors to her four bosses. It was very much like her last job and the one before. During her interview with the woman in Personnel, Sharla had modestly mentioned her degree in English and that she had some writing skills. She was wondering, she said shyly, if there might be any opportunity for her to do some writing at the ad agency. The woman had told her that anything was possible, maybe she could work her way up, but Sharla was sure that would never happen. Good things never happened to her.

CHAPTER 2

On Saturday, Sharla went out searching again, knowing that she had better find a place to live soon. The Y wasn't good for her. Her depression seemed to be deepening. She was on her way to look at a promising one-bedroom on Fremont Street when a motorcycle pulled up beside her. The rider greeted her cheerfully. "Meredith Landor! What's happening, woman?"

Sharla stared self-consciously at the friendly stranger who addressed Sharla as if she were her good friend. Another one. I'm not who you think I am, people. I'm not Meredith. I'm not your friend. We must look very much alike, Sharla thought. "Um, it seems..."

"So, am I going your way? Do you wanna lift?"

Sharla could not make out the features too clearly behind the tinted visor. The woman was medium-tall and muscular and seemed very at ease on the black leather seat of the big bike.

"I thought you were out of town." The woman reached into a pocket of her thin leather jacket, withdrew a manila envelope, and handed it to Sharla. "Tell me what you think."

Sharla numbly took what was offered. She wanted to explain, but instead, she opened the envelope. There were photos inside which Sharla looked at, one by one.

5

The biker pushed back her visor and watched Sharla eagerly. "I tried what you said. Check out that shading. Better, huh?"

Sharla was looking at a shot of a tall statuesque woman leaning against a thick-trunked tree staring into the distance. "Much better," she said hoarsely.

The biker's smile was one of the most joyful, open ones Sharla had ever seen. She was Chicana, her hair shiny black, her eyes thick-lashed and burning.

"I'm gonna blow one up for you. I already picked it out. Guess which?"

I'm not Meredith, Sharla thought again to say, but again did not. She wasn't sure why. Perhaps she didn't want the interaction to end. Perhaps she didn't want to see the disappointment on the woman's face, and the change to distant coolness. She looked through the pile once more. "This or this?" she ventured.

"Right, right. It's this one. This is for you. You'll get it soon. Hey, what's with the clothes, anyway, and the make-up? Oh, I know, you're acting in one of your crazy films again." She laughed heartily.

Sharla felt flustered. I'll tell her now.

"You look like you just escaped from Flossmoor." The woman laughed some more, her eyes burning even brighter. "So, are you on your way home or what?"

Sharla nodded dumbly.

"I'll give you a lift. Hop on."

Ride on a motorcycle behind this wild woman in a leather jacket who thinks I'm someone else? I couldn't. Sharla had always wanted to ride on a motorcycle. Andy thought they were foolhardy and dangerous. Fuck you, Andy. So did her mother. Fuck both of you. Sharla climbed on and held the slim waist. They zipped through the streets, Sharla's primly waved hair flying in the wind. In minutes, they stopped in front of a seven-story, red-brick apartment building on Fullerton Avenue.

Sharla got off. "Well, thank you, I..."

"Don't mention it," the biker said, giving a cocky, warm grin. "Any time," and with a wave and a roar, she was gone. Sharla stood dizzily at the curb. I can't believe that just happened, she thought. It was really fun! Smiling broadly, she shook her head. She moved to the sidewalk. I wonder who this Meredith Landor is.

She looked at the apartment building. Maybe she's there now, she thought. Whoever she is, she sure has some unusual friends. A woman driving a motorcycle! Weird...in a way, but...how free she must feel! Staring dreamily off in space, Sharla slipped into fantasy, no longer aware of where she was, oblivious to the curious glances of passersby.

She pictured herself in the leather jacket and helmet, taking the big bike dexterously around curves, leaning into each turn, then tearing speedily down a straightaway, flying past cars. She kept going until she left the city and rode deep into the countryside, through giant snow-peaked mountains, along wide beautiful rivers. Sharla's smile grew as the fantasy continued, as she saw herself soaring faster and faster, free and wild. Then the joyful expression changed to a puzzled frown.

Now, why should something like that interest me, she asked herself. Riding around on a silly motorcycle. That's definitely not my sort of thing. It's out of character for me, right? I'm the type who likes to knit, am I not? She thought of the sweater she'd made for Andy. I wish I could have another ride, a longer one, maybe cross-country. She did not move from her spot on the sidewalk. Maybe that woman and I could take a trip together. Maybe I could get my own bike. Smaller than that one, though. Sharla straightened up her back. No, a big one. A real big one.

The sounds of traffic brought Sharla back. She blinked and looked again at Meredith Landor's apartment building. I wonder what sort of person she is. Sharla wished she could get a look at her, and considered hanging around the building until Meredith showed up. If we resemble each other so, Sharla thought, maybe she'd even be interested in meeting me. The dreamy look came again. Maybe she'd introduce me to her friend and I could go for another ride. Sharla shook her head. She was leaning against a light post now. No, that wouldn't happen. Her friend would probably be angry at me for not telling her, for letting her think I was Meredith Landor, and she'd want nothing to do with me. I wouldn't blame her.

Sharla began to walk away, west on Fullerton toward Clark Street, but in less than a half block, stopped and looked back toward the apartment building. There'd be no harm in trying, she supposed. What do I have to lose? She started to return, then stopped again. No, I couldn't, I'd be too embarrassed. Again she turned to go, then back again, completing the circle. Her expression grew contemptuous. Here I go again. Afraid, always afraid. Go on, you coward, go ring her doorbell and introduce yourself and see what happens.

She continued toward the building, struggling to defeat her characteristic resistance to anything new, to taking risks, to meeting people. Take a chance, bitch, she angrily cajoled herself. She had reached the entrance door and made herself walk right into the lobby. Her eyes swept the names. Meredith Landor, 303. No husband, apparently, Sharla thought. No roommate. Ring the bell, she told herself. Her finger would not move. Coward! She rang the bell. The familiar anxiety came and Sharla, trying to overcome it, began rehearsing what she'd say. *Sorry to bother you, but I just wanted to meet you. You see, several people mistook me for you and my curiosity got the best of me.*

She rang again and waited, feeling miserably uncomfortable, excruciatingly shy, wanting to leave, to run away, to go hide in her barren room in the Evanston Y. She was about to do so when the inner lobby door opened and an elderly man in a trim tan suit came out. He nodded to Sharla as if he did so frequently, holding the door for her. Sharla felt she had no choice but to go in. "Thank you," she said and walked to the waiting elevator. She was sure the man was watching her.

Inside the elevator, she felt a moment's relief when the doors closed. What now, she wondered. I could wait a few minutes 'til the coast is clear then get out of here. She pressed "3", instead, stirring the elevator into motion. On the third floor, she walked along the quiet, carpeted corridor until she stood before the door with the little "303" above the peephole.

I could knock. No, she'd wonder how I got in the building. No, she'd understand because she'd see how much we resemble each other. No, she isn't even home; she would have answered the bell if she were here. Sharla was turning away, about to leave, when the door to the next apartment opened. She attempted not to look afraid or guilty.

The woman smiled. "Forget your key, Meredith?"

Licking at her lips, Sharla tried to think what to say. The woman's smile was large, with flame pink lips bordering golden-edged teeth, and friendly.

"Yes, but I'm..."

"You're in luck. Mr. Borgman is on his way up to fix my tub again. Damn old drain." The door at the stairwell opened. "Here he comes now. Meredith forgot her key," the woman called out cheerily.

The paunched little man trudged toward them, rested the wrench against the wall and tucked the plunger beneath his armpit. He shuffled among his keys, then opened 303 without a word.

"Thank you," Sharla said softly. *Please go away. I have to get out of here.*

"Oh, I see you have one of those cute little lamps," the pink-lipped woman said, peering into Meredith Landor's living room.

Sharla nodded. She knew she would have to go inside. She stepped across the portal, then, turning, mumbled, "Well, I hope your drain is OK," and closed the door.

CHAPTER 3

Standing stiffly, her back flush to the door, Sharla decided to wait sixty seconds and then leave the apartment. The living room looked warm and inviting. *God, what if she's home?* "Hello," Sharla called out meekly. *One-two-three-four...* She looked around the room, at the soft earth colors, the tasteful decor. "Is anybody home?" *...ten-eleven-twelve...* Two of the living room walls were covered with photos, dozens of them, framed and varied. She took a step forward, stretching her neck, peering intently at one of the photographs. Swiftly she strode across the room for a closer look. She was breathing heavily, staring with disbelief at the haunting face. "It's me!" she said aloud. The woman in the photo was wearing a hat and had her arm over the shoulder of a woman Sharla had never seen, but the features were absolutely identical to her own. Sharla's face was inches from the photo. *That's not just a resemblance.* She blinked her eyes tightly. *Unbelievable. Meredith! Who are you? I have to know. She'll be amazed, too,* Sharla thought. *I'll call her, that's what I'll do. I'll take her phone number and then I'll call her later and...* Sharla scanned the room for a phone. Seeing none, slowly, cautiously, she began to walk to the hallway that surely led to other rooms, past the john to

9

a partially closed door which she pushed open gingerly with her finger tips. It was an office.

Sharla scanned the room, taking in the slightly choatic scene. There were reels of film—in boxes, and on them—and stacks of papers everywhere, and numerous other objects. Who is this woman? Sharla thought, the telephone forgotten. How could we look so alike? Even her next door neighbor couldn't tell us apart. I've never heard of such a thing. Strangers looking that much alike. Who is she?

It's none of your business.

I have to know.

It's none of your business. You must leave! Right now! Walk to the door and leave. You don't belong here.

I have to know. I have a right to know, don't I? She's not just some stranger; she's my double, my *doppleganger*. Sharla said the word out loud, playing with it, letting it roll around her tongue. "My doppleganger." It's OK if I just look around a little. We look alike; that means we're connected. It's all right to look.

Sharla walked slowly, curiously, from room to room around the apartment. *You don't belong here,* she admonished herself with every step. *Housebreaker.* What a homey place. There were plants everywhere. *Intruder, violator, home invader.* The apartment was almost neat, though not quite, certainly not meticulously orderly like her own had been in Portland. The office, in fact, was rather cluttered, but Sharla thought it the most interesting of the rooms. The bedroom was rich and cool-warm; the living room bright, gay; the kitchen, with unfinished wood and copper and ceramic, was almost cute. But the office fascinated her, with its little brass statues and wooden boxes and books, film and photos piled everywhere. While the books tempted her, the pull of the photos was much stronger.

I shouldn't look at them.

Sharla opened a cardboard box on the desk.

You're being bad.

The box contained more photos. She began going through them, one by one, frightened by her behavior, but also somewhat delighting in her audacity.

There were a few shots of buildings and trees, though most were pictures of people, attractive, interesting-looking people, laughing, clowning, standing around or sitting in groups, women mostly. At the tenth print, Sharla stopped. She stared at it, her lower jaw hanging. It was what she was looking for but it shocked her nonetheless — another picture of herself! She brought it closer to her eyes. In the photograph, she was smiling broadly, wearing clothes she had never worn, talking with a woman she had never met.

Sharla stared a long time, her heart beating rapidly. Unbelievable! Hunched over the desk, she held the snapshot with both hands. Amazing! She knew she should stop this, leave, get out of there, but she could not. She needed to see more. Hard as it was to remove her eyes from the lookalike image, she made herself go on to other pictures. There were scores of people she did not know, and, periodically, startling her anew each time, another one of herself, of Meredith, that is, interacting with the other people, at ease, clearly a part of them.

Sharla felt fascinated, but also a little sick to her stomach. I don't know if I like it, she thought. *Uncanny resemblance.* The phrase kept recurring. *Doppleganger.* She couldn't look anymore, was feeling funny, a little dizzy. A glass of water, she thought, that's what I need. She made her way to the kitchen. The water didn't help at all. She felt feverishly hot. Leaning against the sink, she visualized the images in the photos. *Her* image. She rinsed her face with cold water. The images were still there. Her double. Laughing with people, somber in a huge chair, on a bike, in the center of a group. Always looking happy, self-assured, free.

Almost against her will, Sharla found herself back in the office, looking for more. She went through stacks of things, papers, lots of greeting cards, most of them humorous, receipts, lists. And then, at the bottom of the pile, she came upon an album. She leafed through it. It was full of photos from Meredith's childhood. There was one of Meredith on a swing. That's just how I looked, Sharla thought. Almost. There is a difference, though. She looks more... Sharla squinted her eyes. She looks happier.

Sharla turned the pages of the album, watching Meredith grow, reading the captions written beneath each scene. She stopped at one that said: "Tenth birthday party, Eureka Beach". Hm-m, what a neat thing to do on your birthday. Sharla recalled her own tenth birthday party. The memories were clear; of the party itself and of the day before, going to Kresge's with mother to buy the decorations. She remembered that day very well.

Sharla always tried to avoid the sidewalk cracks on the way home from school. She was not looking forward to her birthday, though

11

she couldn't help thinking about it. Tomorrow would be May 28, 1965; tomorrow she'd be ten years old. Judy and Marilyn had stayed in the playground again and were swinging on the swings and sliding and then they'd go to the school store and get gumballs and Snaps and pumpkin seeds and wax bottles full of sweet sticky juice. Sharla tried to miss the cracks by the slimmist margin possible. Step on a crack, break your mother's back. *She shouldn't go on the slide anyway. She'd get her dress dirty. And mom said it was important to come right home after school. Sharla supposed it was.*

"Hi, mom. I'm home."

"Did you wipe your feet?"

"Yes." She felt a little twinge of guilt from the lie.

Gloria Jergens followed her daughter to her bedroom. "Why do you always run right to your room, Sharla Ann?" Sharla sat on her bed, her back to her mother.

"What's in your bag today?"

"Stuff," Sharla mumbled. "My spelling book."

"What else?"

"Nuthin'."

Gloria Jergens rummaged through the schoolbag. "Hey, what's this I see? A ninety on your test. Why just a ninety, Sharla? Didn't you do your homework?"

Sharla loved the feel of the wind flying through her hair, taking her skirt and flapping it all around her legs. She could go almost as high as Judy on the swings. Her mother didn't like her to go high.

"Answer me."

"What?"

"Didn't you do your homework yesterday?"

"I did it," Sharla hissed.

Gloria Jergens towered over her daughter, hands on hips. "That attitude again. I hate that attitude, Sharla Ann. Do you know what happens to people who don't do their homework? Do you? I'll tell you. They become losers, that's what. Is that what you want to be? A loser? Do you want to end up like your Aunt Betty? On welfare. Damn you, listen to me, Sharla!"

"I'm listening."

"Humpf, I don't think you know how *to listen. Straighten up your room, now. Hurry up. We're going shopping."*

"Aw, mom, I don't want to go shopping."

"Yes you do."

"I was gonna write a letter to Ellen."

"Ellen again." Gloria Jergen's hands returned to her hips. "Sharla, it's time you forgot about Ellen. She moved away, left Portland. It's time you accepted that she's gone. I don't want you writing her any more."

"But I miss her."

"That's foolish. You have lots of other friends."

Sharla thought about that. "No, I don't," she said. "Not really."

"Sharla, don't contradict me." Gloria Jergens pushed a strand of hair from Sharla's forehead. "Now, get your room picked up," she said. "Do you remember what we're going shopping for?" She gave a tiny smile. "We're going to buy the favors for your party, dear." She paused, looking down at her pouty child, waiting hopefully for Sharla's happy response.

"I wish I didn't have to have a party."

Gloria Jergen's gray, mascara-bordered eyes widened. "You what?" Her hands clasped each other over her thin waist. "Sharla, I don't understand you." The edges of her drawn lips quivered. "You're the most ungrateful child I've ever known."

"I hate birthday parties."

Gloria Jergens lowered herself to the bed and sat next to her daughter, her face tight beneath the forced smile. "Sharla, dear, it's just that shyness, isn't it?" She started out softly. "You'll get over that. There's no reason to be afraid of people." Her voice grew louder. "They won't bite you, you know. No reason at all. All your friends are coming tomorrow and Sandra's mother will be here and the Guerny kids."

Sharla scooted back across the pale yellow chenille bedspread. "Can't we skip the party this year?"

Gloria Jergen's face clouded, outrage covering pain. "Do you know, young lady, that I never had a birthday party in my whole life when I was a child. Not once. Never. Get up off that bed and clear up that counter and put your school bag on the shelf and change your clothes."

Sharla felt it again, that funny feeling in her stomach. Hate-love-guilt-fear-need. "I'm sorry, mom."

Gloria Jergens smiled. "All right, sweetheart." She reached over to the dresser. "Here, let me brush your hair."

Her mother pulled the bristles swiftly over the fine, tousled reddish-brown strands. It hurt, but Sharla would not let on.

"You'll have a wonderful time at your party, honey."

"I know, mom."

13

You did have a wonderful time, Sharla thought, her eyes wet. She rubbed the tears away, smearing her mascara, then looked back at the photo of Meredith on the beach. Looks like *she* enjoyed *her* birthday party, Sharla thought bitterly. That must be her mother. Sharla scrutinized the photo closely. She looks so relaxed. The next one was Meredith and her mother grilling hamburgers. Actually, Meredith was doing the cooking and her mother was looking on, seeming comfortable and pleased.

I wonder what it would have been like to have an outdoor birthday party, Sharla thought enviously. A party at the beach. Wear a swimsuit at a birthday party! Sharla loved the idea. Of course, she wore a dress to her parties.

"I hate this dress."

"You look very pretty in it, dear. Hold still, let me pull down your slip."

"Can't I wear slacks?"

"To a party! Don't be silly."

Sharla tried not to pout. Her mother said she was always pouting. She tried to stand still and not squirm while her mother adjusted her.

"Am I really pretty, mom?"

"When you remember to stand straight and when you're not chewing that awful gum. Where did you get that, Sharla? Spit it out. Go on, throw it in the wastebasket. You're a young lady now, ten years old, too old to be chewing gum."

The first guests arrived, Sandra Raymond and her mother. "Hi, Sharla. I brought you a present."

Sharla took the package.

"Say 'thank you'."

"Thank you."

The two mothers' high heels clicked to the kitchen. Sharla went to the sofa, took a book off the coffee table, and opened it. She did not look up. After watching her a few minutes, Sandra left the room.

Immediately, Sharla was absorbed in the story, fantasy being, by far, her most comfortable realm. No longer was she in the furniture-crowded living room waiting unhappily for unwanted guests to come and pin the tails all over the donkey and the wall and to drop clothespins in the milk bottle whose opening was too small for her nervous fingers ever to hit. She was in Africa. She was the little girl in the story who wandered away from the safari and got lost, then found, by an elephant. "I wish I had a trunk to reach so high with and spray water with," the little girl said. Suddenly, her nose began to itch. And then it began to grow. And grow. And grow. Until she did have a trunk. And later she got a tail like the monkey and wings like the parrot. Sharla was totally lost in the story, spraying, swimming, flying.

"I said put that book away." Mother-grip on her arm.

Sharla did miss the bottle. She missed the donkey's ass as well, and she blushed when they sang to her, and wished she were in Africa.

Sharla continued going through the album, fascinated, her cheeks shiny from her tears, watching Meredith emerge from childhood to — this one: "May '75 — filming *Radiant Rageout* at Berkeley." In the photo, Meredith was balancing a large camera on her knee while the others, her crew, Sharla surmised, stood behind her.

Sharla thought of her own college days. She had loved her room at Oregon State. She could picture it clearly. It was hard to get a single and when she did she made it a fortress. There were few objects around and few decorations, but each item in view dripped with personal meaning: the latest issue of Oregon State Scribe, containing, on pages 6-8, Sharla's first and only published work — a short story, full of tragic humor; the box with the slim stack of letters, from Ralph, who had broken her heart and taught her to expect less; the brass statue of a seal, a gift from Greta. When Greta dropped out during Freshman year, Sharla missed her more than she would admit.

On the wall was the photograph of the Grand Tetons. Sharla had taken it herself and had it blown up. It was slightly out of focus, but she loved it. And there were the two Renoirs — her favorite impressionist. On the corner of the desk was her pile of literature books.

Sharla rested her head on the books on her desk, a tear in the corner of each eye. She was trying to figure out why she cried so much. The phone rang, then, startling her.

"Hello...Oh, hi, mother." Sharla's voice was flat. "No, I'm fine...This weekend? Well, I have a ton of studying to do. I thought maybe I'd just stay on campus...I know it's my birthday, but...yes...yes...yes...I know...all right...yeah...all right, I'll be there. See you at the train station."

After she hung up, there were more tears. She felt angry, but powerless. Sounds of laughter in the hall interrupted her solitary misery.

*Sharla wiped at her eyes. Go join them, she told herself. Get involved.
No, the voice answered, they don't want you. You're not like them.
Just yesterday, Sharla recalled angrily, that snippy creep, Paula,
had asked her why she's always so quiet. I hate that, Sharla thought.
I hate it! Don't they have any sensitivity? What a thing to say. Of
course, I'm quiet. I'm scared. Don't you understand, you imbeciles!
I'm not like you.*

*A knock sounded at the door. People rarely knocked at Sharla's
door and she opened it hesitantly.*

"Hey, can I borrow your typewriter, huh?" *Paula walked past Sharla
into the center of the room.* "I got this bitch of a history paper due
in the morning."

"Well...I..." *It had to be* Paula. *"I'd really rather not...I..."*

"Oh, come on, I won't hurt your damn typewriter. Don't be so selfish, huh? Where are you hiding it?" *Paula looked around the room.*
"God, it's neat in here," *she said scornfully.* "It's like a nun's cell. You
aren't a nun, are you, Jergens?"

"Hardly," *Sharla hissed. She was still at the door, holding onto it.*

"Oh, oh, you got a confession to make? You haven't been* doing
it, have you?" She laughed crassly. "What about the typewriter?"

"I'll get it," *Sharla said.*

*Later, when she told Larry about Paula's rudeness, he tried to com-
fort her, but Sharla couldn't let it in.* "I'm sick of this place," *she said.*

"You let them get to you too much," *Larry said. He put a record
on the phonograph.* "Relax. Hey, what do you want to do Saturday
night? You want to go see* Doctor Zhivago?"

"I won't be able to see you this weekend, Larry," *Sharla said.*

"No?"

"Uh-uhn. Mom insisted I come home because of my birthday."

"Your birthday? Oh shit!"

"You forgot."

"Shit."

"It's OK."

"No, it's not. Damn. I have a terrible memory. I wrote it down,
too, somewhere." *He grabbed a notebook and leafed through it.* "It's
the same with my history course. I can't remember any of the goddam dates. I know what I'm going to get you."

"It's OK."

"It's uh...it's the 28th, right?"

"Right."

"You won't be a teenager anymore. Twenty years old. So how does it feel?"

"No big deal."

"Yeah, I know. Wait 'til 21, though. You'll feel something then."

"You don't have to get me anything."

"Of course, I'm going to get you something."

"Don't bother." Sharla was pouting.

"Don't be like that, Sharla."

"I am what I am," she said coldly. Larry stood up angrily. "You're a real pain sometimes."

"Thanks."

"You're so fucking negative."

"I know. I'm a real bitch. That's what you think. You might as well admit it."

Larry was silent.

"You think I'm awful," Sharla said.

He still did not respond. "You hate me, Larry."

"Shit."

"You do."

"Sharla, what is it with you, anyway. What's wrong with you?"

"I'm sorry."

"You can be real hard to be with."

"I know. I'm sorry. Everything just keeps going wrong. Sometimes I just feel so..."

"Maybe it's us."

"Oh, no, Larry, it has nothing..."

"I've been thinking," he said slowly. He took the chair across from her. "You know..." He was looking at the floor. "I really think maybe you and I...maybe...I think we ought to start seeing other people, Sharla."

Sharla's eyes, already red-rimmed, looked at him tearfully. "What do you mean?"

"You know. I don't think this is working out that well. Maybe we need to separate for a while, you know, date other people."

Don't cry, Sharla told herself. Be strong. Don't plead. "Oh, no, Larry, please...I...." She was crying.

"Please don't cry. I hate it when you cry."

Sharla continued crying.

"Don't cry, dammit. Come on, Shar, stop. It makes me nervous."

"I'm sorry." The crying continued. She pulled at the hairs behind

17

her neck.

Larry turned from her. Several minutes passed.

"I'm thinking of quitting school," Sharla said at last, wiping under her eyes with the palms of her hands.

"Oh, come on, that's a little..."

"It would probably be best. Nothing's working out right for me here." She was crying.

"Stop crying!"

Crying.

"Stop crying!"

"You hate me!"

"Oh, God, Sharla. You're such a baby."

Sharla stood. "I'm leaving," she said angrily.

He did not try to stop her. Sharla closed the door of his apartment and ten minutes later the door of her room. I hate people, she thought. Stop crying! But she didn't.

Now, almost a decade later, in Meredith Landor's apartment, Sharla Jergens was crying. It will never change, she thought. I hate life.

CHAPTER 4

Sharla's eyes were dry. She had pushed her life aside and was again absorbed by the photos and letters spread over Meredith's desktop. They were streaked by slivers of sunlight, one patch falling across a profile close-up of Meredith's face. It continued to amaze her. They say everyone has a double somewhere in the world, she thought. I never believed it. Striking resemblance, maybe, but not like this. She picked the photo up. The arch in the eyebrow, the way the lips turn, the eye color, everything, every detail, identical.

Sharla took her mirror from her purse, trying to see herself in profile. We couldn't possibly be twins, she thought. She held the photo of Meredith up trying to see both their faces at once. Why would mom have twins and only keep one of us? It doesn't make sense. She put the mirror away. Mother would have loved having two of us to nag at and overprotect, she thought. Sharla wanted to laugh at that, but a laugh would not come. She would have loved it. She'd have dressed us in identical clothes and paraded us around for the world to admire what she'd produced. Sharla leaned back in the chair. Maybe we are twins, and I'm adopted, she thought, smiling sardonically. Maybe I was right all along.

As a child, Sharla went through periods when she was convinced she was adopted, that she did not belong in the Jergens family, but was from some other, better stock, somewhere far away; good people whose baby girl was kidnapped. As it had in the past, the thought now brought guilt and fear. I love mom. I do. Sharla's eyes teared again. That nagging bitch, that nasty pinched-face hag.

Painfully uncomfortable now, guilt-pain, Sharla shifted her thoughts back to Meredith Landor. She began reviewing what she had learned about Meredith so far. Born June 1, 1955, four days after me. Raised in Eureka, California. Mother, father, older brother, younger sister...The phone rang then, startling Sharla. She jumped, guiltily uttering a stifled squeak. In the middle of the second ring, there was a click. Sharla looked at the phone and the machine next to it, then an electric voice came. *Hi, Meredith, it's Nikki. I just found out you already left. I wanted to say good-bye and tell you how much I envy you. Three months in San Francisco! Far out. And getting paid for it. Anyway, call me when you get back in town. August, right? In fact, by the time you hear this message it will be August. Happy August. Hope you had a great time. Bye.* Beep. Buzz.

Sharla let her breath out noisily. She was smiling. So, she's gone; she's out of town. Sharla began to laugh. She felt gleeful. She's out of town! San Francisco. Far out. Far out of town. The laugh had turned to giggling. "She's far away so I can stay," Sharla sang.

She leaned back in the chair revelling in her good luck, humming to herself. Now, let's see, where was I, she thought. She has a brother and sister. Went on vacation in Hawaii in 1961. Birthdays on the beach. Lotsa friends. Swimming champ. Rugby player. Filmmaker. Berkeley University, 1973-78. God, I've learned a lot. Columbia College in Chicago after that. Lots of women friends. Unmarried. Presently residing in San Francisco, to return in August. Reader of many books, taker of many pictures. Filmmaker.

Maybe she makes films for a living, Sharla thought. Her fingers ran among the letters on the desk, selecting one which she began to read. It was a warm newsy letter from a friend of Meredith in San Francisco. My God, Sharla thought in the middle of a sentence, as if just struck by the realization—I'm reading a stranger's mail. This is terrible! It's immoral. She turned her eyes away from the letter. I don't do things like this. Never. No. I should get out of here. But she did not move to leave. Instead, she picked up a reel of film and held up a section to the light. I'd love to look at some of these. It wouldn't hurt anyone, would it? She shook her head, answering herself. And she *is* my doppleganger, maybe even my long lost twin or something. That gives me the right, doesn't it? No one will ever know, Sharla added, searching for a projector.

The first reel contained unedited shots of outdoor murals, bold, colorful paintings on building walls and under viaducts; shots of the murals and of their creators talking ponderously of their work. It interested Sharla only mildly. This was not what she was looking for. She craved more information about Meredith Landor, feeling the excitement of the quest livening her. In fact, she realized she was feeling very alive and energized, rare feelings, indeed, for her, almost foreign ones.

The next reel was more of the same. Sharla watched only a few minutes of it, then rewound and returned it to its tin. In the office closet where she'd found the projector, she discovered a box of reels that seemed much more promising. Each of the round tins was labeled in Meredith's quick sprawling handwriting. Similar to my own writing, Sharla observed, but not quite as neat. The first reel was labeled "Broadway Prostitutes—Interviews". Sitting on the floor, Sharla looked through the rest of the reels in the box: "Lavender Loonies", "Scenic Clips", "Androgyny Panel Discussion", "Travel and Play Footage", "Michigan Festivals". Thinking that "Travel and Play Footage" would be a good start, she was removing the 16mm film from its case when she heard a noise. Her muscles contracted involuntarily. Her widened eyes darted around the room, surveying the mess she'd made. What if she's coming back home for some reason? Sharla flushed with guilt and skin-crawling embarrassment. She shoved the film back into the tin and quickly stacked all the reels back in the box and back in the closet. Gathering the photos and letters, she replaced them, hopefully, in their original locations. Her heart was pounding. When she finished, she stood still, listening. She could hear nothing. It had probably just been someone passing in the hall, she thought, relaxing some. I should leave, though. I have no right to be here. I'd die if I got caught. Yes, I should leave.

She started toward the front door, but stopped midstep, remembering something she had seen in the desk drawer—keys, five or six of them. Dashing back to the study, she grabbed the three that looked like they might be house keys and went to the front door. Slowly, she pulled it open and peered both ways down the hall. No one was around. She tried each key, but none turned the lock. What am I doing? Leave, she told herself harshly. You don't belong here.

Go back where you belong. The YWCA. Ugly little room. She tried the keys in the back door. The second one fit.

No one was on the porch when Sharla made her way down the three flights of back stairs and into the alley.

CHAPTER 5

Sharla did not sleep well that night, but it was not her usual insomnia of depression or anxiety. In fact, she felt energized and alive and excited. Her wish to explore the life of Meredith Landor was growing from a curiosity-inspired desire to an impelling need. I think it's destiny, she thought. I think I was meant to go there, to learn about her. Yes, even to come to Chicago in the first place. It was meant to be. Sharla ached for tomorrow to come so she could go back and probe some more. Tossing restlessly on her bed, pictures of Meredith Landor paraded themselves before her eyes, vividly, while the facts she had learned about Meredith Landor's life lined themselves up for her review.

We *must* be twins, she concluded. Two people could not look so completely alike just by chance. She's my twin sister and I was drawn to her by the power of our connection. I'm *supposed* to pursue it. Sharla turned over on the squeaky bed, smiling. She felt as she had years ago in her journalism class when she was working on that article about runaway children—revved, bouncy, happy. My God, happy! I haven't felt happy in... The gloom threatened a return, but she skirted it with memories of the photos, and of how the woman in the vest, Pam, had looked at her, thanking her, and of the fas-

22

cinating motorcycle woman.

That must be how people treat you when they really like you, Sharla thought, when they *respect* you. A car horn sounded outside reminding her of Andy. He used to announce his arrival by honking the horn, a behavior which always annoyed Sharla but which she never mentioned. Had Andy respected her? Had Ralph or Bill or Larry or any of the men she'd known? Some of her women friends had, Sharla thought; Greta especially, the one person Sharla had allowed in. Greta knew her well and continued to like and respect her, but Greta... Sharla shuddered, feeling that same unpleasant sensation along her back and neck that came every time she thought of Greta's death. Her suicide. It had happened four years ago, but still she could not bring herself to scratch Greta's name from the ragged old address book she kept in her purse.

It was during Freshman orientation at Oregon State that they had found each other, each sensing immediately that she had a needed friend. It was painful for Sharla when Greta dropped out during their second semester. Greta felt alienated, she said, among all the coeds and frat boys, and couldn't stay. She went back to Portland. Sharla understood. They maintained their friendship with phone calls and visits until Sharla, too, dropped out of the university and returned to Portland. Her friendship with Greta deepened then. She felt closer to her than she ever had to anyone, so close, in fact, that it began to seem wrong. They were both scared of it. Sharla's mother nagged incessantly about her spending so much time with Greta.

"You should be dating," she'd say in the way she said such things. It almost sounded dirty. "Meet your future."

Sometimes Sharla would have bad thoughts about Greta, obscene thoughts that made her feel sick and unclean. Her psychiatrist seemed to agree that the fantasies were not healthy. He, too, pushed her to date more and so Sharla did. Although she always felt awkwardly shy around men, they seemed to be attracted to her, initially, at least, and asked her out. She often got hives on her inner arms when she was with them. She never really relaxed. Of course, she rarely relaxed with anyone, women either. People made her nervous. Nonetheless, she dated then and saw less and less of Greta.

Sharla shuddered again thinking of her dear friend coldly alone in the gunmetal-gray box in Greenview Cemetery; still there since the day Sharla cried painfully to the syrupy words of the hired eulogist, and said goodbye.

When Sharla finally slept that night in her third floor room at the Evanston Y, she dreamed not of Greta and sadness and death, but of flying through mountain roads on a huge Harley, arms wrapped around the leather-covered waist of a strong vibrant woman, a woman totally different from her, a woman named Meredith.

Sharla hated Sundays because the next day was always Monday which for the past eight years had meant going back to work, going to some demeaning lackey job where she felt shy and out of place and interchangeable. The job with the publishing company three years ago had seemed the most promising. At last she was in the middle of where it happened, but, not unpredictably for her, nothing happened. She typed and Xeroxed and filed and, occasionally, on the sly, helped out a proofreader, Julie, whom Sharla knew was using her. Nothing more than that happened.

This Sunday, Sharla felt none of the usual dread and heaviness. She felt light, alert, itching with anticipation and curiosity, the way she thought a detective might feel when hot on a case. She put on jeans and a green print polyester blouse, a birthday present from mom. Although she hated the blouse, she felt it suited her. She added a green scarf, adjusting it in the wavy mirror over the plastic-coated chest of drawers.

"You look like Meredith," she said to her face.

For breakfast, Sharla stopped at a corner greasy spoon. Instead of her usual coffee and toast, she got two eggs, basted, with bacon and home fries and rye toast and two cups of cream-loaded coffee. She knew she wouldn't look for an apartment today, and she wouldn't walk along the lakefront and envy the people in pairs or groups who had someone and seemed happy. She knew she would go straight to apartment 303 at 286 West Fullerton Avenue even though she knew she shouldn't.

Again the back porch was empty. Sharla let herself in. Everything was just as it was when she'd left the evening before. She put the pop she'd bought and the sandwich meat in the refrigerator and went to the phone answering machine, rewinding it to the beginning of the tape.

Hi, Meredith. Paula. I heard you were leaving town for a while. If you haven't already left, give me a call before you do. It's about the Wasteland film. If I've missed you, call me when you get back and welcome home. 975-0774, in case you lost it. Ciao.

Beep. Buzz.

24

You pile of shit, why aren't you ever home? Miss you, need you, want you, fuck you, darling.

Beep. Buzz. *This is the Perrault Camera Shop returning your call. 274-3684 before six.*

Beep. Buzz.

I hate your machine. No, I will not leave a message. I refuse. Suffer. Heh! Heh!

Beep. Buzz.

Hi, Meredith, it's Nikki. I just found out you already left. I wanted to say goodbye and tell you how much I envy you. Three months in San Francisco! Far out. And getting paid for it. Anyway, call me when you get back in town. August, right? In fact, by the time you hear this message it will be August. Happy August. Hope you had a great time. Bye.

Beep. Buzz.

This is the big bopper speaking. I just tried to call you in Frisco. How dare you be out. Don't you know I need to tell you I miss you. You've been gone exactly three days and ten hours. Hurry back. I'm lonely for you.

Beep. Buzz.

There were no more. Sharla flipped the switch back to "incoming messages", feeling an odd satisfaction from this bit of aural voyeurism.

Next she went to the bedroom. She chose a black t-shirt that said "I know you know" in light purple letters. Know what, Sharla wondered, taking off her blouse and scarf and pulling the t-shirt on. She looked at herself in the full-length mirror on Meredith's closet door. This plastic belt is wrong. She found a leather one among Meredith's things. Much better. She continued her investigation of the closet. Not a single dress but there were about six or eight vests hanging in a row. Sharla took the denim one, then inspected herself again. Not bad, she thought. Certainly not Sharla. She laughed, thinking what her mother would say. "What kind of get-up is that supposed to be, Sharla Ann?"

On Meredith's dresser was a carved wooden box which Sharla opened without a second thought. Possessively, she fingered the silver chains and turquoise bracelets and rings. She found a pendant among the other pieces. Unusual, she thought, similar to an axe but with two blades. Hanging it around her neck, she took another look in the mirror, and then at the close-up photo of Meredith she had brought with her from the office. Close, she concluded, but the hair's not right. It's long, too neat and too school marmish. Andy loved her hair. She found scissors in Meredith's top dresser drawer and also several letters. The letters, she put on the bed, then standing before the mirror, she began to clip, feeling almost as if in a trance. She trimmed a good four inches all the way around, cutting off the curled edges she and the curling iron had carefully created that morning. Seeing the locks lying in curly clumps on the carpet gave Sharla a strange, pleasurable feeling. She combed her hair, which now fell just to her shoulders, combed it back, away from her face, and smiled at herself. She looked at the photo then again in the mirror. "Not bad." Her teeth were white and straight. They looked good despite their propensity for holes which Sharla had to have plugged repeatedly. Usually she wasn't crazy about her nose, perceiving it as slightly too big, but right now it looked just right, straight, narrow, rather regal, she thought. She knew, objectively, she was an attractive woman, and for once, she was actually feeling it.

"Do you really need that eye make-up?" she asked her reflection.

She had large brown eyes which, she now decided, did not require the mascara bordering. From the pictures, it seemed that Meredith used no make-up at all. We don't need it, Sharla thought. In the john, she filled the sink and, using Meredith's rust-colored washcloth, re-naturalized each eye and washed away the base and blush and lipstick, too.

Next, Sharla took a stroll around the apartment, going slowly from room to room examining everything with her eyes and allowing her fingers to run over the contours of a vase or feel the smoothness of a table. She checked some of the book titles. They included mystery stories and other fiction, including some erotica, anthropology, astronomy, filmmaking, feminism, art, politics, social criticism. Broad interests, Sharla thought. The furniture was soft and comfortable-looking, the colors warm. I like it here, she thought. It feels like home.

Returning to the bedroom, she picked up one of the letters from the bed and began to read. *March 29th. Dear Meredith. It was good to hear from you. I know you prefer the phone so a letter's a real treat. Dad and I are excited about seeing you when you come the end of April. Let me know exactly when you'll be making it up our way. I'm delighted that you got the grant, and I know you love San Francisco so it will be a labor of love for you, right? Sorry to hear about the delay on the mural film, but maybe it's just as well since you'll be here in California most of the summer anyway.*

Guess who came by last week—Hedda. She was in town for a meet-ing. We had a very pleasant visit together. Even dad joined us for a while. He's always liked Hedda. Well, there was that brief period, when he learned about you two, but that didn't last long, did it? She stayed for dinner and even made a sugarless dessert. It was quite good.

Phil is on another trip, Japan this time. He's presenting another paper. Jean and the kids are going to join him there for a vacation. The kids will be on Spring break. We had a peace march and rally in town, anti-nuke. I couldn't get dad to go, but that didn't stop me. I've enclosed a button to add to your collection, and also several arti-cles I thought might interest you.

I'm glad you decided not to get a motorcycle. I try not to worry about you, but I do make some exceptions. I picked up a little some-thing for you at an antique shop. I was going to send it, but since you're coming soon I'll be able to give it to you in person. Are you excited?

Love you, Meredith. Miss you. Love, Mom.

Sharla couldn't prevent the crying. She'd been trying all her life to cry less. Her crying seemed to grate on people, but she was never very successful at controlling it. She cried now because she liked Meredith's mother. She cried because she could feel the love and respect between them. She cried because never in her life had she gotten a letter like that from her mother and she never would.

The other letter was from someone who was living in Europe, an artist, apparently, and a very good friend of Meredith. Sharla was returning the letters to the dresser drawer when, impulsively, she picked up one of her fallen locks from the floor and slipped it into the envelope with the letter from Meredith Landor's mother. She put the letters back and gathered up the rest of her hair to flush away.

In the bathroom, she looked over Meredith's toiletries. There wer-en't many, several bars of unusual soaps, though, avocado, straw-berry, things like that. There seemed to be few clues to Meredith's character in the john, though Sharla did consider the presence of can-dles in candle holders interesting. The tub was sparkling clean. Sharla liked that, and she liked the pulsating shower head, thinking she might want to try it. On the wall was a section of photographs, all women. Each of the photos had something to do with water, she realized. There was a shot of someone swimming in a pool and one of several women splashing on the shore of some beach. The one Sharla liked best was a close-up of a face, chin raised, with sparkly water trickling down over it—very sensuous, she thought.

She was ready to look at the films now. Threading "Travel and Play Footage", she thought gratefully of David MacLean who had been taking a film course when she was dating him and who insisted she learn how to run the projectors. She'd been all thumbs, at first, especially with him watching over her. He always seemed disapproving though he rarely actually criticized her. He ended up teaching her quite a bit about filmmaking, which she was glad of now, though, at the time, she only learned it to please him. Sharla wondered why their relationship had never taken off. He had just sort of disappeared after a while leaving her puzzled, but not especially surprised. Besides, she had never felt particularly close to him, anyway. He made her nervous.

Sharla darkened the room as much as she could to block out the Sunday morning sun. The vacation shots were filmed on Super-8 without sound instead of 16 mm. like the others, so Sharla searched for and found the right projector. She watched with fascination. The scenes seemed to span maybe ten years and several continents. Meredith appeared from time to time, but apparently was usually the one behind the camera. It went chronologically, beginning with some California coast shots, some San Francisco scenes, and then what looked to Sharla like Oregon.

Sharla enjoyed the challenge of trying to figure out when the shots were made. Cars helped. For some reason, she was good at recognizing cars—year and make. Probably because mom had emphasized how enthralled boys were by automobiles, so Sharla should tune in. There was a '75 Dodge Dart going over the Bay Bridge. She saw none that looked newer than that. Meredith appeared in the next scene, hanging on the outside edge of a cable car, waving, clowning. Sharla had ridden a cable car in San Francisco once. She sat inside between her mother and father. They had just had a fight and everyone was stonily silent.

From San Francisco, the shots moved to the coast again. Dunes. It's Oregon, Sharla thought excitedly. I wonder if Meredith has ever been to Portland. Maybe we passed on the street without seeing each other. Maybe she was wandering through the Japanese gardens while I was up the hill at the zoo. Maybe she... Sharla's eyes widened at the next shot. It showed two women, young women, in their 20's, both with very long wild hair. The women were embracing and kissing. It happened so quickly Sharla wasn't sure she saw what she

28

thought she saw. She stopped the projector, rewound a few feet, and set it on slow motion. They were kissing all right and not a little cheek brush either. Sharla missed the next scene, river and canoeing shots. She was inside herself, conscious of feeling repelled by the kiss and also aroused.

She thought of Greta. Many times, she had imagined herself kissing Greta like that, and more, a lot more than kissing. Her shrink had labeled it a narcissistic fixation. He said she identified so with Greta that, at times, their boundaries merged. Sharla's erotic attraction, he declared, reflected her attempt to get the self-love she'd always denied herself. Sharla had assumed the psychiatrist was right.

She backed up the film once more and again watched the kissing scene, this time feeling the arousal more than the repulsion. She let it pass, not wanting to think about it right now, and continued watching.

Meredith was in a canoe going through whitewater, skillfully maneuvering the slim craft between rocks. Her muscles seemed very powerful. Sharla flexed her arm and looked at her own biceps, unimpressed with the meager bulge.

Next was Greece. Meredith danced lightly between two natives linked by white handkerchiefs. She dances well, too, Sharla thought. What doesn't she do? Actually, Sharla danced well herself, though she'd rarely do it publicly. It embarrassed her to be on display. Alone in her room, however, she often let herself move freely with the music, swaying with it, her body flowing loosely, sometimes even gyrating rather wildly. No eyes but her own ever saw her move so uninhibitedly. Meredith seemed totally without self-consciousness as she moved along gracefully with the rest of the line of dancers.

From Greece, there was Italy, Spain, then countries in Northern Europe. Sharla was beginning to look for several women who seemed to be in many of the shots—a curly-headed blond with an unbelievable tan, a very tall, Asian woman with very long black hair and a short woman with short dark hair and glasses who never bothered to smile for the camera. Two of them had been on the canoe trip and now they were all in what might be Hong Kong.

The vacation reel went for about an hour, the last scenes being recent ones, many of them shot in Chicago. Sharla leaned forward excitedly when a fade-in of a woman on a motorcycle appeared. It was she, the one with the glowing eyes. Sharla got a rush seeing her. Then the scene shifted to Meredith throwing a frisbee on a beach.

29

There was no sand, just rocks. It looked like one of the beaches Sharla had stopped at several times, the one at Belmont Harbor, and then the reel ended.

Sharla did not move right away. She was picturing herself sitting at the beach with the motorcycle woman, throwing stones in the water, laughing. It was a good fantasy and several minutes passed before she rewound the film and put it in its box. She was hungry for more, enjoying every second of her quest. Unable to find any other Super-8's, she chose next a reel labeled "Panel on Androgyny". It was a 16 mm sound film. She set up the other projector and was ready to run it, but decided she wanted a can of pop and a cigarette.

Doesn't Meredith smoke, Sharla wondered, looking around for an ashtray. Of course not, only assholes do. Climbing on a kitchen chair, she poked around in the upper cupboard shelves. She looked through drawers. When she finally located an ashtray, she found something else as well, a book, not a printed one; it was handwritten, a journal. Sharla's heart jumped. What a find! She hugged it to her chest, but then, as quickly as the joyful feeling had come, it was gone. I can't read this. It's her *journal*. Her private thoughts. Journals are sacrosanct. If I read this, I'm truly evil. She held the book at arms length, then laughed a dry croaking cackle. Mother said if I didn't change my ways, I'd come to no good. So, I'm no good. Right again, mom. I'm a prying, snooping, evil intruder. She held onto the journal tightly as if someone might grab it from her. Meredith will never know, she thought. It won't hurt her if I read it. She stroked the smooth gray cover. I think I'm supposed to read it, anyhow, she thought. Her eyes had a glazed look. It's meant to be. The films forgotten, Sharla took the journal to the living room, settled into a soft easy chair with her cigarette, and opened the volume to page one.

September 15, 1973. Berkeley—First Impressions. Sharla skimmed a few pages then leafed through the rest of the thick book. About four-fifths through, the writing stopped. The last entry had been made two months ago. Over a decade of Meredith's life is in here, Sharla thought eagerly. This is perfect. She went back to *Berkeley - First Impressions* and read, slowly, savoring each scene and thought, each description of emotion and idea that Meredith had written. She read without stopping, for over a year, taking a break in the winter of '74, when Meredith took some time off to go to Paris.

The pages were much more filled with Meredith's thoughts and feelings than with events. A journal entry was made every month or so, most of them fairly lengthy. There were several poems interspersed here and there, and a few quotations; many of the entries related to Meredith's growing feminism.

Sharla certainly advocated equal pay for equal work and thought that fathers should help more in raising the kids and that more career opportunities ought to be available for women, but this stuff Meredith was talking about seemed rather extreme. She said things about the basic institutions of society needing radical altering; she criticized capitalism and went on and on angrily about the oppressive injustice of the patriarchy. Sharla didn't really understand all that Meredith was saying or, at least, why Meredith thought this way. She categorized it as "bra-burning radical women's libber" thinking.

Sharla went into the kitchen, made a sandwich and thought about what she'd been reading. She had known some people like Meredith at Oregon State, not really known them, but been aware of them. They frightened her, she realized. They didn't seem particularly concerned about what others thought, for one thing, and they were very opinionated people. Sharla had felt secret admiration but avoided them. They seemed very free, very different from her. No, she was not like them, and they would want nothing to do with her. She associated with people like Kristin Carney and Jennifer Stone, a small circle of friends that was neither free like the libbers nor "popular" like the other crowd Sharla avoided. I guess my friends in college were losers, Sharla thought. Like me. She felt the sinking drop in her stomach. Putting the barely-touched sandwich aside, she lit a cigarette and brought her thoughts back to Meredith, to Meredith's first years in college.

Some of the allusions in the journal, Sharla did not understand. Meredith clearly was not writing for others. One entry she found fascinating. Meredith went into much more detail than usual and Sharla read the story twice.

September 29, 1974. Taking Back the Night *It was still dark, an hour yet before dawn, when my alarm pulled me from sleep. We gathered in pairs, pairs of women, a can of paint per pair, climbing into cars or vans around Berkeley, Oakland, San Francisco. Each pair knew where to go. I had on my grubbiest jeans and my hair was tied back. I was really feeling eager and a little scared. We went in Kat's car, drinking coffee as we drove to the Sunset District in San Francisco, our "territory". The morning was cool and foggy, but at least it wasn't raining. Not many people were out at that hour. We knew the police were close to shift change. The neighborhood was quiet, row after row of pastel townhouses, all neat and still. We parked at the corner of Twenty-second Avenue and Noriega. The can of paint was open now, sitting on a piece of newspaper on the car floor.*

Kat asked if I was ready. I gave her the thumbs-up sign and opened the car door. I felt this incredible mix of nervousness and excitement. I went to the first sign and started to paint. I was working so fast, the paint got drippy, but when I was done and stood back to admire my work, it looked great. That familiar STOP sign saying what had to stop: R-A-P-E. STOP RAPE. Kat said it felt like it took me forever to finish. It actually took about five minutes. I jumped back into the car and we took off. I did the next few signs and then we switched, and Kat painted while I played lookout and drove. We were on stop sign fifteen when someone spotted us.

"Hey, what are you doing there?" this guy yelled. He looked like a banker or a stock broker or something. I was real cheerful. I said, "Good morning. Trying to stop rape. How do you feel about that, sir?" "You're defacing city property," the guy said. I answered, "Men are assaulting women." "I'm going to call a cop," he said. I told him I wasn't surprised. I finished painting the sign then I walked back to the car, nice and slow and easy. I was feeling kind of scared, though, but angry, too. We got the hell out of there.

We wondered if we should stop, but then we decided no way. Anyway, we still had lots of paint left, and to tell the truth, it was feeling great to be doing what we were doing. We drove about ten blocks then started again. We did two signs and I was just finishing up the P on the third when I heard the signal—three short little beeps. I looked at Kat and then up the street. There was the cop car. I grabbed the can of paint and ran. I ran up somebody's walkway and then through some bushes. I could see that one of the cops was after me. My heart was banging like mad and I wondered if people my age can have heart attacks. I stashed the can of paint under a porch, and then I ran into a back yard. Luckily a lot of houses have backyards in the Sunset. I kept running from yard to yard, and every once in a while I caught sight of the cop running after me. I went between two houses and then back out front to this yellow garage because I could see the door of the garage was slightly open. I slipped inside and I crouched behind the car. I was having a lot of trouble breathing and I was worried about Kat, wondering if they got her. She told me later that she'd crumpled up the newspaper with the paint all over it and shoved it under the seat, then she said to the cop, "I have no idea what you're talking about, officer....Doing here? Just enjoying the morning. Writing a poem, actually." She held up a piece of paper... "What friend?" I thought that was great.

Anyway, I waited as long as I could stand, in that garage, and then I figured I'd circle around the block back to where Kat was and see what was happening. Unfortunately, I didn't get that far. As I was turning the corner, there was the cop, standing there, not ten feet from me.

What really bothered me was the matron at the police station. She treated Kat and me like total trash. She could give a shit about our motives. It's like because we broke the law—no matter why—then we automatically were bad and had no right to dignity or respect. That was the most upsetting part about the whole thing, the way that woman was. Why do some women remain so unaware? Women denying woman. God, I hate that. We need to help each other.

They caught six other women besides us. We got out right away on the bond money that was part of the fund. We'll probably be convicted of a misdemeanor. That's what everybody says. Probably a $25 fine. I'd say it's well worth it.

The story fascinated Sharla. I'm sure it didn't do any good, she thought, but I have to give them credit for trying. I'd never have the nerve to do something like that. That kind of thing isn't going to stop rape, but...I don't know. The story fascinated her.

Sharla read on in the journal, reading and fantasizing and identifying with Meredith more and more. At one point, she became painfully aware of how fast the time was passing. The morning was almost over already. She began reading faster, her body tight, hunched forward in the chair, both hands gripping the journal. She had developed a headache from the pressure she felt to absorb everything she could about Meredith Landor's life as quickly as possible. Absorb her life, Sharla thought. That's it. It's as if the more I learn about her, the more her life is mine. Sharla rubbed at her throbbing temples. That's bizarre, she thought.

She looked at her watch again. There was so much she wanted to do before the day ended and she would have to go back to her own life. Tomorrow she must return to Media One Productions. Her stomach churned. She had hoped that this time it would be different.

She had hoped she'd be more assertive and not end up being taken for granted, discounted and ignored as she'd been on every other job she'd held, but the familiar pattern was developing again. She had worked there only a week and a half and already was slipping into the pigeon-hole-for-nonentities that seemed to wait for her. Her bosses were cordial but essentially oblivious to her unless they wanted something. She felt like a tool, a functional object to them, an extension of the typewriter and the telephone. It had always been that way. She had a bachelor's degree in English, could construct syntax better than most, if not all, of the people for whom she worked, had excellent editing skills, and yet they composed and she transcribed. And answered phones and took messages and filed. So, do something about it, Sharla chastised herself in the sunstreaked living room of Meredith Landor's apartment, but she didn't know what, nor how. And she was afraid. She went to her purse for some aspirins, then changed her mind. There was a bottle of generic aspirins in Meredith's cabinet. She took them instead, two of them, feeling pleasure in the literal ingestion of something that was Meredith's. She returned to the journal.

From what Meredith wrote, Sharla gleaned that she had spent about six months in Paris. Mostly her writing of that period consisted of cultural comparisons and more feminist stuff. The repetition and the constancy of Meredith's views, as well as the power of her arguments, were beginning to reach Sharla, as if tapping an awareness already there but dormant. Then Meredith was back at Berkeley. Stretching, her headache beginning to ease, Sharla started reading the entry entitled, "Leaping Out". By the time she was half way through it, her head was pounding with sharp excruciating pain and angry tears burned her eyes.

"She's a lesbian!"

Sharla's stomach revolted violently. A queer, my doppleganger is queer. She clutched at her churning gut. No! How could she? How could she do this to me! She threw the journal on the floor. "Ech!" She shuddered, a spasm, chilling her, her teeth on edge. "A sicko! Pervert!" Sharla wiped her hands on her jeans. "I'm getting out of this place." She began picking things up putting them away, moving in rapid jerky motions, then abruptly she stopped.

Why bother cleaning up? Why should I bother? She stomped to the kitchen. Let Meredith *Homo* Landor deal with the mess. Tears soaked her face. How could she do this to me? Let her get scared that somebody was in here going through her queer things. Let her think there was a burglary. Sharla paused. She was almost to the back door now. "A burglary? Why not?" she said aloud. Why not take a few things? The movie projectors, for example, and the TV. The stereo. Sharla knew she had no way to transport these objects as well as no wish to have them. I'll smash 'em, then. Destroy them. I'll burn her letters, her films, her disgusting journal.

She began carrying armloads of things to the fireplace—photos, papers, the journal, yes, that for sure. She ran back and forth frantically, leaving a trail of dropped books and papers and reels of film. She was sweating, and crying. The crying escalated to sobbing. She dropped the load she was carrying in the center of the living room floor, grabbed her purse and ran out the door, down the steps, into the alley. She ran until she noticed people looking, then slowed to a fast walk, then a very slow walk until she sat at the edge of Lake Michigan and the crying had stopped.

CHAPTER 6

Somehow Sharla got back to the Y. Her eyes were swollen, her face lined and haggard. On the el, she had avoided looking at the two young women who sat across from her, convinced that they were lesbians. Safely in her room, she swallowed several valium, crawled onto the bed, and lay there numbly, staring at the dirt streaks on the window. Are they all lesbians? Pam, too, and the motorcycle one? They don't look like lesbians. Do they? Meredith obviously doesn't. Sharla got up and looked at herself in the mirror. What does a lesbian look like? She took more valium.

When she awoke it was dark. Her watch said three a.m., her head felt lead heavy. She slept again. Meredith was there, in her dreams, or was it herself?

She was entwined with numerous bodies, women's bodies, all naked and warm. She moved among them, cushioned between them, sliding over them and under them. And there was water, lots of clear, soft, flowing water. The water carried her away, her and another. The other could have been Pam. It was quiet then, just the two of them, wearing men's clothes. Sharla undid Pam's belt and pulled the pants down enough to reach inside.

She squirmed in her sleep. Would there be a penis? She felt around.

No, no, of course not. It was soft and rounded and warm there, and moist.

Sharla moved her fingers eagerly around and in. She awoke, panting, her hand between her legs, her fingers wet. A moaning kind of stifled painful cry escaped her throat. She turned over, hiding her hand beneath the pillow, and crying softly until sleep finally returned, without dreams this time.

It was early morning when Sharla awoke again, just after sunrise. She sat up in bed, knowing immediately that she would not go to work today. As much as she'd always disliked her jobs, Sharla rarely ever missed a day. She leaned against the pillow and, stretching out her long legs, allowed the memory of the dream to come back. She did not fight it, but let herself remember and even let herself extend the dream with fantasy. She was with Pam, making love, warm and caring and loving, feeling good, feeling valued and wanted—and excited. Unbidden images of Greta intruded and a quick tremor caught her, shooting down the curve of her spine. She pushed the memories away and Pam was there again, alive, accepting, tender and sweet, speaking lovingly to Sharla and looking at her that way, that special way, and holding her. It felt good. Sharla was smiling with the fantasy, her whole body warm, her head light. But isn't it sick, she questioned. She twisted and tugged on the hairs behind her neck. Isn't it wrong? She was sitting cross-legged now on the creaky bed, the pillow in her lap. Everyone says it's wrong. That it's not natural. She thought of Pam again. I don't know. She was rocking on the bed, confused and torn. Meredith, I need to know.

In the shower in the communal john where, before, Sharla had worried about getting athlete's foot, she now wondered if the woman in the next stall was a lesbian. The possibility frightened her, but it was not only fear she felt. At 8:45, she went to the lobby and called Media One Productions. She told them she was sick.

That done, Sharla itched to get started. Though she couldn't say exactly what it was she had to do, she felt driven to begin. Her feet took her along the street, automatically, her actions seemingly undirected by her will, until she arrived at the el station and, twenty minutes later, at Meredith's Landor's living room. Sharla picked up the journal first and carefully placed it back in the drawer where she had found it. She stacked the photos neatly, picked up the letters and papers, and kept working until, gradually, all the physical signs of her rage were gone. The eager feeling of anticipation did not leave her. When she was finished cleaning up the mess, she found herself in front of Meredith's bookshelves. Almost immediately, she saw what had only vaguely registered yesterday, what she had probably come here to find—books on lesbianism.

Sharla read all day, hesitantly at first, almost as if the words might attack, then more boldly, rapidly, hungrily. She took few breaks. At some point in the late afternoon, she ate a sandwich. At another point, she tried to watch TV but only managed ten minutes before being pulled back. She read about the myths. She read about the oppression, about the love and joy, and about separatism. Initially, she resisted, bringing forth the arguments everyone knew. They were aberrant, pathological, psycho-sexually fixated. It was against nature, perverted, anti-social, wrong. But the more she read, the weaker her resistence grew. She read "coming out stories" and cried and laughed. She read about Sappho and other right-on women. Feeling the anger, the pain, the strength and the softness of the women and their struggle, she became more and more drawn in until she was totally captivated. There was another whole world, she was realizing, a place where women (they seemed like strong, whole women), loved and supported each other and knew it was right. Could that be wrong?

In the early evening, Sharla made a quick trip to the grocery store. Although there were cans of food in Meredith's cupboard, she would not consider touching these. She got a frozen pizza and other prepared foods, and almost bought cigarettes, but at the last moment decided not to. Maybe I'll quit, she thought. She felt as if she probably could this time. At the apartment, she went straight back to the books, reading well into the night.

When Sharla finally slept, it was in Meredith's bed, and when she awoke, she read some more. She read about wimmin and womyn and women-loving-women, and nearly forgot to call into her job, finally remembering at 9:45. The more she learned, the more intrigued she became, and, at times, delighted, yes, and excited. Gradually, as she read more, digesting it, thinking deeply about it, a warm feeling began to grow in her, eventually enveloping her. The feeling reflected a sense of completion, perhaps, as if she were finding something vital that had been lost. Part of her was amazed at this reaction. Part of her was clearly seeking it.

She read about goddesses and witches and matriarchy, and then it was Wednesday. Sharla did not go to work. She had not left

Meredith's apartment since Monday evening when she had gone for groceries. She read sections from the *Joy of Lesbian Sex* and began a novel by Jane Rule. She let herself have many fantasies, feeling happier than she had in a very long time. At four in the afternoon, she took a break to do some exercises, jumping jacks and situps, and to tidy up the apartment. After washing the few dishes in the sink, she had just sat to read some more when she heard someone at the front door.

Oh God!

The someone had a key.

Oh shit! What should I do?

Sharla ran into the study.

She can't be home yet.

Sharla hid, listening, her heart pounding, listening to the footsteps. The footsteps went into the kitchen. Sharla could hear water running. In her hiding place behind the study door, she was perspiring through Meredith's shirt, her hands slippery wet against the wall. More footsteps sounded, and whistling. Don't come in here, Sharla prayed. Then, through the crack in the door jamb, she caught a glimpse. It was a woman, but Sharla couldn't tell if it were Meredith or not. A moment later, she got another glimpse. It was not Meredith. The woman was holding something in her hand and moving around the room from place to place, whistling.

The footsteps went back to the kitchen and there were more water sounds, then footsteps to the living room. Sharla remained frozen, staring through the crack in the door. This time she could see her clearly, a young woman, in jeans and a bright pink blouse. She was stretched up on her toes pouring water from a sprinkling can onto the huge rhododendron.

I can't let her find me. Are there any plants in here? Sharla looked around the study. Shit, yes. Hanging at the window were two spider plants and, on the small bookcase, a fern. She backed out from behind the door and tiptoed silently toward the closet. Don't creak. Slowly opening the closet door, she slipped in among the boxes of film, pulling the door softly almost closed behind her, and held her breath. In less than a minute the footsteps came into the study. They stayed for a short time, accompanied by sounds of pouring water, and then were gone.

Sharla hoped there was no sign of her presence in the apartment. Thank God I didn't smoke today, she thought. My purse, where did

I leave it? The bedroom, yes, it's in the bedroom. Please don't notice it. Were there plants in the bedroom? The sweat covering her body was cold now. She shivered. A moment later, she thought she heard the front door close. Listening, barely breathing, she could hear nothing more. She waited. There was silence but for the thumping in her chest. She waited in the dark silent closet for ten full minutes before finally easing the door open. She listened, still hearing nothing. The living room, she cautiously discovered, was empty. No one was in the john, the kitchen, the bedroom. Her purse was where she'd left it, on the floor in the bedroom. Sharla assumed it had gone unnoticed and sighed with relief, wiping her forehead with the sleeve of Meredith's blue cotton shirt.

Sitting in the bright kitchen that was not hers, she thought about what she was doing—trespassing, invading another person's privacy, snooping unconscionably into her life. Reprehensible behavior, Sharla knew. Ordinarily. But this was not ordinary. Her probing did not seem all that bad to her, somehow. The fact that Meredith and she looked exactly alike made it all right, she felt, or if not all right, at least understandable. It was as if she were investigating her own parallel life rather than irreverently probing into that of a stranger. Meredith Landor was hardly a stranger. Meredith Landor was her doppleganger, her alter ego, her shadow self, her sister. Suddenly a compelling need grabbed hold of Sharla. She had to get back to the journal, right now, to put the other books aside and find out more about who Meredith Landor was. That she was a lesbian clearly bothered Sharla less and less over the past couple days; in fact, at this point, it actually pleased her. She shook her head with the realization, and, smiling, retrieved the journal from its drawer and continued reading where she had left off three days before, at the entry called "Leaping Out".

Before, what Meredith revealed had thrown Sharla into a terrible frenzy. Now, as she read, she responded very differently, identifying with Meredith's feelings, understanding, even rejoicing with Meredith as she moved to woman love.

June 3, 1975. I love Hedda. I think it's the first time I've ever really been in love. Pat was wonderful, my first. She'll always have a special place, but Hedda, Hedda, Hedda. I love you. Neither of us could pay attention at the meeting yesterday. We kept catching each other's eyes and smiling. I think I might have even blushed. That's a first.

I love being in love. At the meeting, somebody asked me what I thought about the feasibility of a women's hotline based on what Leslie had just said. I didn't even know Leslie was there. I hadn't heard a word of it. I think I covered pretty well, though, and it looks like we really might get the hotline going. I told them my ideas about it, about how to do the training sessions and how to support the people taking the calls.

After the meeting, Hedda and I went to the pool. It was great. We kept sneaking little grabs and touches under the water. She has great skin. I love Hedda. We had dinner afterwards at Squeakies. She was talking about looking forward to the weekend, and I blew it. I couldn't help it. I said I love surprise birthday parties and she called me a brat. I wouldn't tell her how I found out, but I told her not to worry because I'd be surprised anyway. She pouted then. I love how she pouts. Her mouth just looks so cute and adorable and I want to kiss it. I did kiss it, but later. Anyway, after I blew it about the party, she said, well, I suppose you also know that we're all taking you to the beach on Sunday. I said, "I know now," and I cracked up and then I gave her a big hug. We were supposed to study after dinner, but somehow we ended up in my room with about ten candles burning and we smoked some dope and made wonderful, wonderful love. I love Hedda.

Sharla read until 1979. Each year, Meredith seemed to experience more than Sharla had in her whole lifetime. But they did have something besides looks in common, Sharla realized; both she and her double were serious, contemplative ponderers. While Sharla rarely committed her own thoughts and speculations to paper, fortunately for her, Meredith did so regularly. In addition to the personal, diary-type entries, much of what Meredith wrote delved deeply, sometimes wrenchingly, into serious philosophical questions and life issues. Meredith analyzed, critiqued, developed and redeveloped her ideas, focusing especially on value-related topics. Sharla felt as if she were actually witnessing the development of Meredith's character, seeing her basic beliefs and philosophy of life emerge and alter and grow. She was growing fonder and fonder of this complex, deeply caring, bright, energic woman, who was also a lesbian.

41

CHAPTER 7

It was Saturday. Sharla had not gone to work all week and by Thursday she had stopped calling in. She had checked out of the Evanston Y, an act which gave her significant pleasure, and brought her possessions to Meredith's. She had finished reading the journal, identifying with each event Meredith described and with each thought and feeling. She had also gone through Meredith's files, looked at her school yearbooks, read much of her correspondence, and continued to read her feminist and lesbian literature. Not for a moment did Sharla tire of it, having no desire to do anything but what she was doing. She slept in Meredith's bed, cooked in her kitchen, bathed in her bathroom, wore her clothes and she looked at the photos over and over again, and the films.

She kept the apartment as it had been when she first arrived, knowing watergirl would surely come again. She smoked very little and kept the rooms aired. At 5:30 on Wednesday, watergirl did come. Sharla hid in the closet.

Each day and each evening, day after day, it continued. Sharla spent nearly every moment reading the books Meredith read, thinking about Meredith's life, absorbing her thoughts, examining her possessions, and becoming more and more possessed by everything that was

Meredith. She left the apartment only for groceries, shopping rapidly, hurrying back to delve some more. She related to no one.

The more saturated Sharla became with the details of Meredith's life, the more remote her own began to seem. There were times when she actually believed she *was* Meredith Landor, that this was her apartment, that the life she was immersed in was her life. She wondered some more about the possibility of parallel lives. Could it be that she and Meredith really were the same person, two manifestations of one person, who simultaneously lived two disparate lives, one good and fulfilling, one empty? Most of the time Sharla retained enough objectivity to reject this, but there were moments when she thought it might be so. Maybe I was brought to Chicago to reclaim my good life, and Meredith no longer exists as a separate person. Maybe she isn't in San Francisco at all. Maybe I'm supposed to learn about her part of my past and let that part merge with the Sharla part and take over? It makes sense, doesn't it? Why else do we look exactly the same? Why else did I end up in Chicago and in this apartment free to explore everything here? That can't just be coincidence. Why else would Meredith's ideas, so different from mine, make such sense to me, so much sense that I'm actually becoming a feminist! Sharla shook her head. It was meant to be. Yes. It's coming so easily, all of it. I understand how she thinks; I agree with it even though I never would have before. I'm woman-identified now, Sharla thought, like Meredith. I think I might even be a lesbian.

Other times, Sharla would reject this sort of thinking, concluding it was just by chance that she came to Chicago and discovered Meredith's existence. At those times, she attributed her obsessive fascination to the fact that they looked so alike and that Meredith had the things Sharla had always wished for.

The next Wednesday, when watergirl came again, Sharla was ready. She made sure no evidence of her presence was apparent. At 5:15, she went to the study to wait. At 5:34, when she heard the door, she took to the closet.

The following day, after re-reading parts of the journal and looking again at some of the films, Sharla stood before the mirror, hands on her hips, looking very pleased with herself. It was Thursday, May 17. She had been in Chicago a little over a month. Nearly half of that time she had spent at Meredith Landor's apartment, losing herself in Meredith Landor's life.

I'm a lesbian, she thought, looking at her reflection, a proud strong woman. I'm powerful. I'm confident. I'm competent. I'm free. She was wearing a pair of Meredith's jeans and a Meredith blouse and necklace. I love my life. I love myself. She smiled broadly, pulling her shoulders back even further.

A knock on the door interrupted her. I wonder who that could be, Sharla thought with interest and anticipation, still thinking she was Meredith. She bounced cheerfully to the door in Meredith's running shoes, and opened it confidently.

A stranger stood there, a young man in a sports shirt and dress pants. "My name is Dan Corrigan," he began. "I'm with the Illinois Conservation Committee. We've been talking with people in the neighborhood to gather their opinions on topics related to ecology in Illinois. Would you mind responding to a few questions?" He spoke rapidly but pleasantly.

Immediately Sharla was clutched by the familiar discomfort. Confronted with a real live person, the Meredith confidence disappeared, immediately and totally. And he wanted her opinion! Oh, God, why that? She hated to be asked her opinion. What should I say? I'll probably say something stupid. What do I know about ecology? I shouldn't have opened the door. "I...I can't right now, I..." She struggled with what to do with her arms, finally folding them across her chest.

"It would only take a few minutes..."

"No, I..."

"...but if you prefer, I could leave this material with you and possibly stop by another time."

"Yes."

Smiling, the young man handed her some pamphlets and walked away. Safe again behind the closed door, Sharla dragged her body to a chair and slumped into it. She felt sick to her stomach. She threw her head back, her face full of pain and self-loathing. Who do I think I'm kidding, she thought. Her mouth was a sneer. Me, a proud strong woman, what a laugh! She looked less like Meredith now, her features taking on expressions Meredith's never knew. I'm a weak nothing woman, that's what I am, just like always. She was biting at her fingertips. I'm afraid of people, for Christ's sake. I'm afraid of life. Her lower lip trembled. I'm afraid even to answer a few questions. Sharla pulled at her neck hairs. I don't feel like a person at all. She crouched further down into the chair. And you think you're Meredith! She looked around the room. What a stupid dreamer I am. Her face twisted into an expression of pain and revulsion. A strange gutteral sound came from her throat and then she began to laugh.

"You're nothing like Meredith Landor, you asshole!" she said aloud through croaking laughter. Her voice dripped with disgust. One simple encounter with a harmless human being and you turn into a quivering cowardly blob. That's reality! The prideful expression and haughty stance and confidence of a few minutes before seemed ludicrous now. "You— Meredith Landor! What a laugh, you creep!" Sharla was shaking. You're nothing at all like Meredith Landor. Once started, she couldn't stop the attack. You're nothing at all, period. Just the same neurotic, frightened, dull, miserable Sharla Ann Jergens you've always been. Sharla's stomach was burning. And you always will be. She felt nauseated, almost enough to throw up. You're nothing, nobody. Crazy woman. And everybody knows it. Can't even talk to people. Always afraid, afraid. Can't even give your stupid opinion. Deluding yourself. *She's* Meredith Landor, not you! Sharla's eyes were red, the skin of her neck blotchy. We're totally separate, totally different people. She exhaled loudly. Nobody wants *me*. Nobody likes me, nobody worth being with, nobody who counts, just nerds like Andy. Nobody who's anybody wants me. She clamped her teeth together. Why should they? Pam, Carolyn, Beth, Terri, Allison, Jude, they're *her* friends. They never sought your friendship and never would, you loser. She was crying. You never felt their affection and their caring. That was Meredith who did. You never knew their respect. They're *hers*. *You* have no one. What a ridiculous fantasy trip you've been on, Sharla *Jerk*ens. Learn all about her, huh? Her face remained contorted in self-contempt. Become a feminist, a lesbian, become happy, become her, take over, huh? Fool. Fool. Fool. Wake up dreamer, pathetic dreamer of empty dreams. You are what you are. Zero.

Sharla stopped reading after that. She couldn't bounce back, was unable to regain any of the short-lived happiness she had found. No longer did she look at the photos or films. The energized drive and excitement were totally gone and the heavy feeling, so much a part of her, had returned, only more leaden and debilitating now than ever before. She felt depleted, hopeless, demoralized, aimless and absolutely alone. For long periods of time that evening and the next day she just sat in a living room chair or on the couch, staring blankly. When she thought at all, the thoughts were repetitive words and images of desolate aloneness and contemptibility. Her self-hate crushed her to limp passivity and immovability. After a while, her mind began playing tricks on her, conjuring up painful, hurtful scenes—that there

45

were people in the kitchen talking about her, contemptuously, scorning her; that Jude and Beth were there, laughing at her. When thoughts of Meredith came, they were sad ones. Sharla was weighted down with terrible feelings of loss.

At first, she would cry periodically, but after a while, that stopped. Her eyes remained dry and vacant. For days, she barely ate. She stopped washing or grooming herself. Dark shadows edged her eyes. Her mouth was pinched, her face gaunt, skin oily. She did not change her clothes. Sleep came sporadically, off and on, with ugly dreams. More and more, images of Meredith returned to haunt her — Meredith's accomplishments, her lovers and friends, her happiness. Sharla fought the images now, hating them, trying to keep them away. Sometimes she paced. Mostly she sat staring at the wall, feeling the black empty aloneness.

Try as she did to banish them, the images of Meredith pursued her mercilessly.

Meredith in love.

Sharla tried to watch TV, but could not enter the stories.

Meredith's films getting praising reviews.

Sharla did not turn on the lights when the sun left, but stayed without moving in the darkness.

Meredith's friends, so many, caring about her, respecting her, seeking her out.

Sharla found some liquor and tried to get peace that way, but it only grew worse. The thoughts of Meredith would not stop and Sharla was beginning to feel a growing anger toward her double. We live in different worlds, doppleganger, different universes. You know nothing of what life is like for someone like me. What do you know of loneliness, Meredith Landor? Nothing! Have you ever been depressed? I mean for more than five minutes. Hell no! You're a stranger to my world. And yours is just a dream to me. Mine would be a nightmare to you. You know nothing of alienation; it's just a word to you, isn't it? And social invisibility. And inadequacy, and constant rejections, and fear. And shyness. Words. Things other people experience, weird people, abnormal people, not people like you.

The fascination with Meredith and admiration and identification and vicarious gratification that had inspired and motivated Sharla were transforming insidiously to vitriolic hostility. She was coming to despise Meredith Landor. Absolutely loathe her.

Day faded into night and day again. Sharla lost track of time. She sat. Paced. Lay immobile. Her lips were dry and cracked, her hair greasy and matted. Her hatred for Meredith grew to obsession. The light-hearted excitement and self-valuing she had felt temporarily were so far gone now they were not even dim memories.

It was late afternoon of some day, Sharla didn't know which. She stared out the window, not seeing, looking through the plants, not seeing them, through the buildings, not seeing them. She saw only her desperate meaningless past and an empty future she did not want. The plants! Oh, God, what day is this? Is it Wednesday?

She jumped up quickly, making herself dizzy. Her shoes lay on the carpet and a half-empty glass and some crackers on the table. Is it Wednesday? The watergirl. The watergirl's going to come and find me. Oh, God! Images of chains and beatings and ceaseless derision tortured her. She looked at her watch. 4:35. Is it Wednesday? She walked around the room frantically. Is today Wednesday? She put the shoes on, then took the glass to the kitchen and washed it out, almost dropping it, and placed it in the cupboard. Her fingers were shaking. Please, somebody, tell me if it's Wednesday. If watergirl finds me, something...something awful will happen. Something awful. They'll lock me up. They'll... What day is it?

She went to the phone and poked the buttons with shakey fingers.

"Mommie, is it Wednesday?"

"Sharla Ann, is that you?"

"What day is it?"

"My God, Sharla, what's the matter with you? Why haven't you called before? No letter in nearly a month, I've been out of my mind. I can't believe a child of mine could do that, could be that inconsiderate. First you up and leave with no warning at all and then...Now, what exactly has been going on with you and why...?"

Sharla hung up the phone. She paced for several minutes, her lips moving silently, then she grabbed the phone again.

"Operator."

"What day is today?"

"I beg your pardon."

"What day, what day?"

"It's Tuesday, ma'am. Would you like a weather report, too?"

"You're sure it's Tuesday."

"Tuesday, May 22. Are you all right, lady? Do you need assistance?"

Sharla hung up. Tuesday May 22. Tuesday. It's Tuesday. It's not Wednesday. It's Tuesday. Everything's going to be all right. She collapsed on the couch. Everything's going to be all right.

She didn't move from the couch all night. Nightmares, crazy, black, death-filled nightmares tormented her. A bottomless, smelly, tar-lined pit. Slipping, tumbling. A thick jungle with snakes hissing at her. Alone on a ferris wheel in an empty amusement park, then falling, crashing to wakefulness. The next day, all Sharla's energy went into awaiting the arrival of watergirl. She ate nothing. She drank the last can of coke. The TV was on but unwatched. She did not smoke. The apartment was in order. Everything's gonna be all right. At 4:00 she turned the TV off. Every few minutes she looked at her watch. She was shakey, lightheaded. Her breathing was shallow, her head ached, the dirty wrinkled blouse she wore clung to her. The apartment was hot, but Sharla did not notice. She looked at her watch. 4:15. She waited. At 4:30 she crept into the closet.

Sharla remained in the closet long after watergirl left. She stayed crouched on the floor in the corner, leaning against the wall, until after the study was as black as the closet. Surrounded by the boxes of films documenting a life led and being lived, Sharla crouched listlessly, barely moving, listening to her thoughts.

Meredith is in the boxes. Celluloid Meredith. Meredith skiing, Meredith laughing, Meredith talking, Meredith loving women, Meredith loved, Meredith eating up life, knowing how to live it. Meredith. Meredith. Meredith. Sharla was weak from lack of food. Against her right knee was Meredith discussing androgyny, critiquing it eloquently on the panel she chaired, espousing the ideal, the best of the roles, trashing the reality, womanness aspiring to the male ways. Near her left thigh was Meredith clowning in a "Lavender Loonies" farce, acting-out outrageously, making Sharla love-hate her, hate her, hate her.

Sharla's thoughts tossed seemingly without direction, but there was a theme, the underlying theme that seemed to define her—*self-contempt*. Meredith was the Sharla Sharla would never be, but housed in the same shell of dark brooding eyes, lips full, hair touched by strawberry, tall. It ended there. How must it feel to love yourself? "How does it feel, Meredith Landor?" She spoke out loud, her voice harsh and shocking her in the smallness of the closet. "How does it feel to want to live, to feel worthy of it and capable? How? How, bitch? Why you? Why not me?" She pushed the door open with her foot and dragged herself half way out of the closet. She lay on the floor, her thoughts quiet now, her eyes dull and lifeless. The night came and went, and the next day Sharla barely moved. She'd eat a few bites now and then and drink water and go to the bathroom. She did not look in the mirror. She tried not to look inside, but the melancholic remembrances came anyway. Scorned as bookish and too quiet. Feigning indifference to rebuffs, torn inside. The thoughts would not stop nor the contrasts with Meredith, and all the while, she was moving closer to the inevitable, the only solution. More memories came. Snubbing the snubbers and looking for comfort in poetry. Always outside the circle. Writing of love, secretly, never living it. Greta. Could it have been? Marginal edge woman adrift. Needing, and needs unmet. Not knowing how. Not knowing why she didn't know how. Always feeling different, apart, never a part. Lonely painful aloneness, pain deep and wrenching doubling me over pain. Can't remember when the pain wasn't there. Same face. Same body. Like night and day. Ying and yang. Black and white. High and low. Up and down. Meredith and Sharla. Sister. Despicable doppleganger. Sharla sat slouched in a living room chair, barely moving, barely alive. Hateful grasping mother "love" spawning self-hate. Wanting to die. Wanting to die. She was pale and looked very ill. In the world, not of it, floating invisibly on its periphery. Afraid. Wanting in, fearing to try. Trying, missing. Alone again now and forever always without end. Amen.

Her thoughts reeled endlessly as another day passed and another. The pain peaked and then finally, miraculously, it stopped. There was no pain. Sharla felt calm. It was time.

She walked almost briskly to the kitchen. She was hungry. She turned on lights and the radio and listened to music as she ate. She ate the whole can of tuna and the last English muffin and a half-dozen cookies, then took a shower, humming as she washed.

It was so obvious. She smiled. So clear, crystal, tingling, sparkling clear, like the water that took away her dirt. The time is here. It has come. Sharla had known all along that some day it would and that she would know. She knew now and felt relieved and calm.

CHAPTER 8

Sharla had collected the pills over a period of years. The project-ed scene was always the same—a luxury hotel somehwere, in the mountains, perhaps, or maybe by the sea. There'd be a meal, in her room, then the bottle of vodka and the pile of tiny white sleeping pills. She had gotten significant pleasure from the process of col-lecting the pills, a sense of power and achievement. She suffered the sleepless nights to build her cache, hoarding them like diamonds, keeping them safe in the silver Florentine box she had gotten from her parents on her twentieth birthday. The box was padded with soft burgundy felt. Sharla opened it now and fingered the pills. There were twenty-four of them. According to the book she'd found in the Portland Public Library, the amount she had was surely enough. She worried about that nonetheless. What if they turn out not to be enough? What if she just damaged her brain or something? Or what if she panicked before they took affect, screaming and calling for help.

She would practice in her imagination, planning exactly how she'd do it. She would take just two at first and three drinks, screwdrivers. As she began to be sleepy and relaxed, she'd take the rest and turn on the music and lie down to wait. The music changed over the years.

At first she planned to bring her portable phonograph and listen to Bach. The phonograph was long gone, replaced in her plans by her little cassette player with the earphones. It would be a tape of the Grand Canyon Suite she listened to as her painful life faded and she finally got the peace she craved.

She worried about convulsions. She worried about somehow being found, emergency medical procedures, the humiliation of her failure. She worried about feeling fear, but never about regret. She was sure the day would come and when it did she would know. She would feel it. Tonight, as she combed her hair and brushed her teeth, she felt it, and it felt absolutely right. There were no doubts. She had no hopes left. Nothing to postpone it for.

Instead of the luxury hotel, the site would be Meredith Landor's apartment. There was no way she could have anticipated that, but was not displeased with the deviation. She put on fresh pajamas, her own, changed the sheets and crawled into bed. Tomorrow she would have the final meal and listen to the Grand Canyon Suite.

Sharla's sleep was still and deep for the first time in over a week. When she awoke near noon, she still knew it was absolutely right. The heavy feeling was totally gone, not even a trace. She smiled. It was over at last. Good. Thank you, Meredith.

Dressed in bright colors, she went out for groceries, planning cold jumbo shrimp, pasta salad and wine. The sights and activity on the streets were surprisingly enjoyable. Sharla took them in, even letting herself really look at people for a change. They didn't seem threatening now. She noticed the shapes and colors of the buildings and the greenness of the trees, appreciating them. Along the way, she stopped to watch the reflections on a store window, delighting in how clearly she could see the passing scene behind her. She was humming. She felt happy, even chatted with the clerk at the deli. The shopping trip took nearly two hours.

Back at the apartment, Sharla rehearsed the scene once more — the meal, the pills, the music. She would lie on the couch, she decided. Watergirl would probably be the one to find her. Today was Sunday. She supposed she'd be pretty foul and smelly by the time next Wednesday came. That thought sickened Sharla and she pushed it aside. Watergirl would think she was Meredith, of course, and so would everyone else. Sharla giggled. What a confusing mess it will be. In death, I'll make a perfect Meredith. No one will suspect. Then, of course, in August, Meredith will return. Sharla chuckled again.

A stranger will be living here. All Meredith's things will be gone, her friends and family still mourning and adjusting to the loss.

No, no, it won't happen that way. Sharla was in the kitchen. She put a pot of water on for coffee. Meredith keeps in touch with people— friends here, her family in California. They'll be mystified. Whose body could it be? This is impossible! Sharla sat now on the wooden kitchen chair, looking at the copper pans and ladles on the wall. She kind of liked the idea, causing all that confusion, for a while at least, being taken for Meredith. The water was boiling and Sharla poured it over the freshly ground coffee. She set the food out attractively on Meredith's stoneware plates and ate the shrimp, the fresh rolls and butter and salad, slowly, enjoying them, enjoying the fact that this was the last food she'd ever eat, enjoying the fact that only she knew this. Sharla was relishing the control she had. This was all hers. She was doing it for herself, by herself, following her plan, doing it her way with no thought of what others would think, no thought of trying to please anyone so they would like her. She needed no one now.

coffee. She set the food out attractively on Meredith's stoneware plates and ate the shrimp, the fresh rolls and butter and salad, slowly, enjoying them, enjoying the fact that this was the last food she'd ever eat, enjoying the fact that only she knew this. Sharla was relishing the control she had. This was all hers. She was doing it for herself, by herself, following her plan, doing it her way with no thought of what others would think, no thought of trying to please anyone so they would like her. She needed no one now.

She ate all the food, then placed ice cubes in a glass, poured in the vodka and the orange juice. Her cassette player was in the living room, and the pills. She made another drink, and another, and set the three glasses on a tray and carried them to the table where the silver box was. She settled herself comfortably on the couch with her feet up and took a big swallow of the first drink. She sighed. Adjusting the earphones, she pressed the button and leaned back, the first two pills now in her palm. The music filled her ears for a second or two, then became garbled. Sharla laughed. "Oh, God, come on," she said aloud. This wasn't in the script. The batteries were clearly close to dead. Sharla laughed some more. She took the earphones off, got up and went to the desk in the study. She had seen some batteries in the middle left drawer. Meredith helps me out again, she thought, picking them out from among the index cards and pencils and paperclips. But they were the wrong size. Sharla began to feel irritated. Damn, I don't want to go out again. She considered playing an album on Meredith's stereo instead of using the cassette recorder. No, I want the music to fill me and I don't want the neighbors to hear. The idea of going to the store felt very aversive. She had been through Meredith's things pretty thoroughly and couldn't remember seeing batteries anywhere else. There were a couple of boxes she hadn't gotten to. They were in the bedroom closet with Meredith's camping gear. Even though, logically, the chances were slim, somehow Sharla felt sure she'd find them there.

The first box held some art work, sketches, some water colors, and several ceramic pieces, vases and animals. They were signed *M. Landor.* From her college days, Sharla assumed. Not bad but not great. She began to think of Meredith's life again and felt edgy. Returning the box, she took down the other one. There were letters inside, many letters, several thick stacks held together with rubberbands. There was a note with them. *Meredith, I thought you might want these. Loretta Pinski.* Sharla began to put the letters back untouched, her curiosity about Meredith no longer there, but something impelled her to take a closer look. She flipped through one pile. Each envelope was addressed to the same person, Robin Pinski. She spread them on the floor. The early ones had a Boston address, the later ones, Bangor, Maine. They were written in Meredith's free-flowing hand. Sharla checked the postmarks. They seemed to be in chronological order, from November, 1977, through January, 1984. Again she thought to replace them in the box and get on with what she needed to do; but instead she opened the first envelope and began reading.

Meredith and Robin were very close friends, she learned. They had graduated from Berkeley together, then Robin moved to Boston. Meredith missed her already, she said in the letter, and vowed to pester her with a stream of correspondence. The first letter was full of Meredith's news, her feelings, her thoughts, the events and people that made up her life. Sharla found herself irresistibly pulled back into Meredith's life. The woman fascinated her, no denying it. Even now. She picked up the second one and read it, and then the next.

As a source of in-depth information about Meredith, the letters were better than a diary, better than an autobiography, much better than the journal. There were 72 of them in all, many containing photographs as well as page after page of Meredith's self-revelations.

Sharla had moved to the living room. She read throughout the afternoon as the ice melted in her forgotten drinks. She read slowly, spending long periods thinking and daydreaming, about what Meredith revealed, about the world of a fully-alive, complex woman, imagining, once more, that it was she. She read into the evening, took a break for a late dinner, read and fantasized some more. It was nearly two in the morning when Sharla came across the reference. Her mouth opened, her heartrate increased. She read the lines again: "...talking about inheriting it from her. Mom just smiles when I do that and then I remember that I'm adopted. I think it pleases her a lot, that it's so inconsequential to me. That's not to say that I don't still wonder about my birth parents from time to time..." A large smile now covered Sharla's face. More proof that we *are* twins, she thought. But how? Why? She worked on it a while, coming up with no answers. She read on, then slept and dreamed about Meredith. When she awoke, the room was filled with sunshine. It was a new day. Sharla read the final pile of letters, crying at the end when she learned of Robin's illness, and of Meredith's loving support for her dying friend. The last six letters were addressed to Robin in a hospital in Maine. Sharla mourned as if it were her own best friend who was gone.

She sat quietly in the morning sun, thinking. The pallor had begun to leave her face, the darkness encircling her eyes was fading. She thought about Meredith's life, and her character and personality. The letters had filled in many gaps. She felt she truly knew Meredith now. Such a sharp mind she has, Sharla thought, analytical, inquiring, witty. And we're sisters. Maybe I'm like that, too, only something got in the way. The pain threatened to return so Sharla got her thoughts back to Meredith. She asks a million questions, teasing out the answers from her experience and, what seemed to Sharla, her vast knowledge. She quotes novels and poems and philosophers. Some were familiar to Sharla, some not. Meredith had written of some of her problems and conflicts, and in reading them, Sharla had felt her struggles. Sharla felt her joys and sorrows and hopes, as well. And she experienced with Meredith the excitement and creative fulfillment of making films.

Meredith wrote, too, of her friends, her lovers, and what they meant to her. In several letters she wrote sadly of Karin, with whom she'd shared her life for a time and who went away. Meredith's pain became Sharla's. She wrote of Allison and her confused feelings

54

about her. The envy and hate Sharla had felt seemed to be gone. It didn't matter, now, that Meredith had everything Sharla always longed for. Meredith wrote of her brother, Phil, and their competitive, but loving relationship, and of her sister. In the most recent letters, she spoke of Terri, whom she had begun seeing and thought she might come to love.

Sitting calmly on the sofa, Sharla allowed the implications of Meredith being adopted to sink in some more. We're identical twins, she thought. The two of us are one, in a way. I'm really not that different from her, not deep deep inside. Identical genes, carbon copies, both of us from the very same egg in the same mother's womb. Sharla twisted uncomfortably now. But what mother?

She rose impulsively, walked swiftly to the phone in the study and dialed. "Hello, mother. This is Sharla." Her voice cracked from lack of use.

"Oh, thank God! Are you all right, Sharla Ann? I've been sick with worry, literally; I hardly sleep. What happened, baby? Are you ill? Why haven't you written? Your last call was so...It worried me so. Oh, I'm so glad you called on your birthday. I prayed you would. I've been going out of my mind."

Birthday? It had never crossed Sharla's mind. "I'm fine, mom. Sorry about not writing. I've...uh..." Sharla felt dizzy for a moment. "I've been very busy. You see...I..." She wiped at her forehead. "I...well, what happened is I got a new job now, making films. I'm a filmmaker—documentaries." She breathed more easily. "I love it, it's great, and I'm really quite good at it."

"Film?"

"And I have lots of friends here in Chicago." Sharla's voice was animated. "I think I'm finally finding myself, mom."

"Sharla, really? I'm...I'm so glad. You make films?"

"Yes." Sharla looked at her reflection in the window, wearing Meredith's Susan B. Anthony t-shirt. "I'm doing one on street murals now. I interview the people who design the murals and I film their work. It's great fun."

"Well, I knew you had learned some about making movies, Sharla, but I didn't know you were...well, I didn't know..."

"I've learned a lot, mom."

"And you've made friends?"

"Lot of friends. There's Pam. She and I are good friends. There's Beth, and Hedda, Paula, Terri, and Tawn and Karin and Robin."

"All women?"

Sharla hesitated. "No, of course not. Robin's a man and Terri certainly is. He's a doctor, mom. We spend a lot of time together."

"A doctor? My...well, where are you living, dear? I want to write you...and give me your phone number. It's been awful not being able to call you. We miss you, sweetheart. He's really a doctor? Oh, I want to hear all about it. I can't tell you how happy I am that you called." Her voice was quivering. "Dad will be so relieved to hear you're all right. Will you come home for a visit soon? Maybe we can come out there."

"Mom?"

"Dad's been as worried as I. We were afraid something happened to you. I even called the hospitals and the police..."

"The police?"

"It's been ages. That's not like you. Chicago's a terrible city and..."

"Mom?"

"Yes?"

"I have a question."

"What, Sharla Ann?"

"Please answer it honestly."

"Well...of course."

"I need to know."

"What is it?"

"I need to know if I'm adopted." There was silence across the line, across the country. Sharla waited a long time. "Am I, mom?"

"All kids go through that fear."

"Tell me."

"We love you very much, Sharla. You're our chosen child, the very one we wanted more than anything. We wanted you more than anything, Sharla. But this isn't something to speak of on the phone. We need to arrange a visit. Tell me..."

Sharla let the phone hang limply from her wrist. She could hear the sharp crackle of her mother's voice, high-pitched endless words. The receiver lay on Sharla's lap. She stared unseeing across the room, then hung up the phone.

She went to Meredith's stereo, found the album she sought, and listened. *Sister, take care of sister. Don't leave any woman behind. Sister take care of sister, we need every woman, we need every woman we find.*

Sister. Sister. Ying. Yang. You're not my mother, mother. No blood ties us, not a drop. Sharla felt a floating sense of liberation. Sister take care of sister. Lean on me, I am your sister. I am my sister. Exact identical genes. We're not so different after all. Sharla went to the bedroom and stood before the mirror. She did not regret having cut her hair. It looked better that way. She pulled off the t-shirt and tossed it on the bed. Her shape was good; muscle tone a little loose, though, and she'd lost some weight. She needed exercise, and she was pale and pasty-looking. Meredith always had a healthy fresh glow. Sharla went to the closet and put on a sleeveless gray-green blouse of Meredith's and a pair of Meredith's jeans. Identical twins. Separate, but linked. This is the same outfit Meredith had on in the beach shots, Sharla realized. No one could possibly tell us apart. I could go anywhere you go and pass, Meredith Landor. We're not so different. I can hold my head like you. She lifted her chin. I can get rid of that darkness under my eyes. Same genes, sister. We are one. Ha! And you don't even know it. You have a way of smiling, though. Sharla tried it. It was difficult to get that self-confident look. She practiced before the mirror. Think Meredith, she coached herself. Think about your new love, Terri, and how much she adores you and how she respects you and how everyone else does too. Think pride. Think self-respect. The smile came, then. Self-satisfied, self-loving. Like Meredith.

I'd like to call my friend, Pam, Sharla thought. Maybe she'd want to go for a walk by the lake. She giggled. God, that would be fun! I could fool her, I know I could. She'd look at me that way she did before. I can still hear her words: "Meredith, what a pleasant surprise!" She seemed so glad to see me. I'm glad to see you, too, Pam. Are you free for dinner tonight? I know she'd say yes, people always say yes to Meredith. I'll give Pam a call. She left the bedroom and her eyes fell on the silver box of pills on the living room table. She felt suddenly confused. I'm supposed to kill myself. It was all planned. I wanted it. It felt right. She picked up the box and opened it. Yes, the peacefulness. Her head was beginning to throb. I don't know now. I don't know what to do. Maybe it's not time yet. Maybe tomorrow. Yes, I think I'm supposed to call Pam. I'm supposed to be Meredith for a day, just for a day, one good day. I can die tomorrow.

Sharla found a "Pam" near the end of Meredith's address book. Pam Wholey. There were no others. She began to dial, but felt a sudden clutch of fear. It won't work, she thought, replacing the receiver. I could never pull it off. Old creep Sharla would come back. I'd stammer and blush and get tongue-tied. Pam would laugh at me. "Why, you're not Meredith," she'd say. "You're a fake."

In high school, Sharla had joined the Drama Club. It had taken all her courage to do it, but somehow she sensed that on the stage, being someone else, she could transcend her inhibitions and insecurities. She was right. She got the leading role in *Mrs. Reardon Drinks a Bit* and did very well. On the stage, she was not Sharla anymore. There had been other plays, then one that was a terrible flop, and she never acted again.

Maybe I could do it, she thought. Have my one day, my one truly happy day, and then I'd be ready to go. I'll *act* the part. For one day, I could play the role and I'd feel the thrill, the joy of having their respect, their admiration. She was reeling with excitement. But, I'll have to rehearse. Really seep myself in the character. I'll have to practice and practice. She went to the mirror and tried the smile again. It came easier this time. "Hey, woman, come here," she said, trying to copy Meredith's tone and voice inflection. It didn't sound quite right. She went to the boxes of film.

Sharla listened to Meredith talk and practiced saying the same words in the same way. She watched her move, her walk, her gestures, and imitated these, too. She watched and practiced in front of the mirror and watched some more and compared. She had a way to go, but it was improving. You have to think like Meredith, she told herself.

"What's your basic philosophy of life, Meredith?"

Sharla began to answer. Standing before the mirror, she spoke the ideas she'd heard Meredith express on film and had read in letters to Robin and in her journal. There was often humor in what she said.

"Life is like a river," Sharla proclaimed, emiting her Meredith smile, and chuckling her Meredith chuckle. "A flowing river with bags of shit you can drown in or flower petals and a canoe if you can grab it. You gotta have a strong arm and a little help from your friends."

"Why are you a lesbian, Meredith?"

"Why are you straight, Sharla Ann Jergens? You have such potential."

Sharla was pleased. She kept it up. She practiced non-stop for nearly three hours and, at the end, actually seemed to be thinking and feeling like Meredith.

I *will* call Pam, she decided, but not yet. I need a lot more practice. Then not only will I call Pam, I'll...I'll do other things, too. Maybe I'll go to that bar Meredith likes—The Found. Sharla was tingling with excitement. I suppose I ought to learn more about filmmaking, too, if I'm going to pull this off. It may take a while but that's OK. You can die later, Sharla, first you're going to live a bit. You deserve that. A final fling. Sharla was smiling broadly. Today's my birthday. Happy birthday, Sharla. Happy birthday, Meredith. *Our* birthday. Or is our birthday June 1? That doesn't matter. What matters is that Gloria Jergens is not my mother. My mother is Meredith's mother. Lean on me, I am your sister.

CHAPTER 9

By June 20, Sharla was ready. For the past three weeks, she had spent nearly every moment preparing. She had studied the films until she fully mastered Meredith's gestures, voice inflection and phraseology. She had the journal and the letters to Robin Pinski practically memorized. She had also worked hard on increasing her knowledge of filmmaking, reading Meredith's books and magazines on the topic. Nearly every waking moment, she practiced moving, thinking and feeling like Meredith Landor. It had been a wonderful three weeks.

On June 1, Sharla had celebrated their birthday, hers and Meredith's, with a crab leg dinner she caringly prepared for herself and a glass of wine. A week after that, she had begun taking short trips out of the city, ready to begin relating to people in her Meredith role, but not yet sure enough of herself to meet anyone who knew Meredith.

Her first venture was to a suburban shopping mall, in Morton Grove, where she spoke to the salespeople the way she knew Meredith would. As she suspected, it felt very much like being on the stage. People responded to her with friendliness, courtesy, and respect. She bought a pair of shoes, the kind Meredith would get, and a book on sex roles. At lunchtime, she stopped at a dime store counter and struck up a conversation with the silver-headed woman sitting next to her. For the first time in her life, the small talk came easily. They discussed the high price of everything these days and how humid the weather had been. The older shopper seemed pleased to have company with her chicken salad sandwich and, when she left, thanked Sharla for the enjoyable conversation. Sharla glowed with pleasure and pride in herself. I'm doing it. I'm doing it.

A few days later, wearing her new shoes and dressed in clothes from Meredith's closet, she took a Greyhound to Milwaukee. On the bus, she conversed freely with the young mother who shared her seat. She listened and asked questions and talked about traveling and raising children and about many other things, including herself. She spoke of films she'd made, of growing up in California and attending Berkeley University, and she took the opportunity to express at some length her views on ecology and conservation. At no time did Sharla feel any of the usual inhibitions and self-doubt. It was quite apparent that her seat-mate regarded her as an interesting conversationalist and likable person. When they parted, she shook Sharla's hand warmly and wished her a pleasant time at the zoo. Sharla's goal was to remain always in character and she was succeeding. When a Sharla thought came, she banished it with an actor's willful determination, making herself maintain the role even in her most private little thoughts.

Sharla had always liked zoos but had stopped going years before because of the pain of seeing everyone else with friends, lovers, family and she so alone. At the Milwaukee Zoo, she had a totally enjoyable time. She talked about the big ears of the African elephant with a wide-eyed five-year-old, and made comments to adult zoo-goers every chance she got. She found that people were very friendly in Milwaukee.

One sunny day in the middle of June, Sharla took a movie camera to the campus of Northwestern University. She had written a treatment for a short silent film and, that day, began the filming. For a couple of the scenes, she needed people. Sharla had no problem asking several students to toss the frisbee back and forth and do the hide-and-seek sequence. As Sharla, she would never have dared do such a thing. As Meredith, it felt almost natural. The students seemed flattered to be recruited for the roles, not doubting at all that Sharla was, indeed, the filmmaker she claimed to be.

To Sharla, the people she met seemed to be acting too, playing out scripted parts, as much as she. Never before had she known people to relate to her this way. It was as if she had entered an entirely different social world. People liked her! They obviously genuinely liked her. But of course they do, she thought. I'm Meredith Landor.

The dress rehearsals successfully behind her, Sharla felt ready for her debut, for opening night, or day, in this case. She was ready to put herself to the real test, to contact people who knew the real Meredith Landor. It was June 20. With her chin high and a cocky bounce in her walk, Sharla set out for her appointment with Meredith's hair stylist.

"It's been so long. We missed you." The beautician's name was Norma. She was Cuban. The sparkle in her eye when she greeted Sharla was clearly genuine.

They talked of light things, Norma more than once asking Sharla's opinion, about a movie or some fashion fad, and listening closely to her replies, as if they really mattered. There seemed not a trace of doubt in Norma's mind that this was the Meredith whose hair she'd cut for several years.

They even joked together. "So you tried the scissors yourself. Maybe I should try making a film."

Sharla laughed. "You could film me cutting my hair."

"Using a pair of hedge-clippers, like you must have done on this."

"Then you could get a shot of me shaving my legs with a meat cleaver."

"You shave your legs?"

Sharla smiled broadly, looking at Norma in the mirror. "Of course," she said. "Ain't I a woman."

"I don't think you do."

"You're too smart, Norma."

Sharla stayed in character the whole time and left the shop soaring. I did it! And it was easy! Norma was friendly and chatty. I love it. In the past, beauticians never seemed to have much to say to Sharla.

She was dressed in Meredith's jeans and a short sleeve sweatshirt. She caught her reflection in a window as she walked along Broadway. It was Meredith. Unmistakably. The walk was right, the gleam in the eye.

After her haircut, Sharla took a bus to Meredith's Health Club where she swam in Meredith's black tank suit, worked out for a while

61

on the Nautilus equipment and then enjoyed a relaxing ten minutes in the sauna. From there, she went straight to the beach. She needed color badly. She chose the Belmont rocks where Meredith often went, hoping to run into some friend of Meredith. Many of their faces were familiar to her now from the films and photos. Sharla appreciated that compulsive part of Meredith that made her label her photos, name the people and the places. She knew what Tawn looked like, and Beth, a black woman, and Karin, an ex-lover of Meredith. There were no pictures of Pam, however, nor of Terri, Meredith's present love interest, but there were many others including several of Jude, the woman on the motorcycle. Sharla felt tremendous gratitude toward Jude for bringing her to Meredith's home and giving her the chance to have this fling.

No one Sharla recognized came to the rocks, but she got an excellent start on her tan, and was feeling very good. As she was walking home through Lincoln Park, she saw a familiar face, a woman named Allison, another "ex" of Meredith. Allison was walking her dog. Sharla felt excited, eager for the challenge. She waved to her.

"Hey, haven't seen you in ages, Meredith," Allison called back.

Sharla leaned casually against a tree in one of her favorite Meredith poses and watched as Allison approached her. She was a slim woman, wiry, with full curly hair and a slight hint of sadness in her blue-green eyes. "I know. It's probably because you've been here instead of San Francisco."

"So, that's where you've been. I've been thinking about you." The dog sniffed at Sharla's ankles. "In fact, I was planning to give you a call."

"Were you?" Sharla rubbed the gray terrier sensually behind its ears. "Yeah, I just got back." She continued petting the dog.

"San Francisco, huh? You know, I need to do some traveling myself." Allison looked at Sharla teasingly. "Maybe you can come, too. What do you say?" Her eyes glinted mischievously.

"Sounds good," Sharla replied, her own eyes equally mischievous. "If you promise to be gentle."

Allison chuckled. "Seriously," she said, "would you like to get together sometime? Not a date, I promise. No flowers, no candy, no passes, just a good talk, a bottle of wine, and a couple of laughs. You up for it?"

Sharla looked at Allison flirtatiously. The expression was from a scene in "Lavender Loonies". "Name the time," she said.

Allison seemed pleasantly surprised. "Tomorrow night."

"You're on."

"Well, good."

They arranged to meet at the Chicago Claim Company, a restaurant down the street from Meredith's apartment. Sharla was high from their interaction. She had often heard others doing that kind of playful repartee, but never never had she done it herself. It was fun. Silly, pleasant, moderately witty, good fun, and now they had a date.

Sharla skipped down the street. Could she really handle it through a whole dinner? She tried to remember everything she could about Allison. She and Meredith had had a brief relationship a couple years ago, no, more like three years ago. Meredith was confused about her feelings for Allison and ended up deciding not to continue seeing her. Allison was hurt. There were some bad feelings, but in time things got smoothed out, and they got together occasionally after that, though not often. Allison was some kind of biologist at the University of Chicago. She worked in a lab, "sticking pins in mouse brains" as Meredith had put it to Robin. She was also a musician, Sharla recalled. It was pretty obvious that Allison still had a crush on Meredith. Maybe I'll surprise her, Sharla thought. Maybe I'll seduce her. She giggled mischievously as she floated home, reeling with her successes and the astoundingly wonderful feeling it gave her to be treated as she had been today. So, this is what it's like.

The plants had been tended in her absence. Watergirl was so faithful. Sharla wondered who she was. There were no pictures of her among Meredith's things. Sharla knew she was going to have a relationship with a woman before Meredith returned... Maybe watergirl. Or Allison. Or Pam. Yes, Pam.

Sharla dialed the number.

"Hello."

She recognized the voice easily. "So, how's the job going? Beth still happy with you?"

"Meredith?"

"Did you miss me?"

"Hey, welcome back! I was afraid you'd decide to stay in San Francisco forever like all the other deserters."

"It was tempting, but I had to get back to ask you a question."

"Oh, right. That's why you came back, huh?"

"Seriously. I gotta know."

"Know what?"

"Whether you like poetry."

"What? You're too weird. Yeah, I like it. In fact, I like it a lot. Why do you ask?"

"I wrote some stuff. I want to show it to you."

"You write poetry? I didn't know that. Well, I guess I shouldn't be surprised about anything coming from you. Yeah, I'd love to see your poems. I'll show you mine, too."

"At the beach," Sharla said.

"What?"

"We'll go to the beach and read our poems."

"I'm flattered by all this."

"You're sweet. So what's new in renovation?"

Sharla didn't know much about Pam Wholey. Meredith mentioned her a couple of times to Robin, but that was all. She assumed they didn't know each other real well. She did know that Beth renovated buildings, so she figured Pam's job had something to do with that.

"It's working out real well, Meredith. Beth and I hit it off from the beginning. I'm learning all kinds of things. You should see me tape walls. I think Beth's impressed with me. She says she ought to give you a finder's fee. Ha! Ha! She and I may end up forming a partnership."

"No kidding! Well, I wish you well. I want to hear more about it, at the beach, though, between poems."

"San Francisco really mellowed you out, Meredith. Really, I am flattered. I'm serious."

"Now, keep cool, girl. You can handle it."

"You make me nervous."

"No need. I'm really very sweet."

"You're something."

"Saturday morning. Around eleven. That OK?"

"Shall I stop by for you?"

"Yes."

"Great. Then, I'll see you Saturday."

Sharla leaned back hugging herself after she'd hung up. What a kick! She's flattered. Far out! I love it. Far fucking out, as Meredith would say. Hallelujah!

The next night, Sharla met Allison at the Chicago Claim Company. They had a drink downstairs while they waited for a table. Sharla got Allison talking about her mouse brains and the conversation flowed easily. From time to time as she listened, Sharla allowed herself to step back and observe what was going on: Here she was, Sharla Ann Jergens, sitting in a charming restaurant in Chicago, Illinois, with a very attractive, obviously quite self-confident, successful, extroverted woman, who was relating to her, Sharla Jergens, as a peer, with interest, respect, and warmth. It seemed just short of miraculous.

"There's a party Saturday night," Allison said. "A friend of mine, Jodie Claremont, is giving it. I don't think you know her."

"No," Sharla responded, flashing a lusty Meredith grin. "Should I?"

"You hopeless sleaze. She and her *lover* are very nice women. I think you'd like them. Why don't you come. There will probably be some women there that you know. Do you know Sue and Chris?"

"The ones with the sailboat?"

"Yeah, that's them."

"I don't know them well."

"Well, come to the party. They'll be there."

Their table was ready. Sharla had a "motherlode", which was a giant hamburger, and the salad bar. She told Allison about San Francisco, delighting in making up elaborate stories of adventure, gleaned from her own trips to that city, her readings from Meredith's lesbian library, and mostly from her own imagination. She kept Allison either laughing or eager to hear what happened next. Sharla was very imaginative, and for the first time, was allowing herself to use her imagination to entertain and enjoy another person.

"You do have yourself a good time, woman," Allison said, shaking her head. "So, what about your Chicago life? What are you up to here? Are you with anybody now?"

"I thought you'd never ask."

"Hey, honest, I'm not coming on to you."

"Why not?" Sharla asked, smiling.

"What?" Allison drew back dramatically. "Is this you, Meredith? Earth to Meredith, are you there?"

Sharla laughed.

Allison's gaunt face became serious. "Now you wouldn't play with me, would you? You wouldn't raise my hopes, then smash me down again?"

"Would I do that?"

"I don't know. I thought you and I had an understanding."

"I'm understanding," Sharla said playfully. "How about you? Do you understand me?"

"Hell no. I gave up trying long ago."

"Good. But, don't give up everything."

"Mm-m. You're being devilish, aren't you? You know, you're doing things to my blood pressure."

"I've got a little adrenalin rushing myself."

Allison took a deep breath. "Would you like to come to my place after dinner?" she asked.

"Yes," Sharla replied.

Sharla could barely believe she was doing what she was doing and what she was about to do. They were in Allison's apartment on Wellington Avenue, drinking wine, listening to music, talking comfortably.

Sharla took the initiative. She touched the back of Allison's hand, then let her fingers wander up to Allison's shoulder. She caressed her neck softly while looking deeply into Allison's greenish pensive eyes. Sharla had no doubts about *what* to do, about what she wanted to do or *how* to do it. She did have some minor concerns about freaking out over it.

She proceeded nonetheless, kissing Allison softly on her lips. Warm lips. Soft, smooth face. It felt fine, very fine. Woman kiss. Allison responded with the feeling that she had always held for Meredith. The kisses and tender touches went on, building gently and gradually. Sharla continued taking the lead. It was her hand that found Allison's breasts and her mouth that took the nipple in, rolling it tenderly between her lips and around her tongue. It was Sharla who moved them to the queen bed in the alcove surrounded by books and candles, and Sharla who began their mutual unrobing. Allison's soft smooth body felt welcomingly inviting next to her own, and Allison reached back to her, taking Sharla in.

Sharla had felt sexual excitement with the men she'd known, but there had always been a hard edge. Fear was there and always some constraining self-consciousness, and a vague sense of being used. Allison's slim expert fingers caressing, arousing, slipping moistly around and in, carried no message that caused Sharla to fight. The two women gave and received, delighting waves of sensations growing for Sharla to a quaking peak more full than any of the infrequent tremors she had known before. And there was a playfulness to their love-making that added another pleasure to the sensual ones. They chuckled and made comments from time to time. Sharla had never talked during love-making before, and she liked it. It seemed they couldn't kiss enough.

Sharla stayed the night in the queen bed closely nestled with her new friend who thought she was her old friend. Before she slept, Sharla thought about what had happened, about making love with a woman and about how good it felt. Does that mean I really am a lesbian, she wondered. Have I always been? Or could it be that I'd enjoy myself as much with a man now, feeling like I do, strong and whole? She felt uncomfortable then and pushing the questions and confusion from her mind, gave Allison's shoulder a soft kiss and slept. In the morning they ate scrambled eggs and parted warmly with the promise of more to come.

Sharla returned to Meredith's apartment. She couldn't stop smiling. She basked in the good feelings as she changed her clothes and straightened up the kitchen. For just a few minutes, she began really to think about what she was doing, to consider the whole picture. She was acting. She was pretending to be someone she was not, pretending with such conviction that it permeated her thinking and feeling to such an extent that she transcended her real self. And yet, she knew she was pretending. She knew it wasn't real. She knew she was Sharla Jergens, a very unhappy, unhealthy woman. She knew she was deceiving people and that it wasn't right. Meredith will return and I will have to stop, she thought. The heavy feeling started to return. Immediately, she pushed away these thoughts she did not want to think, and pictured Allison and relived the best night of her life. And there was Saturday morning with Pam yet to come, she thought, and then the party on Saturday night. She was smiling again.

Sharla knew some people lived like this all the time, lives filled with fun, pleasure, excitement, friends. She knew some people lived with positive anticipation for what the next day, the next hour would bring. She knew it had to do with self-respect and self-love. People actually lived like this. And now she was.

CHAPTER 10

Stimulated by her phone talk with Pam, Sharla had gotten a thick pad of lined notebook paper and set it on the kitchen table. She sat before it, pen in hand, to see if a poem would come. It had been years since she'd written. The one time she'd generated enough courage to send a story to a magazine, it had been rejected, and she stopped writing after that. Her manuscripts were stored at her mother's house in Portland, in a box on a shelf in the closet of her empty room there. Sharla had shown them only to Greta, who said they were good and encouraged her to keep trying, to submit the articles and poems and short stories to magazines and send the novel manuscript to a book publisher. Sharla never did.

The poems did come. She was at the kitchen table again, working on her third poem. There was a free-flowing quality and a forcefulness to what she wrote that had not been there before. Poem number one was a brief observation about her recent evolution.

Searing hunger, empty hours, and darkly curled in a corner life.
Barely breathing when the bright-eyed dyke on a bike
brought me to you.
I am my sister, therefore, I am.

Your borrowed inner powers, tapped and sapped, mine now.
I leap like you to the sun, eager.
A wide-armed world embraces me in your absence,
Soothing the sharp pin pain and gloom, almost as if
they never always were.

The next was about respect. She couldn't have written anything like it a month or so ago. The one she was working on now dealt with feeling visible and validly present in the world. It was her favorite so far.

Sharla liked her new ways of thinking. She liked her new hairdo, too. And her new wardrobe. Most of her own clothes she had dumped with the other garbage she took down the back steps. Several times as she came and went from the apartment building, people greeted her, thinking she was Meredith, of course. Sharla returned their greetings. They were friendly and so was she; neighbors she supposed. Once she saw the janitor who nodded cooly. The woman in the window of the neighborhood cleaners waved as Sharla walked by and Sharla returned the wave and flashed a Meredith grin. She no longer had to remind herself how to walk when she was out. She walked like Meredith even inside the apartment. She thought like Meredith and felt like Meredith. But not always. There were still those moments when she slipped into Sharla thoughts. It seemed impossible to block them out entirely. Lately, she found herself obsessing over her possible origins and about her connection to Meredith.

Who are my real parents? Why was I adopted? Is Meredith really my twin? How did we get separated? Why did we turn out so different from each other? What would happen if I confronted her when she returns instead of being gone? Could we become friends? Would she hate me for what I've done? Why didn't my lying mother ever tell me? Are my real parents alive?

Each question brought an array of fantasied answers. Her biological father, an irresponsible bum, disappearing; her poor mother killed in a horrible accident; the twins adopted separately; the adoptive parents never knowing there was another. Her biological mother from a wealthy, influential home, Catholic east coast; the shame felt by her family from her youthful, illegitimate pregnancy; the girl hidden away, the pregnancy kept secret, the neonates whisked off the moment they arrived.

Every fantasy contained the assumption that she and Meredith were twins. Sharla was sure of it. The data she had was very convincing. They differed in age by only four days, that minor discrepancy easily being explained by a mistake in dates or intentional subterfuge. They were both adopted. Meredith clearly so. As to herself, while her mother may not have admitted it directly, her response was indicative enough to convince Sharla. But the most telling evidence, of course, was their looks. Two people, one appearance. Especially now, with her metamorphosis. Yes, Sharla was convinced.

Is lesbianism inherited, she wondered. It was Saturday morning. She had gotten up early and put the finishing touches an another poem, her sixth. No, of course not, and yet I feel so powerfully drawn to women now. The sixth poem was about loving women. Allison was very much on her mind. Maybe its just from my identification with Meredith. But no, there was Greta. Sharla shuddered. The doorbell rang and she buzzed Pam into the building.

"I came on my bike. I thought maybe we could ride down to the beach."

Sharla ushered her in. "All right, with me on your shoulders, right?" She liked Pam's looks. The image from their encounter on Clark Street had remained faithful to reality.

"Well, that's a possibility, but it would probably be more comfortable if you used your own bike."

"My bike?" For the first time since she'd started the charade, Sharla felt a sinking dread, the fear of getting caught. Don't let Sharla come back. Think Meredith. "It's been stolen."

Pam set her pack on the floor. "Shit," she said.

"That's what I said."

"Same thing happened to Nora. She had a good lock on it, too. They cut right through it." Pam wore a blue work shirt and wheat jeans. "Your place is looking nice, Meredith. You still got that erotic picture of Carla in the john?"

"I look at it during some of my most moving moments."

They laughed together. "Did you bring some poems?" Sharla asked.

"Probably more than you'll want to deal with."

"I have four to show you."

They were in the kitchen now. "I really had no idea you wrote poetry. I thought film was your passion."

Sharla took two glasses from the cupboard. "I have many passions,"

70

she said.

"Yes, I've heard that about you. So, tell me about San Francisco."

Pam accepted the apple juice Sharla offered. They went into the living room and Sharla told San Francisco stories for a while, clearly pleasing Pam who clearly liked Meredith a lot.

By noon, they were on the beach. They sat on a ledge under a tree and shared their poems. Pam's were mostly angry poems, expressions of rage at the oppressing feet she saw and felt so heavily stamping her and other women and people of color and the differently abled and the politically incorrect. They discussed their work and their ideas and feelings until they were starving for food and went for lunch at an outdoor place on Clark Street.

"You're different, Meredith."

"I am? How so?" The sinking feeling came again.

"Mm-m, I'm not sure. Softer, maybe. Yes, that's it. More open. Definitely a smart-ass still, but mellower. What happened? Are you in love?"

Sharla smiled. "You tell me first. How's *your* love life?" "Oh, just fine," Pam said happily. "No changes. Carla says we're married."

Sharla's chuckle covered her disappointment. "Does it suit you?"

"I don't know. I'm happy, so I guess so. I bought her a Braille typewriter. She amazes me. Sometimes it seems like she sees more than I do."

Sharla nodded. She wanted to change the subject and did when the waiter came. They ordered a dessert and talked of this year's Michigan Women's Music Festival and whether they'd go, and reminisced about previous years. Sharla had good stories to tell. She felt as if she really had gone to the festival all those times that Meredith had with thousands of women-identified-women, naked snake-dancing, cold showering, music-making, peanut butter and half-cooked saltless potato eating, getting lost, stoned, sunned, rained on, chilled, and dusted in tent city-woman city. Sharla felt intimately familiar with The Land, the music, the smelly johns (janes), security/guardians, chemical freedom, Amazon Acres, the jugglers, healing goddesses, the hair cutters, the merchants, tattoos, child care, the boys camp, the music, sober support, the political tent, and always the music.

Pam was delightful. Why have I never met women like this before, Sharla wondered when they parted. Pam and Carla would be at the party that night.

Sharla was eager to go. That was a first. Parties always used to nauseate her. She viewed them as performance tests she inevitably failed. She'd obsess about what to wear and about her hair. By the time she'd finally arrive, late, she'd already be convinced that she was going to have an awful time. She usually did. Conversations she'd attempt quickly dribbled to a clumsy end. People moved away. She'd feel herself perspiring. She'd drink to relax, but it wouldn't help, just make her sick later. She'd find a seat somewhere and notice that everyone else was talking with someone. She'd feel glaringly out of place, would wonder why she had come again; it was always the same. She'd force herself to enter conversations, try to laugh when the others did even though she often was not following what was being said. She'd wish she were anywhere but where she was. Her date would come to her from time to time and ask how she was doing. She always hated that.

Sharla arrived at Jodie Claremont's party at 9:20. She had taken a nap and felt very energized. A half-dozen or so people were already there, and more kept arriving. It was a huge apartment. Allison took Sharla's hands happily and introduced her around. Sharla quickly became an integral part of the group. After a while, the talk turned to film, and Sharla found she had a lot to say. The women listened attentively as she spoke. No one moved away. She sprinkled her conversation with Meredith humor, and lost track of time and liked the people. One of them, Emma, said she'd been trying to get ahold of Meredith for weeks.

"I left a message on your machine."

"I had a hunch I'd see you here," Sharla said, smiling brightly. "What were you calling about?"

"A film I'm working on."

"Oh yeah?"

"You got any time in the next couple weeks. I could use some feedback. It's going OK, but I wonder if you would mind taking a look at what I've got so far. I'll cook you a dinner. You interested?"

"Sure, OK." Sharla felt like she really could be helpful.

They talked about the film and made plans to get together the following Wednesday.

Pam arrived at the party with her lover, Carla. Carla said that Sharla seemed different and Sharla laughed uneasily and said she's always changing. Allison was very attentive and Sharla enjoyed it and thought she'd like to be with her again tonight, to make love with her.

There was one very tense period. It began when a deeply tanned, strikingly beautiful woman arrived at the party. When she saw Sharla, her face changed. She looked surprised, happy, puzzled. "Meredith, I can't believe... What's happening...? How...?"

Sharla had no idea who the woman was. There were no pictures of her to draw on. "Hi," was all that Sharla said, and waited.

The woman looked hurt. "How long have you been back?" she asked softly.

"Not long." *Who the hell are you?*

"I just got a letter from you yesterday."

Sharla nodded. Others were listening to the conversation. The tan woman gestured for Sharla to go with her to the side of the room. Sharla was very uneasy.

"So, what happened?" the woman asked. "Why didn't you let me know, Meredith? What's going on?"

Another woman joined them. "Terri, you wanna hit?"

"No thanks, Lou."

"You?" she asked Sharla, offering her a pipe.

Sharla shook her head absentmindedly, feeling even more distraught now. *Terri. Damn. Meredith's latest love interest. She's one I especially wanted to avoid. Shit!*

The smoker seemed to sense the tension between Sharla and Terri and she moved away.

"It was a last minute thing," Sharla said. "I thought I'd surprise you."

"I'm surprised."

"You seem upset."

"Um...puzzled, to say the least. Confused. In your letter...I don't know. Well, so, tell me, what happened? Did something go wrong with the filming?"

"No," Sharla said. "It's going fine. I'm just in for a few days."

Terri nodded. She looked even more hurt than before. "Something's changed, hasn't it?"

Sharla looked uncomfortable.

"You met someone."

Sharla looked at this stranger sadly, not sure what to do. "I wanted to tell you what's been going on...in person. I had to do some stuff in Chicago, so I thought I'd wait until I got here to..."

Terri nodded. She gave a weak smile. Her eyes looked pained, the lines around her very beautiful mouth looked pained and angry. "Yeah, well...hm-m, so it goes. Does she live in San Francisco?"

Sharla continued looking at her, not speaking.

"It's pretty serious, huh?"

Sharla did not reply. Terri just looked at her for a few seconds, clearly fighting tears, then she turned and walked away. Sharla watched her get her jacket and leave the party. She felt bad. Damn!

Meredith can patch it up, she thought. Damn!

Allison was watching from across the room and, after Terri left, she went to Sharla. "You and Terri having problems?"

Sharla looked at her cooly for a moment, then smiled. "You wanna dance, beautiful person?"

The party continued until nearly two. Sharla and Allison left together. They went to Meredith's. It was obvious that Allison was very taken with Sharla and Sharla was confused about her own feelings. She hardly knew this woman with whom, once again, she made very tender and very exciting love. She felt drawn to her. Were these *her* feelings?

Sharla awoke before Allison and lay with her leg against Allison's smooth thigh and buttocks. Oh, wow, it wasn't a dream. Her eyes were teary, happy tears. She felt warm inside. I can't believe this is me. Feeling this way, content, happy. Being with someone and not feeling afraid. She looked at Allison's soft sleeping face. Being with a woman like this, feeling good and knowing it isn't bad to feel this way. I must be a lesbian. She smiled.

As Allison continued to sleep peacefully by her side, Sharla's thoughts went to the party and to how friendly and talkative the people had been, and interesting. Interested in me, too, seeking me out. That must be why people like to go to parties, Sharla thought. Some of the women flirted with me. She smiled. It wasn't like men; it didn't feel...it felt different from men, like they were seeing me as...what, a whole person, maybe. Yes, that's it, an equal complete person, not a role, not something for them to use or consume.

How easily it came, Sharla thought, being Meredith. It doesn't even feel like acting anymore. It gets easier and easier. We have a good life, Meredith. Sharla stroked Allison's bare shoulder. Allison stirred and Sharla softly kissed her neck. Allison opened her arms to Sharla and later her legs. They stayed in bed until well after noon.

"Remember the time we went camping with Tawn and her weird friend from Denver?" Allison asked.

Sharla hated these moments. It had happened several times at the party, once with Pam yesterday and now again.

"Yeah?"

"It was kind of like this for us then."

"Kind of."

"Does it feel different for you now?"

"It feels great." Sharla kissed her, hoping to stop the words. It didn't work.

"You're hard to figure out, Meredith."

"A real enigma."

"I mean it. Remember what you said on the camping trip? About Karin and how you changed when she left."

"Mm-hm."

"Do you still feel that way?"

"Basically."

"You don't want to talk about it, do you?"

"I don't know."

"You broke my heart, you know."

Sharla looked at the wall.

"I hated you."

Sharla didn't reply.

"Not really. I could never hate you. God, it killed me the way you were after we split. You were so damn *understanding* and *sensitive*. I wanted to hate you but you wouldn't let me."

"That was pretty rough on you."

"Tell me!"

Sharla wanted a cigarette badly but she was pretty sure Meredith didn't smoke. She adjusted the pillow behind her back.

"I can't believe we're together again," Allison said. She pulled her knees up and put her arms around them. "It's scary."

Sharla looked at her, wishing like hell this conversation would end.

"I feel real vulnerable with you, Meredith."

"Yeah...well, it's hard... We all have to protect ourselves."

"Is that a warning?"

"I guess."

"Are you playing games with me, Meredith? Really, I don't need that. Please be straight with me."

"If I were straight, I wouldn't be with you."

"You can't be serious, can you? Am I pushing you again? Like before? You started it this time, remember. All I had in mind was a casual dinner together."

"Can we go a day at a time, Allison? I mean...who knows, you know. Who knows what's ahead."

"You're right. OK." Allison pushed the sheet off of them. "I'm hungry."

"For food?"

"That too." She pulled Sharla into her arms and an hour later they got out of bed.

Sharla made them pancakes and the talk stayed light. At four o'clock, Allison left for a baseball game. She was the catcher.

Sharla watched TV and read *Lavender Culture* until it began to get dark out. She made a sandwich, ate half of it, then got dressed to go to The Found. Her first women's bar.

CHAPTER 11

People eyed them as they entered, three leather-jacketed women and Meredith, who was wearing blue. It was her idea to come, curious about this new women's bar, Silk Scarves, on San Francisco's Valencia Street, game for something new.

Meredith's quick eye caught something new immediately. The woman stood six feet tall, at least. From the center table they took, Meredith watched her leaning over the bar, talking to the bartender whom she dwarfed. Very tall, and lean, with biceps bulging just enough past the burgundy tank top. Cora went for their drinks.

A "leather" bar, they'd been told, so her friends dressed for it, giving Meredith a laugh. One of them, Sarah, was straight and right of liberal; the other two tough as Prell but sexy in their leather.

There were a few older dykes in the corner, flaunting butch, and a young unpolished one with a tattoo on her shoulder and short black choppy hair. She was playing pool, doing the table strut in a way that reminded Meredith of Lily Tomlin playing macho-man. Shiny handcuffs hung from her denim belt loop. Meredith smiled at it and let her eyes drift back to the tall one at the bar. Cora was talking with her.

"There goes Cora again," Meredith said. "Think I'll ever get my beer?"

"She's just friendly," Sarah said smiling.

"She should be careful who she's friendly with," Leslie responded. "There're some weird women in here."

"Oh, you don't think she's dangerous, do you?" Sarah asked, very likely alarmed by the tattooed one's shackles.

"She sure is tall," Meredith said.

Cora brought four beers to the table and one tall woman. "This is Chris," she said. "Meredith, Sarah, Leslie." They nodded around and Chris and Cora sat.

"Chris is a pilot," Cora said excitedly. "How about that!"

"Cora's impressionable," Meredith responded, catching the newcomer's eye. "So am I. You're really a pilot?"

The pilot nodded.

"Impressive," Meredith said.

"I used to be more impressed than I am now," Chris said, drinking. It looked like a Black Russian. "As I was telling Cora, I work for Cascade Consultants, flying executives here and there. It doesn't feel like a big deal anymore."

"I guess anything can become routine," Sarah said.

None of the women much liked the bar, including Chris, and soon they left together, ending up down the street at a taco place.

Meredith saw the potential for a film on women pilots, and told Chris, who liked the idea. Discussing it, Chris, freely once she started, related her own story: High school drop out, fascinated by planes, flying lessons paid for by her parents, logging lots of hours, airport work, teaching, flying short cargo runs and finally the job with Cascade Consultants. Advancement, security, good income, but thinking of moving on. After the food, the other women left for home, but Meredith and Chris stayed and talked.

An hour later, they left, too. "I'll be done with the film I'm working on by the end of July," Meredith said. "I'll be leaving San Francisco then, but I'm serious about doing something on 'women with wings'. That definitely interests me."

Chris nodded. "So we should keep in touch."

"We should. Will you be in town this weekend?"

"Yes."

"Dinner Saturday night?"

Chris looked at Meredith for several seconds, smiling. "OK," she said.

Meredith was leaning against a beat up Buick outside the restaurant. "Pretty sleazy bars you hang out at, Chris."

"My first time there."

Meredith gave a nod. "Looking for anything in particular?"

Chris laughed at that. "What are you getting at?"

Meredith shrugged. "Well", she said, "we start filming early tomorrow and here comes my bus. I'll meet you here Saturday at seven."

Meredith rode, transferred, rode a while more and arrived at Cora's just past midnight. Cora was in bed already, the apartment dark except for the hall light, and quiet.

It'll be hard to leave this city, Meredith thought, removing her boots, and tiptoeing to the kitchen. The film project was going creamy smooth and the social life the same and increasingly interesting. Chris definitely interested her. A classy woman, despite her dressed-down look, Meredith thought, then thought of Terri. She'd written Terri two or three days before and expected a reply soon, maybe a phone call. San Francisco's a good city, Meredith thought, but Chicago is home. She took a beer from the refrigerator wondering if she was homesick. Maybe, a little, she decided. I do miss Terri.

En route to her bedroom, she tripped over a pile of something in the middle of the hallway. Cora's place was a total mess which amused Meredith. Chaos came naturally for Cora, not a stickler for the details of design, except when it came to film. Top notch editor. Meredith was learning things from her and that made Cora very special.

Leslie was another story. She was the only problem on the crew and it had nothing to do with the filmmaking. She had latched onto Meredith in a clinging, ingratiating way that Meredith found extemely annoying, sometimes even repulsive. A talented woman like that being so damn insecure. It bothered Meredith. She tried to be understanding with people who lacked confidence, but it forever puzzled her, especially people like Leslie who had so much going for them. They had long talks, but Meredith was growing impatient and had been treating Leslie coolly lately. Unfortunately, that just made her cling more.

Meredith shed the jeans and blue sweater to sit naked in her unlit bedroom and see how the Golden Gate Bridge was looking tonight; it never grew stale. Tall Chris-the-pilot is going to end up teaching me how to fly a plane, she resolved, scanning the skyline. Always more new things to do, and feel. Meredith smiled and climbed in bed. It's a helluva kick being a person, was her last thought before drifting into deep, undisturbed sleep.

CHAPTER 12

Sharla stayed at the bar until after one a.m. She had a surprisingly good time, a stimulating, exciting time. When she walked in, she had known no one. None of Meredith's friends were there. At first, she felt intimidated, out of place. The squirmy, uncomfortable Sharla feeling threatened to take over. She went inside herself to find Meredith. She pictured Meredith strolling jauntily down a street, laughing with friends, quipping cheerfully, expressing opinions. She pictured herself at Jodie Claremont's party, and with Allison. The discomfort began to fade. I do belong here. Of course I do.

It wasn't long before Sharla found herself conversing with a woman and then with several. Once she started, it came easily. She called herself Meredith and behaved in her Meredith way, but the women she met had never met Meredith. They related to Sharla as if she really were the self-assured, high energy, extroverted person that she presented to them, and she loved it. From Meredith's descriptions, she expected the bar to present a superficial, rather low-brow, though lively scene. That was basically what she found, and was surprised when, in addition to the dancing, the come-ons, the banter and small talk that made up most of the evening, some serious conversation also took place. The group with whom Sharla spent most of the evening, off to the side, away from the juke box, actually got involved in a lively discussion of books. Sharla realized later that *she* had initiated it. They discussed the differences between escapist fiction and "literature" and debated which contemporary authors belonged in which category.

Sharla left the bar with Dana and Adele, who had offered her a ride home, and with three phone numbers in her wallet. She had made plans to get together with several of the women she'd met, to continue their conversation about books and possibly form a book discussion group. The women seemed very pleased to have met Meredith, nearly as pleased as Sharla.

When her new acquaintances dropped Sharla at the apartment on Fullerton, they said they hoped to see her again. They clearly meant it. Sharla went to the kitchen for a can of pop, then to the living room window where she sat looking out at Lincoln Park. What a kick being a person, she thought. "What a kick!" That was a Meredith phrase, wasn't it? Sharla slept peacefully that night.

When the phone awakened her at ten, she pulled herself groggily out of bed and went to listen to the message.

This is Allison. Give me a call when you get home. I'll be at the lab all day except between noon and one when the keepers get to get fed. Talk to you later. Bye. Beep. Buzz.

Sharla yawned and smiled. I like that woman. She laughed. But I like all the women. Am I not being discriminating enough? In the shower, she thought of the women she'd met since coming out as Meredith. There was quite a list. It seemed, though, that along with her fans, Meredith also had her share of acquaintances who weren't crazy about her. There had been a couple of them at Jodie's party. One was Kelly. She was snotty to Sharla, but Sharla quipped with her and then ignored her and was unbothered by it. In the past such treatment would have devastated her.

Sharla had a quick bagel and then took her coffee to the living room with her book on filmmaking. On Wednesday she was going to Emma's to look at Emma's film. Although she already had a fairly adequate passing knowledge of the subject, she certainly wasn't an expert and hoped to learn some more in the next two days. The books turned out not to be nearly as helpful as a notebook of Meredith's that Sharla found on the bookshelf under the windowsill. It was full of notes for teaching film, with dozens of examples. Meredith conducted courses from time to time and this apparently was a resource she used. Sharla studied it thoroughly and felt moderately well-prepared and fairly confident by the time Wednesday evening came.

Emma welcomed her with a royal home-cooked spread, vegetarian. Her partner, Elise, was there and they ate and talked film and Sharla worked at keeping the reminiscing to a minimum, several times needing to make cracks about her lousy memory.

The film seemed good to Sharla. She wished she knew more, but did the best she could, giving some, hopefully constructive, criticism, using Meredith's vocabulary. Emma seemed satisfied and not a bit suspicious. What a kick! But the part Sharla especially focused on was the script. She suggested some rather major alterations and worked on the wording and sequences with Emma. Emma loved her ideas.

"Would you mind doing one more thing for me?" Emma asked.

"Well, that depends, Emma," Sharla replied, smiling suggestively. She loved saying things like that, harmless, teasing, playfully suggestive things. She had never done it as Sharla. She hoped she wasn't overdoing it now.

"Let me get it. I have the treatment..." Emma ran off to another room and appeared a minute later with several sheets of paper. "Tell me what you think."

Sharla read silently. "Clever," she said. "More than clever, really good. Yeah, I think this has a lot of potential, Emma. You going to do it?"

"I need a scriptwriter."

Sharla looked at her.

"Would you, Meredith? I can't promise you big bucks but I'm pretty sure we can get funded."

Sharla smiled a Meredith smile. Inside, she was unconstrainedly joyful. "I could take a crack at it."

They drank some more wine and talked some more film. After a while, Elise went to watch TV.

"I ran into Terri the other day," Emma said.

"Oh?"

"We talked. About you mostly."

"Hm-m."

"She...uh. She's having a hard time." Emma was clearly having a hard time bringing up the subject. "I guess she thought you two had something going, something ..."

"Yeah, well...yeah I can understand that."

"So, you met someone in San Francisco."

Sharla shook her head sadly. "No, its not that," she said.

"Terri thought it was."

"No."

"She's real pissed."

"Yeah, well..what can I say?"

"She said you were only going to stay in Chicago for a few days."

"I'm back and forth."

"Well, the weird part is that Terri's planning to go to San Francisco over the Fourth of July. She thinks you're there. I think she plans to see you there. Something about a confrontation."

Sharla's face drained. "Oh, yeah. Hm-m. Maybe I'll give her a call."

"When are you going back?"

"Soon. Yeah, real soon. Hey, you got any more of this wine?"

"It's none of my business, is it?"

"Not really."

"I know. But Terri's been a good friend. I hate to see her so upset."

Sharla didn't respond and Emma switched to other topics.

The next day Sharla called Terri and they arranged to meet. Terri was surprised that Meredith was in Chicago, and angry.

"So, she's a pilot, huh? That's hard to compete with," Terri said. They were in the zoo, near the sea lions.

Sharla looked at the beautiful Terri, not knowing how to respond, then watched the penguins.

"I called Monday. You were out. I talked to your friend, Cora. She's very nice. She mentioned a tall pilot. I figured she must be the one. Is that how you're managing to commute back and forth from San Francisco as if it were a Chicago suburb?"

"I'm confused right now, Terri."

"You're confused? How do you think I feel?" Her lip was quivering. She bit it. "Two months ago we're spending every moment we can get together before you leave. You're telling me you're falling in love with me. Just a week ago in your last letter, you tell me the feelings are still there, and growing. And then suddenly you turn up at a party in Chicago and you act as if you barely know me. Tell me about confusion!"

"Sorry, Terri." Sharla felt very genuinely sorry.

Terri was close to tears. She was looking toward the sea lions, keeping her eyes away from Sharla.

"Something very strange happened to me," Sharla said slowly.

Terri turned to her, wiping at her eyes with the cuff of her blue jeans jacket.

"You know I'm adopted."

"Yes."

"Well...it's unbelievable, but, Terri, I recently found out something that blew me away." Sharla ran her fingers through her hair. It was a gesture Meredith often did. "I found out I have a twin sister. A twin and I never knew. Can you believe that?"

"You're kidding!" Terri leaned toward Sharla now, her whole demeanor changing. "How did you find out?"

"It was by chance. In San Francisco, two people I ran into...in a Chinese restaurant in Noe Valley...they called me Sharla and began talking like I was an old friend of theirs."

"Sharla's your sister?"

"Yes, that's how it seems. I've been trying to find her. We must be identical twins. She looks exactly like me. It's freaking me out."

"I guess."

"But there's more."

"What?" Terri was clearly fascinated and concerned.

"The dreams. I used to have this dream. I had it over and over. I dreamed I was riding on a bicycle. It always started the same way. I was riding a bike somewhere...in a forest, but not a good forest; it was a misty, mossy, scarey kind of forest. The trees were bare with very armlike limbs, you know, like in the Disney animateds. I'd be riding along when suddenly the bike was a tandem. And there was another person riding behind me, on the back part. I'd turn around to try to see her and she'd shift to the side so I'd barely get a glimpse of her. I'd keep trying and we'd keep riding along through the creepy forest. Finally, I'd see her...and it was...it was me! It was another me. Only the eyes were different. They were staring, like empty, like there was nothing inside."

Sharla shivered at this point and Terri touched her arm.

"Gradually, she'd move closer and closer to me, creeping up from behind me. I'd peddle faster and faster trying to get away but she kept inching up. And then I could feel her leg against mine, moving with my leg, up and down with the peddling, overlapping my leg and then her leg would like melt into mine and our legs would become one leg. Then the same thing would happen with the other leg and then the torso. And the arms. It was like she entered my body, taking it over. And then only her head was separate. And I'd try to get away. I'd move my head way forward, but she'd keep coming. I was terrified and she'd keep coming, coming, until her head overlapped mine and I was gone."

"Gone?"

"That was all. It wasn't me anymore. She had taken me over, totally. Then there was just one person on the bike peddling through the forest. Her. I was gone."

"Frightening dream," Terri said.

"I'd wake up sweating."

"You had it more than once?"

"Dozens of times. Over the past few years. I haven't had it since April, since I left here for San Francisco. Then those women and their story about my double." Sharla shook her head. "It's doing something to me, something to my mind."

"I'm not surprised," Terri said. "That's very freaky."

"They sent me a picture of her."

"Who?"

"Sharla. My double. The women I met in San Francisco sent it. We've kept in touch since we met. They sent me a picture of Sharla and it was me but it wasn't. It was at some place I've never been. She had clothes on I've never worn."

"Looks just like you?"

"Exactly."

Terri slowly shook her head. "You're about the last person I'd expect to be having weird mystical experiences, Meredith."

"It's scaring me."

"What are you doing with it?"

"Wondering about reality."

"Yeah."

"I've been coming to Chicago because they said she lived here. I'm trying to trace her."

"Any luck?"

"None. She's from Portland. I've been there too and made a dozen phone calls."

"Nothing?"

"Nothing. Do you think she really exists?" Sharla asked.

"I don't know, Meredith. Those women, the picture...What did they say about this Sharla?"

"That she's a witch."

"What?"

"That's what they said. She's in a coven. Does witchcraft, whatever that means."

"I know some witches. They're very together women."

"Sharla's not like that. I know some witches, too. That's not how Sharla is... She's..."

"She's what?"

"I don't know. They told me she got real weirded out a couple years ago. Got involved with some very strange people. Men and women. Wizards. Black candles and all that shit."

"This is really getting to you, Meredith. I've never seen you like this."

"It's haunting the hell out of me. But I try to fight it. I keep working on the film and try to keep living like usual. I need everything to be like usual. Do you understand, Terri? It's scaring the shit out of me. I need everything to be like usual. Will you help?"

"Of course."

"Do you understand that I can't stand to talk about it. I had to tell you because...I know I hurt you so I had to tell you, but it tears me apart to talk about it." Sharla had grabbed onto Terri's arm and was squeezing it tightly.

"I understand. Yeah. You gotta just go and...and not let it..."

"Take over."

"Yeah."

"Please don't talk about it with me again."

"All right."

"Ever."

"OK, Meredith."

"Unless I bring it up. Please. I mean it. Nothing that has to do with it. Even these trips to Chicago."

Terri nodded. "All right. But maybe I could help...I mean help you find her, or be a support somehow if..."

"No! I mean it. I have to deal with this my way. Just act as if we never had this conversation, as if you never knew I came to Chicago." Sharla shook her head. "I shouldn't have gone to that party. I don't know why I did. I ran into Allison and she invited me." Sharla shook her head again. "I'm going to San Francisco tomorrow. From time to time I'll probably be coming back here, but just to search...I won't call you when I come. Not 'til I'm back for good in August."

"But why not, Meredith? We wouldn't have to talk about..."

"I *can't*. Don't you understand?"

Terri's face looked very pained. "I guess so."

"We'll go on like it was. I won't allude to it again. I'll just be my usual self. Write me, just like normal. I'll write you just like normal."

"Yeah."

Sharla's shoulders slumped. "Thanks, Terri. I'm done now. Next time we talk it'll be just like normal." Sharla stood. "I'm going now."

Terri stood too and watched Sharla go down the steps at the sea lion pool and away.

As she walked back to the apartment, Sharla felt as if it had all been true and had to shake herself and remind herself that she had made it up, made it all up. She had a headache when she got home. She showered, a long cool shower, and then slept. In the morning, she felt back to normal. She called Allison and laughed and flirted and made plans.

CHAPTER 13

Gloria Jergens had lost eleven pounds. Thin anyhow, it showed badly, especially on her face, gaunt now as well as pale. At work, she functioned so poorly that Mr. Gladstone finally called her on it. Gloria Jergens was never one to cry her troubles, least of all before her boss, but this time she did, confronted as she was with example after example of her egregious errors, rippling the austere corporation.

"You sent an invoice to K.C. McGregor and Company charging them for services never rendered," he said cooly. "We've been trying to get their account for months, Gloria, and this may have ruined it for us."

Gloria Jergens bit down on her lip, while forcing reluctant neck muscles to keep the head up.

"You misplaced the materials we needed to send to Houston. That created a two week delay."

Gloria Jergen's, white knuckled, spoke humbly. "I'm very sorry about that, Mr. Gladstone, I..."

"Half the time when I come out of my office, I find you just sitting at your desk staring into space."

"I know. I'm trying. I...I have the Smith report nearly finished."

"What *is* the problem, Gloria? I never had any complaints before. Are you dissatisfied with your job?"

"No, it's not that."

"Well, what is it then?"

"It's...I...I'm having problems, Mr. Gladstone...family problems."

He nodded. "Your marriage?" His impatience showed.

"No, no it's my..." The tears started. "It's my daughter, Sharla. She's...she's...I don't know where she is." Gloria Jergen's voice would not submit to her control. Jerking sobs dotted the words.

Mr. Gladstone shifted on the leather upholstery. "Well, I'm sorry to hear there are problems, Gloria. Is there any way...Is there anything the company could do to help out?"

"She's been gone for two months. I got a call on her birthday...on May 28th. She was...it didn't go well. I haven't heard from her since. I don't know where she's living or..."

"Yes, well, our kids do go off. Your daughter is well into adulthood, isn't she, Gloria? Do you think you might be worrying unduly?"

Gloria Jergens held her fist against her mouth. "Perhaps. Perhaps she's all right."

"Would it help to take some vacation time, Gloria?"

Gloria Jergens nodded. "Maybe so," she said.

That was now a week ago. She had barely left the house since, bitterly inconsolable. Husband Bud's tries were snapped at so he withdrew, leaving her alone with the pain, except for her best friend, Edna Guersy, who quickly grew as distraught as Gloria and needed consoling herself.

She wondered if it could be the genes, Sharla's unknown past perhaps carrying hereditary ills. What sort would leave a five-week-old infant's fate to chance at the service entrance of Roseland Community Hospital? Bad seed. Tainted. Oh, that's nonsense.

Gloria Jergens recalled her joy when told they had a baby for her, and seeing the tiny rose-cheeked child, with blue eyes; then holding delicately in her loving mother arms the answer to years of hungry dreams and prayers and barren attempts. Bud's sperm count was fine; it was her, something was wrong with her.

Gloria couldn't imagine a childless life. What purpose? Was not mothering the central part of woman's living? Hadn't she prepared for it since age three, cuddling her Susie Doll, giving her the bottle, changing the wet diapers, spanking her when she was bad? And later, playing house, always being the mommie, knowing it was for her. Being a mommie was what she was, the Parker Business School just a step toward work in an office until she married and then to her real work. Bud too was eager, eager as Bud got. He liked children. Two boys and a girl, that was the plan. Each time they were together on the old brass bed from grandmother, Gloria thought "maybe this time", which rendered the sexual intercourse ordeal more palatable, thinking of little eggs and spermatozoa. They tried for four years, Gloria more and more depressed each bloody month, and angry at fate, at God, at Bud. Mostly at herself. What's wrong with me? Am I not a woman?

Putting in their application to adopt lifted drooping hopes again, inspiring plans of just how it would be. She'd raise up the smartest, most capable, considerate son one could, who'd love his mother and father devotedly, be obedient to them and respectful, but independent, too. He'd go far, their son, become an executive like his dad, maybe even a vice president some day.

Gloria's disappointment was only minor when it was a girl they offered her. She'd be pretty and sweet and well-behaved. I'll dress her in cute little dresses and she'll learn to play the piano and give me wonderful grandchildren and live down the street and we'll have coffee and watch the kids grow together. She'll be there for me in my old age. My Sharla, my darling girl. I'll be strict. I'll teach her how to be a real lady, polite and charming. My girl.

But, it never went quite so smoothly as the dreams. Sharla didn't cooperate, at least not so as to satisfy Gloria Jergen's well-delineated needs. So she tried harder, push and poke and prod to shape the clay. Sharla *would* be happy. She *would* be a normal, regular woman and a mother herself.

Floral house robe pulled over her thin legs, Gloria Jergens sat quietly in her living room trying to read a magazine. Tomorrow was the Fourth of July. They always used to go to the high school stadium on the Fourth of July, the three of them. How Sharla loved the fireworks, couldn't get enough, never wanting them to stop. The sounds of the mail carrier's footsteps on the porch stopped the memories. For days, she'd run the moment the mail arrived, hoping for the letter that would make her lost girl finally found. For days, there was none. She tried to wait this time, postpone the disappointment, but, like yesterday, could not, not being made that way. She was at the mailbox before the footsteps left the stairs, slowly going through the pile of bills and ads and...there it was! There actually was a letter from Sharla! Gloria held it to her breast, eyes tearing.

Please be OK. She began opening it with nervous fingers. Say you're coming home, my sweet, that you changed your mind. You'll marry Andy. We'll talk about the adoption. I *am* a good mother. You *are* a good girl.

Dear Mom:

Sorry I haven't written in so long. I'm doing fine. I've been having trouble finding a suitable apartment so I've been moving around a lot. As soon as I get a permanent address and a phone, I'll let you know.

On the shelf in my closet there's a green cardboard box. I need the stuff in there, my manuscripts. Would you please send them to me.

I have a P.O. Box; it's: P.O. Box 1428, Chicago, IL 60614.

Please send them right away. Thanks, mom. I'll contact you again soon. Don't worry, I'm fine.

Love, Sharla

Gloria Jergens read and re-read the letter. "She says nothing!" Throwing the letter on the table, the pacing began. Moving around a lot. What does that mean? P.O. Box. Oh, Sharla, how could you? Gloria Jergens paced rapidly between the tufted sofa and the glass-topped end table. Something must be wrong. Maybe she's in trouble. She wants her manuscripts, I suppose that's a good sign. But, no, it's not right.

Gloria Jergens called the Main Post Office in Chicago. She was told they could not give out the information she sought.

Then I'll go myself. I'll go to the post office and I'll wait. She went to Sharla's room, removed the green box, and began going through the papers.

CHAPTER 14

The script for Emma's film was going well, extremely well considering Sharla's rustiness. She had started on it almost immediately after their meeting, feeling sharp, confident, and enthusiastically equal to the task. It will be a quality work, she determined, worthy of the Landor name. She had done one other piece of writing recently, much more difficult than the script—a letter to her mother in Portland.

She was finding that she rarely thought about her past, rarely thought about Sharla at all. When she got two invitations to Fourth of July picnics, it never crossed Sharla's mind that she had always despised picnicking with groups. One she knew she couldn't attend, the one that would be crawling with Meredith's close friends, including the lovely Terri. The other picnic was sponsored by the Chicago Lavenders, a community group of mostly younger lesbians. Tracy, who Sharla had found at The Found, told her about that one and they went together, with Allison, too, who brought her grill.

Sharla met a great variety of women there, and again, liked them, most of them, even some of the spacey ones who sprinkled their talk with the goddess and seemed to have a thing for the moon, not to mention tofu and menstrual sponges. On a red plaid blanket, Sharla sat talking amicably, joking Meredith-style, with Allison and some women from the lesbian chorus.

"Hey jocks, we need one more player for our team. Come on, Meredith, you want to play?"

Sharla had been checking out the rowdy volleyball game off and on for the past ten minutes, tempted to join, but hesitant. Meredith, she knew, was very athletic, while she had mostly avoided sports herself, heeding mother's assertion of the inappropriateness of such activities for girls, after gradeschool, at least. Brainwashed moron! I can handle it, Sharla thought. In gym class, she had been forced to play volleyball and, though never enthusiastic, had done passably well at it.

"Sure," she said, jumping up from the blanket. Think Meredith, she reminded herself.

She did and did fine. In fact, whenever she "thought Meredith" she did fine, which was most of the time now, automatically. Allison applauded several heroic returns she made. Sharla basked.

From the picnic, they went to watch the fireworks from a twenty-third floor downtown apartment belonging to a friend of a friend of Allison. Each place she went, each group she associated with, Sharla felt at ease. Occasionally, she thought about the contrast. Very occasionally, she thought about the fact that she was living a borrowed life on borrowed time. Mostly she stayed solidly in each "now", and there were many.

The relationship with Allison was deepening, beginning to feel excitingly like what Sharla suspected people called "love". Frequently Allison commented on how Sharla had changed.

"You're more accessible," she said one time. "I mean, you're not aloof at all like you used to be."

"You bring out the best in me."

One day, coming out of a movie theater with Allison, Sharla spotted Jude. She was sitting on her parked motorcycle, looking like the sole owner of Lincoln Avenue.

Sharla waved. "Hi, Jude. What's happening?"

It was clear from their reactions that Allison and Jude did not know each other. Sharla introduced them.

"I haven't forgotten the picture I promised you," Jude said, her bright black eyes gleaming. "It's comin', it's comin'. You are looking good, woman. Your friend must be treating you right."

Sharla thought she detected a note of jealousy. God, did everyone have a crush on Meredith? A friend of Jude arrived and, after introductions and a few minute's conversation, Jude put on her helmet, brought the bike to life and roared off with her companion.

"Wow, so who was *that*?"

Sharla smiled. "An old friend," she said.

"Friend, huh?"

Sharla chuckled and ran her finger over Allison's narrow jaw. "I love it when you're jealous."

"You used to hate it."

"I hate it when you're jealous."

"You're nuts."

Next morning, Sharla decided it was time to get herself to the Lincoln Park Post Office and check her box. There was a short story that she knew was good. She wanted to work on it. A few revisions and she'd send it off. The package has probably arrived by now, she thought, but Allison called and then Emma and Sharla got distracted and didn't make it to the post office that day. Tomorrow for sure.

But the next day, Sharla didn't make it to the post office either. If she had, she would have gotten what she went for, and more. Gloria Jergens took her post out front, across the street. She waited from 8:30 until 4:30, and then went to her hotel to return the next day. She knew the package had arrived and had not yet been picked up. They told her that. She waited.

Sharla didn't go to the post office that day because she was too busy. She was working long hours on the script, hand writing it, then typing, revising, writing some more. She showed what she had so far to Emma who gushed over it.

"God, you can write, Meredith. I mean, I really like your films, but this stuff is super."

Sharla got many phone calls. She always let the machine answer them first. Sometimes, when it obviously was for her, which was most of the time, she'd pick it up while the caller was still there.

"Hi, Pam. Listen to this." She recited two mushily romantic lines from a poem she'd written in a weak moment for Allison.

"M-m, gooey."

"You're so honest."

"Only because I care. Are you busy tonight?"

"Well now, that depends." Sharla used this line every chance she got.

"Carla and I want you..."

"I'm yours...a menage?"

"For dinner, smarty. I mean, to come over here for dinner. Allison too, if she wants."

"Oh, for eating..." Sharla decided she was going too far. "Sounds good", she said, checking herself. She shouldn't out-Meredith Meredith. "I'll ask Allison. What time?"

"Oh, let's make it 7:00 Lesbian Standard Time, so around eightish."

"Pam, you're an adorable person."

Pam giggled. "You're a weird one." She giggled again. "I like you."

Sharla's eyes teared, knowing it was true. "Thank you," she said sincerely.

On Wednesday afternoon, Jude stopped by. Sharla generally didn't respond to the doorbell if she wasn't expecting anyone, but she had heard a motorcycle and went to the window. She buzzed Jude in.

"I told you I didn't forget," Jude said at the door. She held out a manila envelope.

Sharla did a quick review of her mental file on Jude Forerro. "Come in." Friend of Meredith for about a year and a half. Met at the women's coffeehouse. Meredith found her amusing, but a little too butch for her taste. Has a delivery service and makes a good living from it. Likes video games, especially Ms Pac-Man. "So, what's your high score these days?" Sharla asked, opening the envelope.

"High score? Oh, on Ms. One-oh-six. Can you believe it? I actually broke a hundred. That was a couple weeks ago. It's been down hill since then, unfortunately."

"This is great, Jude! Very nice job." Sharla held the photo at arm's length.

"Your advice paid off. Look at the contrast here. Look at that. Perfect, eh?"

"I'm going to frame it. Add it to my wall collection. Maybe there, next to the tower."

"Hey, I'm flattered." Jude reached into her pocket. "You wanna get high?" She pulled out a joint, lit it and passed it to Sharla.

Sharla took a small hit. It wasn't the first time, but it wasn't an everyday event for her either. Meredith seemed to smoke fairly frequently.

"Come on in the kitchen, I'll give you a beer."

Sharla found Jude charming. I suppose she is somewhat "masculine" but it comes off well on her, cute almost. Jude kept Sharla laughing with story after story of her misadventures on her delivery route. She stayed about two hours and her parting comment was, "You like me more now, don't you, more than you used to?"

Sharla was a bit taken aback, but recovered quickly. "I like you," she said, smiling.

It was after 4 o'clock. It was Wednesday. That meant it was time to straighten up the place and get out. Watergirl would be there soon. Sharla put Jude's photo in a drawer, washed out the glasses they had used, did some other tidying up, and took the garbage down the back stairs with her when she left. It was too late to go to the post office today. Instead, she went to the beach. She had her notebook with her, stuffed in Meredith's knapsack which she now used instead of a purse.

She found a comfortable spot on the rocks and sat contentedly enjoying the sight of the sun sparkling on the Lake Michigan water. A poem was forming. She let it play in her mind a while, and then began to write it down. It was sharp and up, a Meredith poem, positive, strong, forward-looking; a clear expressions of how Sharla was feeling these days — content, striving, self-loving, in charge.

"Excuse me."

Sharla looked up. The man was wearing cut-off jeans and a Schlitz t-shirt. He appeared to be about 30 years old, not bad looking for a man.

"This may sound like a strange question," he said, "but I really need to know the date."

"Mildly strange," Sharla replied, smiling. "July 11."

"The eleventh, thanks."

Sharla nodded.

The man stood looking at her, smiling clumsily. "I bet this is a good place to write," he said at last.

Sharla had her notebook resting on her knees, pen in hand. She nodded again.

"I won't ask if you come here often."

"Good."

"I really did need to know the date," he said, still grinning. "A friend of mine's coming to town on the 13th. In the summer I don't keep up with dates or time much."

"I see," Sharla replied, surprised to find herself rather enjoying this.

The man sat on a rock next to her. "I'm a teacher. I have the summers off."

"That must be nice."

"What do you do?"

"What do I do? Well, I write poems."

"Nice. For a living?"

"No."

"What do you do for a living?"

"I fish."

"You fish?"

"That's right."

"I never met a fisherman woman...a woman fisherman. Are you putting me on?"

"Now, why would I do that?"

"I don't know. 'Cause I'm bothering you? Interrupting your work?"

"Lake trout mainly."

"Here, huh? In Lake Michigan."

Sharla nodded.

"You have a boat?"

"An aqua plane."

"An aqua...You fish from a plane?"

"Yes. That's how it's mostly done these days."

"I didn't know that."

Sharla giggled.

"What?"

"You remind me of someone."

"Oh." He looked away.

"A guy named Andy I used to know."

"My name's Bill."

"I'm Wanda."

He nodded. "You're not kidding me about the fishing, are you, Wanda?"

"A lot of people are skeptical at first," Sharla replied.

"Yeah, well, it's an unusual occupation. It's hard to imagine how you would catch fish from a plane."

"Carefully."

Bill laughed.

Sharla looked out over the lake. She was remembering a time she'd been "picked up". It was at the wharf in Seattle. She had gone there after Allan, a man she dated briefly, told her he wouldn't be seeing her anymore. She hadn't been especially attracted to Allan, but the rejection hurt anyhow. It tapped the whole history of rejections and the pain grew tremendously strong, so Sharla decided to take a little trip, a long weekend in Seattle, to console herself. She arranged to take off of work Monday and left for Seattle Friday right from work. She was feeling especially ugly and unworthy and unacceptable and unlikable as she sat on the wharf, when David approached her.

At first, she barely spoke to him, but he persisted. She felt excruciatingly shy and inadequate with this attractive, charming, self-assured man. He persisted, however, and so she tried the best she could to hold up her end of the conversation. She figured he'd tire of her soon and leave, but he didn't. He stayed talking for over an hour, then invited her for lunch. They went to the Spaghetti Factory. She continued to feel uncomfortable and he continued to be pleasant and friendly. They ended up in her hotel room where he fucked her roughly, getting meaner and meaner as time went on, and then, calling her a cheap slut and some other choice names, he took all the cash from her wallet and split. Sharla didn't leave her hotel room the rest of the weekend.

The memory brought the feelings. The feelings brought Sharla and a flood of other memories, of her intense sense of alienation, and how absurd it was pretending to be a normal human being.

"I have to go now," Sharla said.

"Can I walk you?" Bill asked.

Sharla jammed her notebook into the knapsack. "No, I have to go. I'm in a hurry."

She nearly ran back to the apartment. It was after six and predictable watergirl had come and gone. As soon as she closed the back door, Sharla let the tears come. It was the first time she had cried in ages, the first time since deciding to take a crack at living before she died. The sobs wracked her. It was sickening. Of course I have to die, she knew. Meredith is coming back. Will the real Meredith Landor please stand up. She's coming back to take over. This is not me. I'm Sharla. Pathetic Sharla Jergens. Creep. Neurotic. Loser. Suicidal depressive who's going to be dead soon. It's July 11, Teacher Bill. Three more weeks. Three short flying weeks to cram in the rest of a lifetime. What an actress I've been. All an act. Nothing has changed. Sharla Jergens. Sharla Jerk. Loser. Slime.

Sharla had plans to meet Tracy at eight. Why continue the charade? Farce. Ridiculous. If Tracy knew who I really was, she'd puke. If Allison knew...If Pam and Jude and Ilene and Elise and...They'd all puke. If Dana knew and Adele...If Emma knew...and Jodie.

Sharla wiped her eyes. That's a lot of women. She held her chin up. Women I like being with. She straightened her shoulders. I've got three more weeks. I've got a script to finish. By God, Sharla, get back down there! You're not gonna take it from me. No way. Sharla went to the john and washed her face with cold water. She looked at her reflection. "Hi, Meredith." She smiled at herself. "You got some good book talking to do with Tracy and Clair and Paula tonight."

And they did. They discussed *Woman on the Edge of Time*, and picked the next book they'd read. They planned to meet August 8, four weeks from then. At the time, Sharla barely let it cross her mind that she wouldn't be able to be there.

CHAPTER 15

Allison was performing. There's a definite sensual quality to her music, Sharla thought, as she listened from a side table. In fact, Sharla found it very sexy. Maybe she was biased. A moderately large audience had turned out for the show and they, too, seemed to like what they heard and saw. Allison was the lead vocalist, singing mostly songs she'd written herself. There was also a bass guitarist and a drummer. The sounds were repetitive in a haunting, almost chant-like way.

They finished the second set at midnight and stayed at the bar another hour while Allison unwound.

"If I had to give up either biology or music, guess which would go," she said.

Sharla chuckled. "That's easy. Goodbye mice. And if you had to give up either me or music?"

"Oh-h, don't do that to me." Allison gave Sharla a quick hard kiss on the lips. "You love to torture me."

"I love to make love to you."

"Let's go home."

Sharla very much loved making love to Allison. From time to time, she gave fleeting attention to the fact that it had come so easily, her transition from men, such that that was, to women. So had the rest, though, she realized, all the drastic changes she'd made over the past month or so. Of course she had practiced, long and diligently, mimicking each gesture of Meredith, going over and over the phrases, the attitudes, the beliefs, the experiences. But it had so quickly come to feel natural. It crossed Sharla's mind again, as it had some months past, that idea about parallel lives. Maybe we really are one person. Maybe this is part of the plan, for me to pretend to be Meredith so thoroughly and so well that the merging can take place. Maybe Meredith is fading away right now, each day, getting less and less distinct, less and less real, until she'll disappear and I'll go on. I'll go on as her. Ah, yes, that would be nice.

Sharla brought her hand down along Allison's cheek and neck and across her bare shoulder. "I never thought I'd be in bed with a rock star."

"I never thought I'd have another chance with Meredith Landor."

"We're both rather fortunate queer lesbian dykes, I'd say."

Sharla couldn't articulate the vast difference she felt between making love with Allison and the sex she'd had in the past. It was almost as if they were totally different experiences, tapping different parts of her, meeting very different needs.

Allison slipped downward on the bed, resting her head momentarily on Sharla's belly, caressing Sharla's thighs softly with her long fingers. She continued down, an inch at a time, whispering her lips teasingly over Sharla's fuzzy hairs, until her tongue found the tip of Sharla's clitoris. Sharla arched her back instinctively and shivered. Allison's tongue moved slowly, then quickly, moistly, around and over, raising sweeping waves of heat in both of them.

Later, Allison spoke her thoughts. "I'm loving being with you." Her head rested across Sharla's chest.

"It feels good, doesn't it?"

"Nothing ever felt this good. I mean it. I feel very lucky."

"Let me ask you something," Sharla said.

"What?"

"Why do you like me?"

"Wow!"

"Tell me."

"Well... You're serious, aren't you?"

"Mm-hm."

"Don't let this go to your head."

"I'll try not to."

Allison sat up, leaning against the headboard. "I'll do it historically," she said, looking very serious.

"OK."

She took a deep breath. "Well, let me see... At first, I was attracted to you because you seemed so sure of yourself, you know. That was about three years ago, wasn't it? I watched you filming that meeting at the Chicago Lavenders. You just...you were clearly the woman in charge. I like that. I mean, I like that kind of thing a lot. Do you remember what happened that night?"

"What do you remember?"

"I went up to you after the meeting. You were packing up the equipment with that other woman...what's her name?"

Sharla did not answer.

"Oh well, whoever. I went up to you and said something stupid like...what kind of camera do you use? Or something like that. You stopped what you were doing and talked to me. I mean, you didn't brush me off or anything. You were real talkative and friendly."

"Of course. Look who I had a chance to be friendly with."

"Ha! So, anyway, I liked that about you. Then, when I got to know you a little better, I liked your sense of humor, dry and sarcastic though it may be at times. And your deep laugh. Like you did a few minutes ago. I like that. I like the things you stand for. Your feminism, your commitment to it."

"How about lately?"

"Well, all of that still, and how sweet you are to me."

"I'm sweet?"

"Of course you are. What's the matter, are you worried about your reputation?"

Sharla laughed.

"You can be pretty biting when something irritates you, though. But I haven't seen that lately. I remember the time you tore Kristin Gaynor to shreds. She was pushing you about something, I forget what, and you flattened her with that nasty mouth of yours."

"She deserved it."

"I know. But, basically you're real soft and caring. Especially lately. I guess I'm seeing the best of you."

Sharla felt a chill go down her spine.

"You're smart. You're creative. I like that about you. You respect my knowledge, too, and you're interested in my work and you think

I'm a hot singer. How could I help but like you, Meredith Landor?"

Allison shifted her position until her face was over Sharla's. She kissed her deeply. "I like you because I love you."

Sharla concealed the tears that she could not stop and held Allison tightly. They slept that way, in each others arms, through the night.

"Today I've got to get to the post office," Sharla announced the next morning.

Allison was getting ready for work.

"The manuscripts you sent for?"

"Right. They must have arrived by now. I wrote my mom...let's see, it's the thirteenth, I wrote her about two weeks ago."

"They weren't there the other day, huh?"

"I didn't check. I ended up spending the whole day on the script again. I'm obsessed with that thing."

"I think you like writing better than actually doing the filming."

"It does seem that way."

Allison took a last sip of coffee. "Gotta go. Talk to you tonight."

"Have a good one."

It was a long walk from Allison's apartment to the Lincoln Park Post Office. Sharla intended to grab a bus, but the day was beautiful and the walk was feeling good.

Each day that Gloria Jergens spent in front of the Lincoln Park Post Office was worse than the one before. She tried to stop her speculations about why Sharla hadn't shown up yet. She tried to keep calm. The hours dragged unbelievably. She was afraid to read. She had to keep her eyes on the post office entrance door, couldn't afford to look away, not even for a moment. Innumerable fantasies kept her company while she waited, fantasies about reunion: Sharla's surprise, her initial annoyance at her mother's presence, but then warming and talking with her. They would have a long talk at the new apartment Sharla finally found. She would help her daughter arrange things and decorate, would buy some furniture for her and Sharla would be so pleased. I *am* a good mother. My God, I devoted my life to her. I gave her everything—piano lessons, ballet, birthday parties every year, pretty clothes, toys, toys, toys and later the stereo, her own TV, a princess telephone. It would have been such a nice wedding. That was to be the climax, wasn't it? Why did she leave? Not satisfied with her life, she said. Needing to find herself. What does that mean? What nonsense! She had everything. And why is she asking about being adopted? Maybe I should have told her long ago. We'll talk about it. Maybe everything will work out just fine. Maybe she'll marry the doctor. Maybe my dream will come true like it almost did with Andy. Andy is such a fine young man. It almost came true. My dream almost came true.

A woman with hair and a build like Sharla's was coming down the street. Gloria Jergens sat upright on the plastic lawn chair she had bought and watched eagerly as the woman drew closer, straining her eyes, then she stood. Her legs were trembling. The woman continued along the sidewalk, less than fifty yards away now.

Gloria took a few eager steps toward her, then she stopped, her face dropping in disappointment. She could see now that it wasn't Sharla, it wasn't her girl, and so, slowly, she sat herself down again to wait some more. At least a half dozen people had questioned her over the last four days, storekeepers and people who lived in the neighborhood. At first she told the truth, but they asked questions and it was too painful, so then she started saying she worked for a detective agency and was watching the post office for a smuggler, a tall white-haired man with a beard. Those conversations were more fun, even though she felt guilty about the lies.

Gloria went back to the fantasies. They'd sit over tea in Sharla's airy little apartment and talk about the future.

"If things work out with me and Terry, we'll probably move to Portland when we marry. He'll be done with his residency in another year. You'll like him, mom. He's a fine doctor. He's eager to meet you. He'll be so pleased you're here."

I thought it would change after adolescence, Gloria Jergens thought. I thought she'd become more content, but it just grew worse. I raised her well, didn't I? I gave her the right values. Surely she should be happy.

It was 9:45. The opening time crowd had thinned and now there were just stragglers coming from time to time to the post office door. Many of them came with brown paper packages or left with them. Gloria needed to use the bathroom. The restaurant on the corner had a dirty little john with no towels, but it was the closest one and they didn't seem to object to her using their facilities. By the second day of her vigil, Gloria was bringing not only her lunch and chair, but a towel and soap as well.

She tried to ignore the pressure in her rectum, hating to leave for even a second. Each time she did, she'd go right into the post office

103

when she returned and ask if the package for Box 1428 had been picked up yet. She waited for another half hour but then the urge became too pressing. Just before entering the restaurant she looked up and down the street. No Sharla. She ran into the john.

Sharla turned the corner. She was walking slowly, deep in thought about the short story, the one she had written years earlier, six or seven. It was about a woman ending a relationship with a man. What intrigued Sharla was that it could have been written yesterday. Seven years ago, a feminist perspective was one she didn't understand, didn't explore and felt vaguely intimidated by. And yet the story, she was sure, had a very strong feminist perspective. She walked past the corner restaurant, crossed the street, and went into the post office. I've read so much and learned so much since then, and yet, in a way I already knew it, already sensed it even back then. She went to Box 1428. There was a slip inside. She presented the slip to the clerk and got her package. Sharla was excited, eager to go home and look at the manuscripts. A bus was coming. She ran the half block and got there just in time.

From the corner, Gloria Jergens saw her daughter running, saw the package in her arm. She tore after her. "Sharla!" Her voice screeched in her eagerness and her need.

Sharla dropped her coins in the box and took a seat in the rear of the bus.

Gloria, still running, could see the back of Sharla's head as the bus, oblivious to her feverish screams, pulled away. She ran after it. Her heel broke. She took her shoes off, jammed them in her bag and kept running. The bus was getting farther and farther away. She looked for a cab. Where was a cab? She was becoming frantic. Her hair had worked loose from the bobbie pins. She stopped a car.

"Please. My daughter...she's on that bus. I have to get her. Please, would you give me a ride?"

The driver looked at her with contemptuous annoyance, mumbled something under his breath, and drove on. Gloria Jergens could no longer see the bus.

CHAPTER 16

Six more days. Of course, Sharla had known from the start exactly when it would have to end. Sitting cross-legged on the rust-brown carpet in the living room, she drew on her cigarette, feeling nostalgic from the reminiscing she'd been doing. It was odd to be smoking again, but also, not odd at all. A short time earlier, when she'd gone for Meredith's travel agency receipt, she was hoping, somehow, magically, it would have disappeared — a sign that...but the receipt was in the drawer where it had always been. Angrily, Sharla grabbed the fateful reminder, crumpled it into a ball and threw it across the room. It landed at the base of the rhododendron plant.

Over the past few days, the familiar heavy feeling and an edgy restlessness and irritation had been insidiously taking hold of her. At first she wasn't sure why, what the relapse in mood meant. Nothing had changed. She was continuing to live out the rich, satisfying fullness of her life as Meredith Landor; seeing Allison, frequently, loving it, loving the feelings of being loved and feeling love; working on the script, feeling freely creative and capable; being active, involved with people and ideas. Nothing had changed, nothing except the dates, the passage of time. In the background of her mind, in some cobwebby place in the convolutions of her brain, the awful reality was stored, nudging her, subtly at first, and lately, more insistently. Six more days.

Sharla crushed out her cigarette angrily and lit another. The end of the "dream come true". Is that why it's getting hard to stay in the role, why the *Sharla* thoughts and feelings keep intruding? Sharla knew it was. The end was coming much too fast and she did not want to stop. Her hands formed angry fists pressed against the carpet wool. I'm not ready to give it up. She pounded her fists on her knees. I need more time. If only she would stay in San Francisco another month. Just one more month. She lay back on the floor now, her head at the foot of the wooden coffee table, thinking again of Allison and of her new self, her lovable, loving, interesting, alive self.

But you knew it couldn't go on, Sharla reminded herself, that it was all a game, based on deception and destined to end. She thought about her old self now, her self as Sharla. Right under the surface, *Sharla* was always lurking, wasn't she?

She remembered when she'd played the role of Anita in *West Side Story*. She had *become* Anita, strong and sensitive and caring. When she was on the stage, she was Anita and even on the set, socializing with the other actors and the director and stage hands. But as soon as she'd leave, the moment she'd walk out of the auditorium, there was *Sharla*, waiting, scared and alienated. No internal changes had taken place. Of course not. It was just a part in a play, just pretend. Was this play any different? Now, the stage and the set included everywhere she went, even when she was alone, even when she was with people who had no idea who Meredith Landor was. And yet, *Sharla* continued to lurk in the little in-between places, still popped up from time to time, the reminder that nothing was changing inside, that the play, like all plays, would soon reach it's final scene. Six more days.

Sharla felt a spasm shoot through her gut, and nausea. I can't possibly go back to being what I really am! She held her stomach, rolling over on the floor in the pleasant warm living room of Meredith Landor, who was coming home soon.

The sky outside darkened as Sharla remained, crumpled, on the floor. The day was ending. Killing Sharla is the only solution, Sharla thought, sitting up. She moved to a chair and sat with her back straight, her jaw set. I was absolutely correct in that decision. She nodded her head. My final fling, and then the end. That's the plan.

Yes.

But the sense of peace and relief she wanted did not come. There wasn't even a hint of the high that had accompanied her original decision to die. The fling was moving toward its inevitable end and she was not anywhere remotely near ready for it. Maybe the plane will crash, she thought suddenly. She felt a stabbing pang of guilt.

There must be a way. She leaned her head back on the chair, eyes locked on the ceiling as if the white plaster might have the answer. Unconsciously, her fingers reached for the hairs behind her neck. Would it be possible to go on with the act? The ceiling did not respond. It was different this time, different from those high school plays. Maybe it's possible. She's blood of my blood. This is different. It's not like Anita. Maybe I could do it. Maybe the play doesn't have to close. I could move to another city, Sharla thought. She was out of the chair now, pacing. New York, perhaps. I could go there and pretend to be Meredith. I could do what I did here, go places, to bars, and meet women, make friends, start anew. She was smiling now, nodding to herself. I'd take a new name. Kate, maybe. No, no I'd keep Meredith. I love that name, but I'd use a different last name. Stone, Meredith Stone. Sharla frowned then. Yeah, right, sure. Meredith Garbo Stone, the great actor, always on, always performing. The supreme imposter. She leaned against the living room wall, eyes closed.

How long would it take, I wonder, before *Sharla* crept back in? She visualized a snake slinking into her consciousness by way of her ear. I know she'd come back. She's been with me too long to crawl away and disappear. It wouldn't work. People would know. *I* would know. I can't just *act* it, the magic is in *being Meredith Landor*. Sharla felt energized again. Yes, and it was meant to be. I know it was. The other one should not come back. She's not supposed to. This is for me now. It was meant to be. I can't leave. I love this life. Sharla was moving around the room in random jerky motions. She thought of Allison. I don't *want* to leave. She thought of the friends she'd made and how they related to her as if she were someone and how they looked at her. I won't! I shouldn't have to. I shouldn't have to die. I'm entitled to a chance.

Sharla walked angrily, first to the window, then back across the room. Maybe she won't come back. A slight smile softened her agonized face. Maybe she's already disappeared. The smile broadened. Yes, and I'll just stay here forever. She stopped pacing and

107

rested on the arm of a chair, still smiling. I'll write film scripts and be with Allison. I'll live a life where I'm loved and respected and I'll love myself and respect myself. I'll respect myself like I respect Meredith Landor because I'll *be* Meredith Landor. She let herself stay with that fantasy for a while.

I don't want to die! Sharla was crying now. Through her tears, she saw the crumpled up piece of paper on the living room floor. Six more days. Her foot came down on the wadded paper ball with a heavy thud. I hate that bitch! Guilt came again, immediately. It's not her fault; she has the right to reclaim her own life. She's Meredith; you're Sharla. That's reality, asshole, accept it. It's her life, not yours. No! Yes, you have six more days; don't fuck that up, at least, enjoy what you have left, fool.

Sharla went to the study and got the script for Emma's film. She tried to work, but it was impossible to concentrate, impossible to shift back and pretend. She could do it for a few minutes and then *Sharla* would come back. Who am I, anyway? If I did it so well, if I fooled so many people, even myself some of the time, then I must be partly her. The merging is happening, that's it. Sharla's mind raced. She pushed the script aside.

I have to think. Hyperventilating as she walked, she paced back and forth between the hallway and the living room and the hallway and the living room. She paced for a long time feeling more and more stirred up and odd. The phone rang, but she didn't answer it, barely registering the sound. What is identity, she questioned? Are twins actually separate people? What is a person? What makes a personality? Am I still Sharla? Do I have to die? She paced, driven, until she obsessed herself to exhaustion, collapsing finally on the couch and sleeping fitfully with frightening dreams.

The worst of the dreams was almost like the bicycle one fabricated for Terri that time at the zoo. In the dream, Sharla was dancing down the street, lighthearted and free, on her way to meet Allison, when she sensed someone following her. She turned to look. It was a tall woman, gigantic, seven or eight feet tall and she looked just like Sharla, only huge. The woman was angry. Sharla ran from her, as fast as she could, but the woman pursued, chasing her through streets, down alleys, along the beach, in and out of dark and empty bars. Terrified, Sharla kept running, running as fast as she could, pushing herself to go faster, but the giant kept coming. She was gaining on Sharla, getting closer and closer. Sharla could feel the pursuer's hot angry breath on her neck and then a steel grip around her wrist, jerking her to a stop. Forced to face her then, Sharla stared with horror at this overpowering image of herself, and tugged impotently against the vice-like grasp which held her fast. The huge woman smiled calmly at Sharla's struggle. Sharla pulled desparately for her freedom, with all her strength, against a force that would not give. She pulled and pulled until, at last, her constrained arm began to pull away from her body. It tore, and tore some more, finally tearing off completely, ripping out at the shoulder socket. Howling animal-like, Sharla ran, one-armed, away, while the woman, laughing, came after her, catching her easily and taking another piece of her, and then another and another, until all of Sharla, every bit of her was gone and Sharla awoke screaming.

She didn't return any phone calls the next day nor leave the apartment. She spent the whole day alone, thinking, brooding, though she did not forget about her date with Allison that night. Over and over, she tried to force herself back into the Meredith role, to recontact her Meredith self. For short periods, she would succeed. Five more days. I want them, I want to enjoy them. Don't think of the future. She dressed, preparing for Allison's arrival, attempting to be gay, but relentlessly, the painful reality would push upon her consciousness. She struggled back and forth until Allison arrived. Although Sharla tried to be as she had been, Allison noticed the changes right away.

"Tell me, Meredith, what is it? Are you depressed about something? Talk to me."

But, of course, Sharla could not talk to Allison. She could talk to no one about the ache that was returning and why. There was only one thing to do. The pills were ready. She kept them in the top right dresser drawer in her bedroom, in *Meredith's* bedroom. Yes, *Meredith's* bedroom. *Meredith's* apartment. *Meredith's* friends. Respect and love earned by *Meredith*. *Meredith's* life. I have no life.

Sharla struggled through the evening with Allison. It was OK at the movie, but at dinner, it became too difficult to keep up the charade so she claimed a splitting headache and the pressing need to go home, now, alone. Allison was concerned and caring and took her home and offered to stay, leaving only when Sharla insisted she'd feel much better just to sleep, alone, and let the headache go. She slept very poorly, haunted again by disturbing dreams.

She did not pick up the phone the next day when Allison called.

She did not respond to the ring of the doorbell.

She sat, staring, unseeing, by the window, feeling *Sharla's* unbidden, unwelcome return, feeling it taking over.

At one point, as she sat bent over holding her leaden head in her hands, she suddenly started to laugh, to laugh out loud, at herself. Stupid fool! The laugh was ugly. Fake life. Ridiculous fraud. Imposter. Nobody. Spineless disgusting empty zero.

It was happening again, she realized, like the day that preppy guy had come to the door and wanted to know her opinion. Suddenly, Meredith gone; Sharla there again.

Her life came back with unwelcome vividness. Edge life. Outsider. Not connected. Barely real. Not real. Alone. Frightened. Shunning others. Feeling invisible. Untouchable. Unrecognized. Non-being.

And when I'm gone, no one will care. Her face was twisted into a bitter, pained grimace. Mother will cry, of course. Uck. Tears for her miserable self and for her miserable failure. Let her take the blame. Let her suffer, the repulsive sow. And Dad...Sharla's face softened slightly. Closed in, walled off Dad. You'll cry quietly to yourself, won't you, daddy, then you'll go back to the Wall Street Journal.

Should I leave a note? Should I tell Meredith? What about Allison? Poor darling Allison. There were tears in Sharla's eyes. That was the best part, knowing Allison, loving her. Sharla made herself push thoughts of Allison away.

There'll be such confusion. People will think Meredith is crazy. *What do you mean, you never came back to Chicago over the summer,* Terri will say. *What do you mean we never fell in love,* Allison will say. Sharla laughed. It was a strange weird high-pitched laugh. The living room was dark and silent, gloomily silent, except for Sharla's laugh, her strange eerie laugh, bouncing off the walls.

And Emma will want to know how the script's coming. *What do you mean, what script?* More wild laughter, strangling in Sharla's throat and turning to cries. She went to the bedroom. Opening the right top dresser drawer, she took out the silver box and opened it. With shaking hands, she poured the small white disks onto the dresser. She counted them. Twenty-four. More than enough.

Sharla remained standing in front of the dresser, staring at the pills and then at herself in the cold mirror that reflected her deterioration. She knew she was losing it. She stumbled to the bed. Oh, God. She was moaning, lying on her back, the soft light of the warm room highlighting the lines of pain that etched her face. "Welcome home, Meredith," she said bitterly. "Sure, come on back, Meredith. Take it all away from me, Meredith. Take it all, sister. Some sister! Bitch! You're no sister to me. Evil monster." A blob of saliva drooled down over Sharla's lip onto her chin. "Heartless, creeping thief. Self-snatcher."

Her jaw tightened angrily. "No!" she screamed. "No, I won't allow it." She was off the bed now, banging her hands against the wall. "You're not Meredith. *You* are not Meredith, *I am*! I've earned it." Sharla's breath came in deep gasps. "I worked hard. I did it. I've become you. I *am* you. I *am* Meredith and you can't have me." She was screaming it. In the dresser mirror across the room, she caught her reflection and stopped short. "Get away from me, Meredith," she yelled. The image mouthed her words, mocking her. "Get away from me." Sharla's shaking hands grasped a flower pot and threw it powerfully at the offending image, smashing it. "You can't take me away from me. Killer! Soul-snatcher! Get away! Get away!"

Sharla fell back onto the bed, sweating profusely. She writhed and twisted, her face contorted with the hate and pain that ripped her insides. "You have no right to exist anymore, soul-snatcher!" Her voice was hoarse. "It's my turn!" She rocked on the bed, moaning, sobbing.

A harsh buzzing sound came from the living room. The doorbell. Sharla tightened. "Is that she? The evil one?"

It rang again. "Go away, soul-snatcher!" Sharla stayed trembling on the bed.

A few minutes later, there was a knocking at the back door.

Sharla's eyes widened in panic, her whole body going rigid. She's here to take my soul! The panic overtook her. She scrambled from the bed onto the floor and inched herself underneath the bed, dragging bedcovers with her.

Allison peered through the kitchen window, but could see nothing in the darkness.

Sharla lay wedged under the bed, legs drawn up in a fetal position. You can't have me! She lay rigidly immobile for long minutes, then an hour, another hour, and most of the night. The phone rang periodically, horrifying her, and she'd pull herself inward, squeeze her body more tightly into the corner on the floor underneath Meredith's bed, terrified.

CHAPTER 17

Meredith was under the bed. Just her stocking feet could be seen, sticking out from beneath the madras print spread that hung over the edge.

"Can you see it?" Chris whispered.

Meredith did not respond, but in a few seconds, wiggled herself out with the hamster now safely in the little wire cage. Still sitting on the floor, she handed the cage to Cora. "Poor babe's been traumatized," she said. "She needs some of your T.L.C."

"She'll get a slice of lettuce and a lecture about running away from home," Cora said sternly. "Oh, look, she *is* scared. Thanks, Meredith. See you two later." She left, closing the door behind her.

Still on the floor, Meredith leaned against the bed, wiping dust off her jeans.

"How was it under there?" Chris asked. She brought her long frame down to the floor, too, and sat cross-legged across from Meredith.

"It was great. My whole life flashed before me. Past and future."

"Ah, like drowning. Tell me what you saw, especially the future."

Meredith chuckled. "It was very clear," she said. "I saw myself peacefully in my own bed in my clean, neat, orderly apartment, sleeping in, with no hamsters or cats or chaotic Coras driving me nuts."

Chris feigned a pout. "You're eager to leave."

Meredith smiled and put her hand on Chris' waist, pushing up her blouse and feeling the bare warm flesh. "I've got mixed feelings," she said.

Taking Meredith's wrist, Chris stood, pulling Meredith to her feet. "It'll be a long time before we meet again," she said smiling. "I think I'm going to ravage you before we part." She pulled Meredith to her, still holding onto her wrist, and kissed her lips, very passionately, a long long kiss.

Meredith swooned dizzily, laughing. "I think your kind of ravaging, I could get into." She sat on the bed, then lay back pulling Chris with her.

Over the past month, Meredith and Chris had been together on a half dozen occasions. Chris' flight schedule brought her to San Francisco frequently. Several times she had borrowed a friend's plane and taken Meredith flying, short trips mostly, and one to Seattle. Chris had a female lover in Tecumseh who sold photographic equipment and travelled around the country much of the time. She also had a couple of male friends with whom she had sex occasionally as well as a woman or two besides Meredith.

Meredith found Chris to be delightful company, thoroughly enjoyable whether they were talking, flying, or in bed, flying. Chris was an adventurer, Meredith concluded, a very dynamic, interesting, sexually hot, politically incorrect maverick, a perfect person to fling with, with no strings, guilt, fear of recriminations, hidden feelings, or any of the complications she did not need.

Meredith already had some good footage of her for the film on pilots, and Chris, very generously, gave Meredith flying lessons, as Meredith had hoped she would. Yesterday, for the first time, Meredith took the controls. She had lowered the wheels at exactly the right time. Chris nodded her approval. The runway was in view. Meredith concentrated each finely-tuned sense fully on what she was doing, aware of every relevant stimulus, oblivious to cues she did not need. Occasionally Chris uttered an encouraging "good" or "fine, you're doin' fine", and then they were on the ground and braking.

They went to *Mame's*, on Cole Street, to celebrate. Cora was there when they arrrived and Sarah and several other friends who cheered the moment Meredith and Chris walked in the door and broke into a chorus of "Wild Blue Yonder".

"Drinks for everyone," Chris said. "I want you to know I am very proud of this student." She had her arm around Meredith's shoulder.

Cora stuck a beer bottle in front of Meredith's mouth. "Well, Ace, do you have a few words for your fans? What's it like to soar through the clouds without a single flight attendant to fluff your pillow?"

"Ladies and women," Meredith said, taking the bottle from Cora and speaking into its mouth. "It was a peak experience. I felt high, I mean it, like I was flying. It was almost as if my feet weren't touching the earth. Very elevating." She took a long drink from the bottle.

From the bar, Meredith, Chris and Cora went to Cora's. They threw together a dinner, talked and drank their wine and then Meredith and Chris were retiring to Meredith's bedroom when the hamster escaped.

"It was a valiant capture, I must say," Chris said, stretching her endless body alongside of Meredith's. "Now I'm going to capture *you*." She took hold of Meredith's wrist and held it behind Meredith's head, pinning it to the mattress.

Meredith made some mock struggling movements. "That won't be easy. I'm a wild cat, you know, no pussy hamster."

Chris chuckled. "I love a challenge." She ran her tongue over her upper teeth. "I'll tame you."

Chris shifted herself until she was on top of Meredith, still holding her arm flat to the bed. As she kissed her, her free hand went to Meredith's belt buckle, undoing it, and then down to the furry mound, and two strong fingers went inside.

Meredith caught her breath. "I sense that you're feeling especially aggressive tonight, my dear."

"I am."

"M-mm."

They kissed again. Meredith shifted, intending to remove their clothes.

"You can't get away!"

"I'm not trying to ge..."

A powerful kiss stopped her words. "I think I'll have to tie you up," Chris said.

Meredith raised her eyebrows. "Oh?" She smiled seductively.

"Don't move," Chris ordered. She got up and went to the dresser, rummaged through the top drawer and returned with two of Meredith's scarves, a mauve one and a print.

Meredith leaned on one elbow, watching her, amused.

114

"It's clear you need to be subdued," Chris said, dangling the scarves before Meredith, then pulling them softly over her face. "First, the clothes must go."

They undressed each other, smiling, but not speaking, then Chris took a scarf and draped it around Meredith's wrist. "I'm going to tie you."

Meredith shrugged.

Chris looked serious for a moment. "You're OK with it?" she asked.

Meredith shrugged her naked shoulders again. "So far," she said, "kinky woman. I'll let you know if you get too wild for me."

"Have you ever...?"

"No."

Chris molded her face into mock sternness. "You need it," she said. Then her face softened again. "Say, um...let's see, all right, say 'hamster' if you want me to stop."

Meredith felt very aroused. She slipped her hand between Chris' legs. Chris grabbed her arm and pulled it away, once more holding her wrist firmly. "Not yet, woman. Not 'til I say so." She tied a scarf around Meredith's left wrist and attached the other end to the rail on the old iron bed.

Meredith was amused, amused at her own excitement and curiosity and at how terribly politically incorrect this was. She knew the arguments, pro and con. She felt strongly neither way. Chris tied her other wrist to the bed rail.

"There, now I can do as I wish with you."

Meredith tried not to giggle, but Chris caught the glint in her eye and began laughing herself. "This is serious," she said smiling.

"I know. I'm being tamed."

Chris stood back and looked down at Meredith hungrily. "That's a luscious body," she said.

Meredith, lying on her back, naked, arms tied over her head, slowly began moving her hips.

Chris' hands went to Meredith's breasts then slowly downward over the contours of her undulating waist and hips and thighs. "There's nothing you can do but enjoy it," Chris said.

Meredith was oozing. "Oh, all right," she managed to say as Chris spread her legs wide and brought her tongue to Meredith's cunt.

There was no need to say 'hamster'. It was another experience, a stimulating one in many ways, thought-provoking, too, and

Meredith knew she would write about it in her journal when she got home.

Chris left the next day to fly to somewhere in Idaho. They parted warmly, sure they would meet again, but not knowing when. Today, the mix for the film would take place, then feedback from the sponsors, the final editing, and then, on Thursday, Meredith would return home. She would miss San Francisco, but was eager to get home, to see Terri and to get back to the peacefulness of her own apartment.

CHAPTER 18

It had been quiet for hours in apartment 303 on Fullerton Avenue. No sounds could be heard in any of the pleasant, orderly rooms, save one. In the bedroom, from under the bed, came the strained sounds of Sharla Jergen's labored breathing. She had been cowering there for many hours, fading off and on into numb sleep. Her frightened rabbit eyes were wide open now, and had been for some time. Slowly, cautiously, she began to ease herself out from her hiding place.

It was quiet. Maybe it's safe now, she thought. The soul-snatcher must be in retreat, for now. She's coming back, though. I know.

Sharla's leg muscles ached. She could barely support her weight as she made her way to the bathroom where she remained, sitting on the toilet, for the better part of an hour, listening.

I've got to hide.

She started for the bedroom again.

No, she'll find me anywhere. There's no hiding. She'll find me. Soul-snatcher. She's not my sister. She's not even a person. An evil spirit. She wants me. She wants to make me Sharla again so I will die.

Sharla's eyes were swollen, her face lined.

She's coming.

Sharla ran to the front door to check the lock, then to the back. She went from window to window, locking them, drawing the shades.

Stay away from me, Evil.

She felt powerless.

I have to stop her.

Running into the kitchen, her bare feet slapping heavily on the floor, she took a knife from the drawer. And another. She took all the knives, lining them up on the counter. Fight evil with evil. It's the only way. God won't help me. No one will. No one can. God helps those who help themselves. She searched the kitchen for more knives.

Mumbling to herself, she dragged a kitchen chair to the living room, and placed it in front of the door, five feet from it. She sat, a large knife in each hand, and stared at the door, waiting. Fight evil with evil. God and evil. God and devil. If you can't join 'em, fight 'em. If you can't be 'em, fight 'em. She stared at the door, poised, listening for any sound, eyes wild, sweat dripping down her face, waiting for the door to open, waiting for the moment when she would plunge the knives into the evil soul-snatcher's heart.

An hour passed. Sharla's thoughts raced on. Two of us. Identical. Her hands were becoming numb around the knife handles. One with everything. One with nothing. She rocked on the chair as the thoughts bombarded her. Why did it happen? How? It's so unfair, unfair, unfair! Why? How? Her frantic thoughts bumped against each other, mixing, twisted, jumbled, wild.

Then suddenly her eyes narrowed and her mouth opened slightly. It was becoming clear. Suddenly, in a flash, it was all so clear. "Yes," Sharla said aloud. She recognized the truth at last. "Of course."

A huge gush of air escaped her mouth. Now I understand. She brushed back a strand of sweat-soaked oily hair. We were one, she and I. Yes, that's it. The two of us were one. Intertwined. Enmeshed. One person, one complete human being. Sharla put the knives together, holding them blade to blade. That's how it started, yes, now I understand.

But *she* wasn't satisfied. Sharla stared at the knives. No. She wanted it all. Bitch. She pulled out, didn't she? Sharla pulled her hands away from each other, separating the knives. That's what happened. She looked from one knife to the other. She made us two. Two identical bodies...but with opposite souls. Sharla's eyes teared angrily. *She* took it all. Her eyes were riveted on the knife in her right hand.

117

It was in the womb. That's where she did it. She grabbed it all, selfish hog. Left me nothing. Split off from me leaving me nothing. Sharla could picture it vividly. Left me empty. She looked at the other knife which she now held limply in her left hand. Sharla could picture it happening, en utero, one squirming wet fetus pushing out the other. She took all the joy, all the hope, all the love. She took all the strength. The knife in Sharla's left hand dropped to the floor. It lay where it fell on the shiny wood. She took everything. Left me nothing.

"Heh, heh," Sharla cackled suddenly. I tricked her, though. "Heh, heh." I stole some back. Her dry laugh echoed in the room. Now she wants me dead. She's coming. She won't share any of it. She wants it all.

Sharla rocked from side to side in the chair, full of the disgusting insight she had gained. Vile, unfair. She picked up the fallen knife and, still rocking back and forth, her hair wild and matted, waved the knives in the air. It's my turn. That bitch's selfishness will be recompensed. It will be reversed. I must be compensated. Affirmative action. Sharla giggled loosely. It's *her* turn to be Sharla. Sharla nodded her head. Yes, that's only fair. That's how it must be. She and I must switch. "Heh-heh." Switch souls. "Heh-heh-heh." I tasted your soul, bitch sister. Now I want it all! Slowly she moved the two knives towards each other. I'll take you. I'll force it from you. You take me. I'll force me into you, squeeze it in, all the fear and doubt and loneliness and pain. She pushed the two knife blades tightly against each other. I'll extract each drop of you, make it mine, make it me. Sharla switched the two knives in her hands, the left now in her right, the right in her left.

She stood. Her eyes looked clearer now, fierce and determined. It can be done. She took the chair back into the kitchen, and the knives. She lay the two knives blade to blade on the kitchen counter.

A simple shift of souls, mine to you, yours to me. She pictured their souls, misty things, crossing mid-air, passing over and through each other, then entering each other. It can be done, Sharla thought. Priests do it. Priests do things like that. They do exorcisms. They restore souls. I need my soul restored. I demand that my rightful soul be restored unto me.

Sharla went to the bathroom. She made some quick attempts at straightening herself up, ran the brush over her hair, splashed water on her face. She changed her clothes, choosing black slacks, a gray t-shirt and a blazer.

It shouldn't be difficult. They have ceremonies for everything. He'll speak in Latin, say the powerful words that will make our souls begin to stir. Jar them, loosen them. Mine already has a good start. Meredith's may fight it, but they have words, powerful words, for everything. In the beginning there was the word. Soul-switch words.

Sharla had no idea where the churches were. She walked randomly. It didn't take too long to find the first one, Methodist. No, that won't do, she knew. She asked passersby. The third person, a stocky balding man, knew where a Catholic church was. Sharla thought he would be the one to know, the third one, three, like the trinity. The church she sought was just a few blocks north of there.

Sharla waited nervously in the anteroom of the rectory. Finally, the priest bade her come in. He didn't look like a priest.

"You don't look like a priest," she said urgently.

He was young and athletic-looking, with rose glow cheeks.

"I'm Father Arlone," the priest said warmly. "What can I do for you?"

"You're a Catholic priest?"

"Yes." He offered her a chair, then sat across from her. "You're not a parishioner here?"

"I need a soul-switch," Sharla said.

The priest frowned. "A soul-switch?"

"It happened in my mother's womb. I don't know who my mother is. The other one came out there in the womb. We started as one. I would have been satisfied with that. A balance. Strong and weak. Some pain, but happy times. I could have loved myself then, but she took it all. She left me with the dregs."

"I'm confused," the priest said with obvious discomfort. "I can see you're upset, but perhaps, Miss...perhaps you should begin with simpler things. Would you tell me your name?"

"Which name? Which name do you want? The one *she* made me have, the old one? Or the one I should have, the one you're to give me?"

"Just your name, the name you use."

"Meredith Landor."

"I see. And where do you live, Meredith?"

Sharla took a wallet from her knapsack and pulled out a card. It was an old student ID from Columbia College. "See. Meredith Landor." Sharla looked at the card. "But there's no address on here."

119

She seemed quite distraught, as if she were about to cry.

"That's all right," the priest said reassuringly. "You can just tell me where you live."

"You'd think there'd be an address on it," Sharla said absently.

"It doesn't really matter," the priest said. "What do you do, Meredith? Do you have a job?"

Sharla raised her chin proudly. "I'm a filmmaker."

"Oh, I see, um, and what sort of films do you make?"

"Documentaries," Sharla said importantly. "Social issue ones, mostly. Some art ones. Feminist films. I'm a feminist. And a lesbian. I'm a lesbian, too. There's nothing wrong with that, you know."

"No," Father Arlone replied, "God loves all..." He was perspiring a bit, just below the hairline. "But you're troubled, Meredith. You seem very troubled. Can you talk slowly and tell me what it is?"

Sharla wanted to like him. He was gentle, wasn't he? He cared. He would help. "I know you can help me."

"I would like to try. What help do you need?"

Sharla leaned forward, her face now less than two feet from the priest's. "I need a ceremony," she said, "a Catholic religious ceremony." She nodded as she spoke. "There's a woman, she's coming back soon, what she did was, she stole my soul, my rightful soul, you see, and I want it back. I want my soul back. That's only fair." Sharla paused, then smiled slightly, a rather strange smile. "I want you to switch our souls," she said.

Father Arlone pursed his lips. "Meredith," he said softly, holding her eyes with his, "it isn't possible to steal someone's soul. No one can take your soul."

"*She* did. She took it."

"What makes you think that?" the priest asked patiently.

"I know it. She stole the good soul."

"You're not satisfied with your soul?"

"No, I want hers."

"What's wrong with yours?"

"It's...I hate it!"

"Hm-m. Maybe your soul is all right, Meredith, but maybe you need to work on it, make it more like you want it."

"No, no, that's no good." Sharla shook her head vigorously. "I'm entitled to hers. I want nothing to do with my own."

"Have you thought of any way other than switching souls to...?"

"No," Sharla said vehemently, "that's the answer, the only answer.

120

I'm entitled." She leaned further forward. "Will you do it?"

The priest repositioned himself on his chair, crossing his legs. "I'm afraid we don't believe in switching souls, Meredith." He looked very sincere. "But maybe what you can do is..."

"You won't do it?"

"Maybe if you saw a counselor." He folded his hands. "What it sounds like is that you might be trying to take the easy way out, that..."

"Are you saying you won't do it?" Sharla was glaring at him.

"What you're asking for, well, no, I can't do it. It can't be done."

Sharla stood. "Goodbye, priest!" She didn't look at him again.

"There are other options..."

She walked out the door and out to the street. "Useless fool," she mumbled. She walked frantically, without destination for close to an hour, her mind racing. There must be a way. Her throat was dry, her lips rough and chafed. She went into a McDonald's, got a coke and took a window seat. She drank the pop down in a few quick gulps and looked at the people around her. They all had their rightful souls. It wasn't fair.

Across the street was a cleaners, a boutique and a bookstore. Sharla's eyes wandered from one to the other and settled on the bookstore. *Astro Occult Bookstore*, she read. Occult, occult, what does that mean? Mystical. Secret. Magic! That's what *I* need. I need magic. I need it badly.

The bookstore was sweet-smelling and quiet. Astrological charts hung on the walls. Sharla made her way up and down the aisles. I need magic. She picked up a book here and there, at random, leafed through it, put it back. She went to the counter. "Do you have any books on soul-switching?"

"Soul-switching. Mm-m," the clerk said. "Let me see. I'm not sure what would specifically deal with..."

"I need a soul-switch badly. You must have something."

A man stood near the counter, listening.

The clerk rubbed his chin. "I'm not sure I know exactly..."

"Perhaps *I* can help." The man was very tall and very thin. His face was especially thin. His eyes were blue and sparkly.

Sharla turned to him eagerly. "You know about soul-switching?"

The man nodded. "I do, indeed." He looked deeply into her eyes. "Come," he said gently, guiding Sharla toward the exit. "I believe you and I should have a talk."

CHAPTER 19

Sharla made the call to Allison. It took all her strength to pull it off, to stay in character. "I feel terrible that I didn't call you sooner. You must have been worried."

"I was out of my mind! You had that awful headache and then I didn't hear from you in days. I thought about calling hospitals, then I'd think, maybe she's...you know, maybe she doesn't want to see me anymore... But, God, anyway, it's really good to hear your voice. I can't tell you how relieved I am. But what about the surgery? Is your mother going to be all right?"

"Yes, it looks like it now. It was pretty bad for a time. I'll stay with her a while longer, maybe a week or so. I should have called you sooner."

They talked for ten or fifteen minutes, every moment of it a painful strain for Sharla. But it worked. She was sure Allison believed her.

"I'll call you again soon."

"I'm real sorry about your mom. I miss you."

"Yes. Me too. I'll call you soon, Allison. I'll keep you posted."

She did miss Allison. The phone conversation made her realize how much. That fucking soul-snatcher won't stop me. I'll be with Allison soon, she thought. All I have to do now is wait. She remained in the apartment, knowing she couldn't leave, couldn't take the chance of being seen. She left only once, to get the gun and other supplies. Ramal would do it. He was eager to do the soul-switch, and confident. Sharla was ready. She had everything she needed and all she had to do now was wait for Meredith to arrive.

She felt proud of herself, sure that it was truly going to happen, that soon she really would be Meredith Landor, completely, 100 percent. And Meredith, Sharla, could do what she wanted. Maybe she'll return to Portland, Sharla thought. Maybe she'll decide to marry Andy. Sharla smiled and continued brushing her hair. She had taken a shower, eaten a good meal and was feeling much better now. Maybe she'll kill herself. I wouldn't blame her if she did. Poor Sharla. If that seems the only way out for you, I wouldn't blame you. I'd understand. That empty life. No, you don't want such a life. You won't go back to Portland. You'll commit suicide, Sharla, of course, that's your destiny. Sharla felt sad for her soul-sister, but the sadness was short-lived. You had your turn, at my expense. She picked up a magazine and stretched out on the sofa. As soon as the ceremony was over, she would pick up where she left off. She'd get back with Allison. Sharla felt a warm tender glow at that prospect. She'd finish the script. I'll be what I was meant to be, she thought, have the life I'm entitled to.

It was July 31. Just two more days. The phone rang occasionally. Sometimes it was for her; sometimes for the other Meredith. Sharla never picked it up. The tape should be erased, she realized. She backed it up, back to the day she got her first phone call, and erased everything after that. Two more days. Tomorrow's Wednesday, then Thursday and she'll be here. Ramal is ready. Wednesday. Watergirl day, I can't forget about watergirl.

Sharla spent an hour of Wednesday afternoon in the office closet, just as she used to when she first came to the apartment. When watergirl left, there was a note and a key. *Welcome home. Your plants were lonely for you. Hope you had a great time. Your car's all gassed up and ready. It's parked up the hill from the Conservatory. Call me soon. Bobbie.*

So watergirl has a name, Sharla thought, fingering the car key. She recalled the lies she told as Meredith about why she was without a car. Repair problems, hard-to-get parts. No one had pushed her for details. It had been easy being Meredith, unbelievably easy. It would get easier yet. She was all ready. Everything was ready.

The next night at 7:35, Sharla pictured the plane landing. One more hour, she figured. The only good hiding place was the office closet. She was sure Meredith would have no reason to open it tonight, but was prepared for that, too, in case it happened. At 8 o'clock, she took up her post in the closet. It hadn't been difficult getting the 45. She acted as she was sure Meredith would; asked around, made a contact, bought it quickly in the back room of a barber shop. No problem. She was hardly even nervous during the process. She held the gun now, loosely, feeling confident. Eight thirty came and went. Sharla began to feel slightly uneasy. At 9:00 she felt nervous. By 9:30, agitated. The bitch better not try to betray me again, she thought angrily. Or, maybe... Her eyes widened in the darkness. Could it be? She was smiling wickedly. Maybe she's not coming back. Ever. Because maybe she doesn't exist anymore.

By 9:45 Sharla had nearly convinced herself that Meredith really had disappeared, that there would be no homecoming for there was no other Meredith, and then she heard a sound at the front door. It was the familiar watergirl sound, but Sharla knew it was not watergirl this time. Her heart pounded in the dark closet. She listened, listened to the door open, and then...there was talking. No! Goddamn her eyes, she's not alone!

She could hear Meredith's voice clearly. It sounded just like her own. That felt strange. And the other voice—Terri's. Of course, Terri had picked her up at the airport. Damn! Sharla was enraged, breathing in hisses. Shit!

It's OK, she told herself moments later, trying to find a more comfortable position in the cramped closet. Terri will leave soon. She strained to hear their conversation.

"I *really* missed you."

Silence. "Absence makes the heart grow rounder."

"No, blonder."

"Tubby albino heart."

"Is it too early to go to bed?"

Laughter. "Never."

"Maybe a glass of wine first."

"You're eager to taste my going-away present."

"I'm eager to taste everything." More laughter. "Do you want me to help you unpack?"

"No, I'll get to it tomorrow."

"Or the next day."

124

"Or sometime. Everything looks the same. It feels good to be here. Did I tell you I missed you?"

"You mentioned it."

The conversation was muffled then. They must be in the kitchen, Sharla thought, or the bedroom. I wonder if she saw the broken mirror yet. She'll blame Bobbie Watergirl, no doubt. It sounds like Terri will just *have* to stay the night. The bitch. Damn, damn! Sharla wished she had brought a pillow or something soft into the closet. It looked like she was going to be there a long time. She leaned her head back against the wall. The pistol rested on her lap.

There were a few more snatches of conversation, then footsteps into the office. Sharla gripped the gun nervously, her finger on the trigger. Don't open the closet, Meredith, whatever you do, don't...then she could hear Meredith listening to her phone messages. She felt relieved, but still held the gun ready. I hope she doesn't get suspicious that there are no more messages after...Sharla took a deep breath. Relax, she told herself. She heard Meredith leave the room. Everything's going to work out. There was silence in the apartment then, no more sounds came for over an hour. It must be close to midnight, Sharla thought. She was tempted to proceed, even though Terri *was* there. But, she made herself wait. She slept some, waking frequently. Her neck was sore. She patted the gun and the bag next to her, then dozed again. Finally, through the doorway crack, Sharla saw the room begin to lighten. It must have been around six when she heard the first stirrings. A few minutes later, there was conversation.

"I *want* to be up with you. Stop trying to send me back to bed. Believe me, I'll crawl right back in as soon as I send you on your way. Coffee, sourdough bread and orange marmalade. Admit it sounds good."

"I admit it. You want to take a shower with me?"

Meredith laughed. "I'll pass this time," she said. "I don't want to wake up completely yet." She yawned loudly. "This is my morning to be very lazy. God, I've been looking forward to it for days."

Sharla waited. It took them an eternity. Finally, she heard the front door open, more conversation, and then it closed.

Slowly, silently, Sharla lifted herself from the floor. Her legs were painfully stiff. Go to bed now, Meredith. Close your eyes. Fade away. The prospect of seeing her double churned in her. Curiosity was there, of course, but also disgust. Sleep, Meredith. Sharla had the gun stuck in her belt. She held the bag in her hand. Everything was ready. Slight postponement, but no matter. The apartment was totally silent. She waited ten more minutes then slowly and soundlessly stepped out of the closet and to the office door. The living room was empty, quiet. Two leather suitcases stood near the doorway. Sharla tiptoed past them, and down the hallway. The bedroom door was ajar. She crept silently toward it.

Meredith lay beneath the peach-colored sheets. She had one pillow wedged under her head, her arm resting on the other. Her hair lay loosely across the pillow, the auburn highlights shining against the darker strands. Sharla stood in the doorway. Meredith's eyes were heavily shut, her jaw loose. Sharla absorbed it all through her alert, darting eyes, her teeth clenched tightly.

She had removed the bottle from the bag. She opened it now. The odor filled her nostrils. She backed away a few steps and poured the clear liquid onto the cloth she held, wetting it just enough.

The gun still in her belt, Sharla made her barefoot way into the bedroom, inching step by step toward the peaceful, unsuspecting sleeper. She stood at the head of the bed, holding the cloth by two corners and moved it slowly closer and closer to the face that anyone would think was her own.

Sharla lowered the cloth. Meredith stirred. Sharla let the most saturated part fall over Meredith's nostrils. Meredith moved, opened her eyes and started to sit up. Sharla pressed the cloth firmly over her face. Meredith struggled groggily for a moment, then went completely limp. Sharla held the cloth in place for another half minute, then pulled it away.

She looked at Meredith's slack face. She couldn't stop staring. It was exactly what she expected to see and yet she was astounded. She stayed, bent over the unconscious figure for several minutes, digesting the sight.

Then she moved into action. Quickly, she left the room. She ran into the kitchen and opened the bottom drawer of the cabinet under the sink. The chain jangled in her hands as she removed it from the drawer, along with the handcuffs.

Meredith's return to consciousness was gradual. Her head felt heavy, clouded. I must have slept half the day, she thought. My head. She reached for it. There was a clanging, metallic sound. She opened her eyes fully. Around her right wrist was a silver shackle, and attached to the shackle was a chain.

"What the fuck!"

She bolted upright, grabbing onto the chain, looking around the room.

"Good morning."

Meredith's jaw dropped wide, her eyes saucered. She closed her eyes tightly then snapped them open again. She shook her head vigorously, banging on her forehead with her fingers, her eyes closed again. Then, again, she looked at Sharla. "Are you real?"

Sharla smiled. "More and more every day."

"Who are you? What's going on?" Such a realistic nightmare. I'm ready to wake up now.

"Don't you remember?"

Meredith narrowed her eyes, piercing directly into Sharla's. Sharla did not flinch, though she had to force herself not to look away. Meredith threw the sheet down and jumped out of bed in a swift angry motion. She pulled on the chain. The slack stopped suddenly. The other end was attached to the radiator pipe.

"What the fuck is going on?" she demanded.

Sharla smiled.

The chain allowed Meredith about a six foot radius of movement. She went as close to Sharla as she could. There were still about four feet between them. Sharla was leaning on the doorway. Meredith stood angrily facing her, wearing only her loose brown tank top and a pair of underpants.

"Will you explain this, for Christ's sake?"

"Do you notice a resemblance?"

"Who are you? Why are you doing this? Take this goddam chain off of me!" Meredith flung her arm around vigorously causing the chain to clatter dully against the carpeted floor.

"Calm down." Sharla moved back a few steps.

"Who are you?"

"Can't you guess?"

"I can't believe it!"

"What?"

"You. You...me. Are we twins?" Meredith spread her arms in angry confusion, her eyes fiery, glaring.

"Seems that way."

"Tell me! What..."

"You're curious."

Meredith backed toward the bed and sat on it heavily. "I'm curi-

127

ous. Good," she said sarcastically. "Will you talk to me?"

"Yes."

Meredith looked at Sharla, waiting.

"You stole my soul in mommy's womb."

"What?" Oh, God. The woman's insane. Fear joined Meredith's anger and confusion.

"I've come to take it back."

"You're crazy!" Meredith jumped to her feet again.

Sharla glared at her. "Don't say that!"

Meredith gauged it. "All right," she said. She took several deep breaths. "Why this? Why the chain?"

"I don't trust you."

"You don't trust me. What do you want from me?"

"Your soul."

"Good God!" Meredith lowered herself to the bed, and sat there speechlessly, staring. At last she spoke. "Well, how did you...how did you get here? Tell me how you discovered me. Are we really twins? Did you know you had a twin?"

"Not until recently."

"How did you find out?"

Sharla seemed willing to talk, even eager. She told her captive about Pam mistaking her for Meredith, and about Jude driving her by motorcycle to the apartment. She told Meredith about the photos and her conclusion that the two of them must be identical twins.

Meredith's eyes stayed riveted on Sharla throughout her discourse, listening with obvious fascination. "It's amazing!" she said when Sharla paused. "Twins! God." She kept shaking her head and staring at Sharla. "I can't believe it. I want to hug you and cry and rejoice but, this chain..." She raised her wrist. "This nonsense about taking my soul..."

"It's not nonsense." Sharla's eyes took on that strange look again.

"OK, OK. Tell me more. Tell me about yourself. Your life. Where have you lived all these years?"

"I haven't."

"What do you mean?"

"I haven't lived. I'm going to be born tonight."

Meredith felt a chilling fear, and anger. "It's hard to talk to you sometimes."

Sharla laughed. "When I don't say what you want?" Her expression became angry. "You're done, girl. You're done having everything. You're going to become Sharla."

"What are you talking about? Who is Sharla?"

"The name my fake mother gave me."

"Oh."

Silence.

"Sharla what?"

"Jergens. Ugly name, don't you think? But you'll know all that stuff soon enough. You'll know all about Sharla Jergens because tonight you will become Sharla. You'll know just what it's been like for me all these years."

Meredith forced herself to contain her anger and her fear. "You've had a rough life, Sharla?"

"Don't call me Sharla."

"Your life's been hard?"

Sharla went to the chair near the door and sat. She was still out of Meredith's range. "It's been miserable."

"How?" Meredith's eyes were soft. "How so?"

Sharla looked off into nowhere. "Unhappy. Lonely."

"Mm-mm. Will you tell me about it?"

"I always felt different..."

Meredith waited for Sharla to continue, her own mind racing. An identical twin. Mind boggling enough. But she's...unbalanced. Mentally ill. Delusional. Am I awake? Can this really be happening? Dangerous. Maybe very dangerous. Keep her talking. Gain her confidence. Then get her to unlock me. A twin sister! I wonder if mom knows. No, of course not, she'd have told me. A twin. Who could our parents be? Was Sharla raised by them? Why didn't they keep me? God, she looks exactly like me. Exactly. Even the way she's frowning now. And her hair. And her clothes. Hey, that's my t-shirt she's wearing.

"...ever since I could remember. At times I thought it was because I was better than everyone else. Unique. Special. But, mostly I felt inferior. I was always afraid of people. Mom said I was just shy and I'd outgrow it." Sharla looked at Meredith then. "But I never outgrew it!" she said angrily. "I wasn't shy. That wasn't the problem. *You* were the problem and I never knew it." She looked away again. "I sensed that something was missing and now I know what. You stole it from me. My soul. You left me a shell, a frightened, empty shell."

"How could I have done that?" Meredith asked softly. "I don't understand."

"You don't remember, that's all. It happened before we were born. You split me and took the best part."

"How?"

"I don't know *how*. That doesn't matter."

"You think you've been unhappy because I took something from you."

Sharla nodded. "That's what happened."

"Aren't there other possibilities?"

Sharla didn't answer. Her face was taking on that demented look again so Meredith changed the subject. "What are your parents like?"

"You wouldn't want to know."

"I would."

"Dad's bland."

"Bland."

"Quiet. Remote."

"He didn't relate to you much?"

"To anyone. I guess he can't. He's not bad, just...unavailable."

"Emotionally, you mean."

"Yeah. He's a businessman. Office furniture. He's an expert on office furniture. He's great with business deals, accounts, mergers, projected sales, overseas markets. He likes that better than anything."

"Better than you."

"Better than anything. You know..." Sharla's eyes were wet. "Deep down I think he's a kind man, caring. He just never knew how...how..."

"How to show it?"

Sharla nodded. She wiped at her eyes with the sleeve of Meredith's t-shirt. "Then there's mom."

Meredith waited. She was feeling hopeful. As long as Sharla kept talking rationally, she felt there was hope.

"Sometimes I thought she hated me."

"Mm-m."

"She always said how she loves me more than life itself, how I mean everything to her. She's a mess. She didn't know how to raise a kid. She was overprotective, nagging, critical...I was scared of her. I wanted her approval so badly, but no matter how hard I tried..."

"Couldn't please her."

"Never."

"I almost married Andrew Borman to please her."

130

"But you didn't."

"No." She looked up at Meredith. She smiled. "I'm a lesbian now."

"Oh, yeah? That's a recent change?"

"Recent. Mom would die. She would. She'd probably kill herself. She'd feel like an absolute and total failure."

"Too bad."

"I know. Ignorant. I really like being a lesbian. I'm in love with a woman now."

"You are?"

"An old friend of yours."

"A friend of mine? Who?"

"She's in love with me, too. Really in love. I think it's the first time I ever felt loved. She respects me."

"Yes."

"She calls me Meredith."

"She thinks you're me?" Meredith's heart was pounding. What had this woman done? Was what she was saying true?

"I will be soon."

Oh, oh. Get her off of that. "So, it was hard to get your mother's approval?"

Sharla shook her head. "Impossible. It's as if she had this complete detailed idea of exactly how I should be, and I never quite fit. Actually, I think I never even came close to it."

"Did she reject you then?"

Sharla thought about this. "In a way. She hovered over me, always wanted me around, but, in more subtle ways she rejected me. She kept trying to make me into someone she could love, *the* one, the image she had."

"That sounds really rough. Is she still that way?"

"Always. You'll meet her soon."

"I will?"

"Yes, after the switch. I imagine you'll go back to Portland for a while."

"Portland. Is that where you're from?"

"You've been there. We could have passed on the street without seeing each other."

"It's really exciting discovering you have a twin," Meredith said. It was, but Meredith was not interested in that now. She had to keep this odd, disturbed woman calm, listen to her and talk to her until she could talk her into unlocking the fucking handcuff.

Sharla smiled at her. "Isn't it amazing! It's just...amazing. I mean, I'm sure there were times, as a kid, that I wondered what it would be like to be a twin, but I never suspected that I really was."

"Me neither."

"But, we're not like regular twins. In the womb, you took my..."

"How did you happen to come to Chicago?"

Sharla shook her head. "I don't know. It was probably destiny. I bet it was. I think we were meant to meet because it's my turn now."

"You're turn for what?" As soon as she asked, Meredith wished she hadn't.

"To have the good life. To be you."

Meredith squirmed. How crazy is she? "Maybe you could come to have a good life as *you*," she tried.

"Ha! You won't say that after tonight. Once you see what it feels like to be me, you'll understand."

"Boy, I could sure use something to drink. I bought some orange juice last night. Would you like some?"

Sharla shook her head. "No, but I suppose I could get you a glass if you're really thirsty."

"I'd just as soon get it myself. I wish you'd unlock this. Really, it's killing my wrist."

"Can't. I'll go get the juice."

While she was gone, Meredith examined the chain. There was no way she could get free without the key. She wondered if Sharla had the key on her. In her pocket, maybe. Her mind raced with possible maneuvers. Maybe if she gets within my reach...

Sharla brought the juice, setting it on the floor where Meredith could reach it, then moved back. "I've enjoyed being you so far," she said.

"Being me?"

"I've been impersonating you. People think I'm you. Your friends. I fooled them all."

"You've actually been pretending to be me?"

"It won't be pretend much longer."

Meredith drank some juice and looked closely at Sharla. "You know, I feel very moved looking at you. I mean, realizing it. You're my sister. My blood. We could get to know each other. Trace our backgrounds together, find out how we got separated. I wish you didn't have this idea about switching. We could get to know each other and be friends, do things together. What do you like to do?"

Sharla kept her distance, not moving from the doorway. "Make films," she said.

"You're kidding."

"Well, that's a recent interest. Actually, I write."

"You do? And I make films. Maybe we could work together. Did you ever write a filmscript?"

Sharla's face lit up. "I'm working on one now. With Emma."

"Emma? Emma Greigh? You know her?"

"Yes, I told you I know your friends. Some of them. I know all about your life. Soon I'll know even more."

Meredith frowned pensively. "Do you hate me?" she asked.

Sharla jerked back as if she'd been punched. "Hate you? Do I...? As a matter of fact, I think you're great. Yes, I hate you. I hate you for what you did to me."

"You don't have to believe that."

"Yes I do! It's the truth. You stole my soul and I hate you for that. That can never be forgiven. It was totally selfish and unfair of you."

"What if I didn't do it?"

"You did."

"What if I didn't?"

Sharla backed a few more steps away from Meredith. "You're trying to trick me or something. I can't trust you. I have to remember that. I can't trust you."

"Maybe you can."

"No!"

Sharla left the room.

"Where are you going?" Meredith called after her.

Sharla went into the office and dialed the phone. "Ramal. It's me, Meredith...We're ready...Tonight, tonight for sure...Yes...She has no choice. I told you I'd make sure of that. She'll be here...Good. Yes. 11 o'clock. Yes."

"Could you come here," Meredith called.

"No. I can't talk with you anymore. I can't trust you."

"I can't hurt you. Just come here."

"No." Sharla stood in the hallway.

"I have to go to the bathroom."

Sharla went to the doorway. "Do you really?"

Meredith nodded. "I'd like to take a shower, too."

"I don't trust you. I have to stay away from you until Ramal comes."

"Who is Ramal?"

"You'll find out." Sharla started to leave.

"Hey, what about the bathroom?"

"I'll bring you a bucket."

"Oh, please."

"That's my offer."

"Goddam it, this is ridiculous." Meredith moved toward the bedroom window. The chain wouldn't let her get all the way there. "Hey, out there!" she yelled as loud as she could. "Phyllis. Phyllis Tremaine, call the police. A burglar..."

"Shut up!"

There was panic in Sharla's voice. Meredith shut up. "All right. It's all right, I won't yell. But, listen, I really hate this chain. Why don't you undo it. I'm not going anywhere."

"No."

"Why?"

"I can't trust you. I'm getting you a pot to piss in and then I'm leaving. I'm going to the other room. You stay quiet in here." Sharla closed the window, brought a plastic pail, then left the bedroom without looking at Meredith.

CHAPTER 20

Meredith stayed chained to the radiator for endless anxious hours. Sharla did not respond when she called out to her. She tried threats and pleading; she tried reasoning with her, but Sharla did not respond. At noon, she finally appeared, bringing Meredith a sandwich and a can of Pepsi. She neither looked at Meredith nor spoke, but set down the food and quickly left.

Meredith lay tensely on the bed, eyes narrowed in a troubled frown, struggling to make sense of what was going on and plan something. Who is this Ramal, she wondered. What the hell do they have in mind for tonight? She considered writing a note, fastening it to the wooden box where she kept her jewelry and throwing it through the window pane. She considered screaming and yelling until she got some response from Sharla. How crazy is she, Meredith wondered. How dangerous? Not once had Sharla gotten close enough to touch. She's not dumb. Of course not, same genes as me. But, so different, in ways. So similar, too. Uncanny. How does her mind work? By what process would an insane mind think souls could be exchanged? Meredith sat up, cross-legged, at the head of the bed. I can't imagine. Who could Ramal be? Ramal, strange name. Is he a swami? A religious nut?

Meredith's bedroom window faced the alley. Next door on the left was Phyllis Tremaine's apartment. The first window would be her john. On the right, nothing, the corner. Down below was the alley. People passed. The jewelry box might do, Meredith thought. Someone would pick it up, hopefully not an illiterate kid. They'd read the note, then call the police. Meredith had the jewelry box in her hand now. Of course, Sharla would hear the crash, she thought. She'd probably figure out what I did. Meredith tapped her fingers on the box. I could do a lot of crashing around first. False alarms until she started ignoring them. Of course, she might not ignore them. She might panic. She might drug me again...or worse. Meredith lay on the bed again. She was exhausted but knew she couldn't sleep.

Sharla was asleep. She lay on the couch, almost peacefully. The hours passed. When she awoke, she thought happily about the future. Sharla would leave, she thought. I'll see her off, put her in the cab myself. She'll go away and die and I'll stay here and live. There's money in her bank account. I'll use that and I'll earn more making films and writing. Sharla smiled. It will be wonderful. The phone rang several times, interrupting her reverie. Sharla listened to the messages from friends of Meredith and one for her, from Emma. Soon, I'll be able to return my calls.

At six, Sharla brought Meredith dinner. Again she didn't look at her and moved to leave the moment she set the tray down on the bed, but Meredith grabbed for her with lightning speed and caught her wrist before Sharla could get away. They tussled on the bed, shifting who had the advantage, their strength about equal. Meredith fought dirtier. She jabbed her elbow into Sharla's throat and pushed, trying, with her other hand to enter Sharla's jean's pocket. She did. She searched them all. There was no key.

Her hands were now around Sharla's neck. "Where's the fucking key? Answer me or I'll choke you. I'll do it, I swear."

Sharla's eyes were bulging.

Meredith loosened her grip slightly. "Speak."

"In the kitchen," Sharla gasped. "In the silverware drawer."

"Promise you'll get it or I'll choke you and not stop."

"I'll get it."

"You better." Meredith released her.

Sharla coughed and breathed heavily. Her face was red, her neck splotchy.

"You better."

"I'll get it."

Sharla walked slowly toward the door. At the doorway, she stopped, turning to Meredith. "Evil bitch," she said. "I knew I was right. You deserve what you're going to get."

"Get the key."

"Get fucked." She said it just the way Meredith would have, then slammed the door and did not return. Meredith cursed.

It was dark out now. Meredith lay motionlessly on the bed. She had turned the dresser lamp on giving the room a warm glow. The reflected light highlighted the reddish tinge in her hair and the lines of worry on her face.

The doorbell rang.

Meredith moved toward the bedroom door, as close to it as she could get. A minute or so passed, then she could hear a soft knocking at the front door.

"Who is it?" Sharla asked.

Meredith couldn't hear the reply but she heard the door open, then a soft-spoken male voice. She put on a pair of jeans and was just zipping them when the pair entered the bedroom. Ramal was tall and thin with blue eyes and a wispy dull black beard and moustache. His hair was about as long as her own, and Sharla's, but stringy. He wore a loose gray blouse with a pattern of small diamond-shaped figures up and down the sleeves and along the neck line, and he carried a large satchel.

Sharla stood next to him looking very excited. Ramal stared at Meredith then looked at Sharla and back at Meredith. His lips broke into a small smile showing gray teeth, some gold-rimmed.

"We must prepare the room," he said. He moved soundlessly to the window and pulled the drapes across it. On his feet, he wore gray suede mocassins without socks.

"Would you mind telling me what's going on," Meredith said to him angrily. "You're aware that I'm being held against my will. You're a party to an illegal act. You should stop now before..."

"Sh-h." He placed a finger of his ringed hand over his pursed lips.

From his satchel, he removed candles and vials, large pieces of print cloth, a scalpel, a cassette tape recorder, more candles, and incense sticks.

"Who are you?" Meredith demanded.

Ramal placed the tape recorder on the dresser and turned to her. "Be silent," he said sternly.

137

His authoritative air caused Meredith to pause, but only momentarily. "Do you realize you're being a cohort to a very mentally disturbed woman?"

"Shut up!" Sharla screamed.

Ramal raised his hand slightly to calm Sharla. He turned to Meredith. "Atmosphere is very important. We need calm for the ceremony. Quiet calm. I do not want to gag you. Hold your tongue, please."

It seemed so reasonable the way he spoke it. Meredith watched him silently. He continued his preparations, draping a patterned cloth over the bed, covering it entirely, the headboard, too.

"Another chair please," he said to Sharla.

She left the room.

In the center of the cloth-draped bed, he placed a thick mat, milk white, about two feet square.

Sharla returned with the chair. Ramal positioned it on the side of the bed, its seat facing the bed, and draped a cloth over it. He placed the other chair on the opposite side of the bed and draped it, too.

Ramal then distributed candles around the room, six of them, and chanted a string of undecipherable words as each candle caught the fire from the long stick he used to light them. He turned off the lamp. The room took on an eerie glow and soon the sweet smell of incense filled it. He beckoned for Sharla to close the door. She stood, eyes wide and hot with excitement, watching each move the strange man made.

Around his neck Ramal hung a large medallion, the center stone ruby red and huge. He turned on the tape recorder. Haunting, eerie strains of music began, high-pitched, flowing, with a chant-like rhythm. He gestured for Sharla to sit on one of the chairs. She did, bolt upright, ready.

He gestured for Meredith to take the other chair. She hesitated, then did so, mumbling, "mumbo-jumbo".

Standing behind Sharla, Ramal held up a thick, heavy black cloak. He recited some strange sounds and draped the fabric carefully over her shoulders. Around her neck, he hung a silver chain which held a piece of black polished wood with a blood red center. He continued his incantation as he worked.

He approached Meredith then, taking a position behind her. She turned to face him. Gently he turned her back. Reciting the strange phrases, he carefully placed a snow white, thick, embroidered cloak over her shoulders, and around her neck, he hung a smooth white wooden circle suspended from a golden chain. In the center of the white circle was a drop of red.

Ramal went to the dresser where he had placed a small stained glass vial. Uncorking it, he walked to Sharla.

"Foh-hoo-rah-me-aye-ee," he chanted. He poured some of the vial's contents into a tiny ceramic cup. "Drink," he said, handing it to her.

Sharla raised the liquid to her lips, her eyes closed, and drank.

Ramal went to Meredith.

"Foh-hoo-rah-me-aye-ee," he chanted. Again he poured from the vial into the little cup, and passed the cup to Meredith. "Drink," he said.

"No way."

He nodded calmly. "Drink."

"What is it?"

"It is for you to drink," he said softly.

"I'm not drinking that. How do I know it's not poison?"

Ramal held the cup up to the ceiling and then to his lips, drinking it all. He poured again from the vial. "Drink."

Meredith looked at Sharla. She seemed calm and happy. Meredith considered her options, holding the little cup in her fingers, and then she drank.

Ramal took the cup and vial and returned them to the dresser. He went to the foot of the bed and stood there, ramrod straight, between the mirror-image women. No one spoke. No one moved.

Within a couple minutes, Meredith's head began to feel fuzzy and pleasantly light. She stared hypnotically at a candle, entranced by the flickering soft yellowness of it.

Time passed. Meredith was not sure how much. Ramal began moving, almost floating it seemed, around the room. The music sounded louder, more freeing, and Meredith found herself swaying with it as it entered her ears into her mind and moved circling around and around within her head.

Ramal again stood at the foot of the bed between the two swaying sisters. He reached over and took hold of Sharla's hand, pulling it gently toward the center of the bed and placing it softly atop the white mat. He did the same to Meredith, taking the arm that was unchained and placing it next to Sharla's. Meredith did not resist.

Their hands were close together on the soft white mat, fingers nearly touching.

Bending over the bed, Ramal loosely wound a gold braided cord around each woman's wrist, attaching their arms together. Meredith could see that he was holding a scalpel and inside her head heard herself protest, fight him off and move away.

With the scalpel tip, a quick slit was made in the fleshy part of the middle finger of Sharla's hand. One round drop of blood rose out and rested there where she held her hand limply, palm up. Ramal took Meredith's finger between his own. She did not try to pull away but watched the drop of blood Ramal released growing on her finger tip.

The pungent incense filled Meredith's nose sweetly, the music her ears, along with Ramal's melodic sing-song chanting. He placed Sharla's finger atop of Meredith's and their blood mingled as he spoke the special words, his eyes closed, holding their fingers together, flesh on flesh.

The lightness in Meredith's head grew even more pleasant as she felt and listened and watched with removed fascination the two bloods being one. The scoffing thought, *soul-switch — ha!* came, but held no sway. She felt neither skeptical nor convinced, just neutrally there and not there.

Sharla was totally absorbed. When Ramal once again brought a cup for her to drink, she took it in like freeing nectar, feeling the changes happening. Meredith, too, drank unthinkingly, and soon the two soul-sisters faded further until they were quite asleep.

Ramal moved slowly about the room, tugging the patterned cloth free from under the dozing pair, folding it up, then pulling and pushing the two gently until each was fully on the bed, one identical body stretched out next to the other; one free woman, one in chains.

He finished his cleaning up and packed his things away. The music stopped. The candles were gone. Ramal had left and the odor of incense faded as the night wore on.

Maybe neither woman dreamed, or maybe Sharla dreamed of her soul finally freed, she possessing it at last, and perhaps Meredith dreamed of death.

CHAPTER 21

Sharla awoke first. The morning sun barely entered the room, kept out by the drapes. She rose to let it in, and stood there looking at the sky.

I feel good.

She closed her eyes. Yes, yes I do. I feel strong, very strong.

She began to smile, but the smile transformed into a pensive frown. She shook her head, her eyes still closed tightly. The memories...that shouldn't be. The memories are still there. I thought they'd be gone. Didn't Ramal say they would? Am I Meredith or not? She tried to feel deeply within herself to know.

I feel good.

I feel strong.

I must be Meredith.

But Sharla's too vivid. That shouldn't be. I remember everything about her. And Meredith, yes, I remember, but not enough, not everything. I should remember everything. I want to touch and wrap around the memories; to know how it was on the beach on my tenth birthday, to feel the pain for my dog I loved and lost. I want to think of Terri and fill with tender love; but Allison comes to mind. That shouldn't be. It should be Terri. The beach is from the photos and my fantasy. It's not mine. Sharla bit her lip feeling the tears of frustration coming. It didn't work, she thought, I'm still Sharla. The old memories are still in me; the new one's aren't. It didn't work! Her whole body was tight and shaking with the disappointment and anger.

She looked down at Meredith who was beginning to stir. It didn't work for me, but...Oh, no! For her? Could it have worked for her? Sharla buried her face in her trembling fingers. Then I'd have no soul at all! She moaned.

Meredith moved again; her eyes were half open now.

But no, that couldn't be. Surely, that's impossible. Sharla stared at Meredith. Maybe we're both sharing the same soul. Are there two Sharlas now? An ugly squeal of a laugh escaped her throat. Irony.

Meredith sat up. She looked at Sharla looking at her. "How are you?" she asked, rubbing at her eyes.

Sharla did not speak but a sound almost like a growl came from her mouth.

"That fucker drugged us," Meredith said. "We must have slept all night. Are you all right?"

"Who *are* you?" Sharla hissed.

Meredith's eyes looked very sad. "You want me to answer 'Sharla'."

"Well?"

"I feel no different."

"Nor I."

"It can't be done by magic, Sharla."

"Don't call me that, you bitch!"

"Learn to love her."

"You learn to love her. I don't want her." Sharla stomped across the room, then turned back to Meredith, her arms folded defiantly in front of her. "There's more we can do, you know. Ramal told me. There are many ways. He can use the dolls. He talked about that. He said he might use two identical dolls and that's how he'd do it. He should have used the dolls." Sharla had begun pacing and her talk was pressured. "I'll call him. He'll come again. He'll use the dolls and that will work."

She ran to the phone.

"May I speak to Ramal, please...Well, where did he go?...That's impossible...When will he be back?...That's impossible, he said we could try the dolls. I don't believe you. How can I reach him? You have to tell me how I can reach him...No! I don't believe you." Sharla slammed down the phone.

"I don't believe that bastard. I'll find him. I'll find Ramal." Her voice was panicky. Several minutes passed. She dialed again.

"Information...yes, would you give me the number of the Astro Occult Bookstore on Clark Street...Thank you..."

Again Sharla dialed the phone. After half a minute she slammed it down and returned to the bedroom, but she did not look at Meredith. Her movements were frantic. She got some shoes from behind the door and clumsily tied them with her shaking fingers. She stayed out of Meredith's range.

"Sharla, sit a minute. Let me help you."

Then Sharla did look at Meredith. Her eyes were wild. "Help me!" she screamed. "*You*. Help me. *You*, the curse of my life."

"I can be your friend." Meredith's voice remained calm and soft. "Let me try."

Sharla's shoulders slumped. She stood away from Meredith still looking at her. The wildness began to leave her eyes. "I don't have friends," she said.

"Let me try."

"You just want me to let you go and then you'll get rid of me. I know you hate me. You'll have me arrested."

"No."

"You think I'm crazy."

"You have some crazy ideas."

"I'm not crazy." Sharla's eyes were wet.

"You're desparate."

"I don't want to die."

"You don't have to."

"I want to be you."

"You want some of the things I have. You can get them without being me."

The two held each others eyes for a long time, Meredith sitting quietly on the bed, Sharla standing away from her near the door. Meredith's eyes were soft and sincere and inviting. Sharla wavered.

"Do you think so?"

"Yes."

"But I never have before."

"That can change. It will take hard work."

Sharla gripped the edge of the door, her face distorted. "I don't know."

"Let yourself try. Let me be part of it."

"You want to?"

"Yes."

Suddenly Sharla shook her head. "I don't believe you. You'll say anything. You're trying to manipulate me. No, I won't fall for it. I know how you people are. You'll just take what you want from me and then dump me."

"That's not true."

"Why would a person like you want to be *my* friend? I don't believe it."

"You're my sister."

"I don't believe you!" The wildness was coming back. "I'm not done. I'm not giving up." She was not addressing Meredith now, but talking aloud to herself. "I'm going to find Ramal. I'm going to the Astro Bookstore. We'll do it, I know we will."

Sharla left the bedroom slamming the door behind her.

"Shit," Meredith hissed. She pulled against the chain, venting her anger, knowing the metal would not give. Running her fingers through her hair, she shook her head. "This can't be happening," she mumbled. She poured herself a glass of water from the pitcher on the dresser and sat down angrily on the bed.

Sharla waited at the bus stop, nervously shifting from one foot to the other. She couldn't stand still so she began to walk. The rush hour was ending, traffic beginning to thin. Sharla kept walking, her mind filled with plans. I'll find him, she thought. He'll help. He promised. He talked about dolls. He said that was one way. He'll do it. He'll do it that way. He hasn't left town. That man was lying. Ramal wouldn't desert me. I paid him $1000. He had no doubt that it would work. He wouldn't leave. He'll do the dolls.

It was 9:30 when Sharla arrived at the Astro Occult Bookstore. The door was locked. She banged angrily on it, peered inside, cupping her hands around her eyes to see, then banged some more. The sign on the door said, "Open 10-8 daily". Sharla did not see it until 9:45. By then her hands were sore from the banging, her throat scratchy from yelling.

She looked at her watch. Fifteen minutes. For fifteen minutes, she paced, and when the proprietor finally arrived, she ran up to him before he even reached the door. "Where is Ramal?" she demanded.

"I beg your pardon?"

"Ramal, Ramal. Where is he?"

"Ramal? Oh, you mean Winkleman. The tall guy with the beard?"

"Yes, Ramal."

"His name is Ronald Winkleman."

"Where is he?"

The man opened the door. Sharla followed him inside. "I haven't seen Winkleman for a couple of days. He might have left."

"Left?"

"He was talking about going to L.A."

"You're lying."

The soft-spoken, pale-complected bookstore owner looked angrily at Sharla. "Look, ma'am, I can't help you out about Winkleman...Ramal. I have no reason to lie to you and I resent..."

"I have to find him."

"Well, I hope you do." He went behind the counter.

"You don't understand," Sharla said.

"Let me give you a warning, for what it's worth," the man responded. "If I were you, I'd be cautious around Winkleman. I don't know what you're into with him, but...uh...don't count on him too much."

"Liar!"

"All right, lady, I'm just trying to be helpful. So forget it. Do what you want. You can't hang around here, though. If you want to leave a message for him, OK. Write it down and I'll give it to him if..."

"I'm not leaving. He'll come here. He told me he comes here all the time. He says you give him tea."

"I give him tea."

"In the back room."

"Yes."

"Is he there now?"

"No, he's not. I told you I don't know where he is."

"You want him for yourself. I know he's back there." Sharla's eyes had the wild look. She started moving toward the rear of the store.

"Hey, where are you going?" The man followed her, blocking her way.

Sharla shoved him. He grabbed her arm. "Lady, you're going to have to leave."

"He's back there. I know he is." Sharla pulled her arm free and tried to push around him.

"Get out! Now!"

"Ramal!" Sharla screamed.

Two customers had entered the shop.

"You're making a scene. Please, just leave."

"Ramal!"

The customers stared.

"He promised to switch our souls," Sharla said to the people. "He tried but it didn't work." She began screaming. "Ramal, it's me. We need you again. We need the dolls."

The owner succeeded in ushering Sharla out the door of his store. "I don't want to have to call the police," he said. "Please, just go away. Don't make any more trouble."

"Go away. Always go away, go away. Ramal!" People on the street turned to look.

The bookstore man shook his head and walked inside the store.

Sharla paced, mumbling to herself, then finally disappeared down the street. Soon there was banging on the back door of the store. The owner could hear the shouts.

"Ramal!"

Sharla was still banging a few minutes later when the police car pulled into the alley.

"What's the problem, lady?"

Sharla barely looked at him. "Ramal is in there, I know he is. I have to talk to him."

"You're making a disturbance. You'll have to leave."

"I won't leave until I see Ramal."

"You'll have to leave, lady, or we'll arrest you."

"She stole my soul. Only Ramal can get it back for me."

The officer looked at his partner.

"Ramal!" Sharla banged again on the metal door. "We need the dolls. She's waiting. We're ready. The blood didn't work, we need the dolls."

"What are you talking about?" the officer asked.

Sharla turned her wild eyes on him. "You couldn't understand," she said hatefully. "You have your own soul, don't you?" Her voice was very loud. She stared into the officer's eyes. "The bitch stole it from me, in the womb before I ever had a chance. Get it? She looks so much like me, you'd be amazed. You couldn't even tell us apart, you fool, but don't you see, she has the good soul and I'm going to get it." Sharla turned her back to him. "Ramal!" she screamed. Bang! Bang!

146

CHAPTER 22

The room where they made her wait was mustard yellow with peeling paint and a flickering overhead fluorescent light. An attendent sat across from her examining his fingernails. Sharla was quiet now. She no longer yelled for Ramal. Her hands ached from the pounding and her wrists were sore. They had used handcuffs. She tried to explain that she didn't need to see a doctor, that she couldn't possibly go to a hospital, but they insisted. When she hit them and tried to run, they put the handcuffs on her. Did they get them from a leather shop like I did, Sharla wondered. No, cops got them other ways, she was sure.

The hospital was big and ugly, full of strange people and bad smells. Maybe it wasn't a hospital at all, Sharla thought. Did that sickly-looking, lying bookman set this up to keep me away from Ramal?

The door opened and a small, pudgy man entered the room.

"I'll be down the hall, doctor," the attendant said, leaving.

"Ms. Landor, I'm Dr. Eventon. I'd like to talk with you, ask you a few questions. You don't have to answer, but it would help if you do." He took a chair across from her. "I want to determine your mental status. What you say could be used in court. Do you understand what I'm saying?"

"My mental status is fine."

"Mm-hm. How are you feeling now?"

"I'll answer your questions."

"Good. How are you feeling?"

Sharla glared at him. She rubbed her wrists. "Angry," she said.

"You're feeling angry. Do you know what you're angry about?"

Sharla looked sad. "Everything," she said.

"What sorts of things?" the doctor asked.

Sharla took a deep breath and sighed. "Ramal disappearing." Her eyes looked very sad. "The soul-switch not working." She started to look angry then. "Those men making me come here. What is this place? Are you a wizard, too?"

"I'm a doctor, a psychiatrist. This is a hospital. Do you know why you're here?"

"So I don't find Ramal, I think. They don't want me to find him. They don't want the soul-switch to succeed."

"Soul-switch? What do you mean?"

Sharla looked at Dr. Eventon, from his balding head down to his scuffed black shoes. "Tell me, mister," she said. "Is there someone somewhere in this world who looks exactly like you, in every way, exactly like you?"

"Is there someone who looks just like you?"

"Exactly."

"Who is that?"

"She calls herself Meredith."

"Same name as yours."

"Exactly."

"So, there's another Meredith Landor who looks just like you?"

"Yes, she stole my soul."

"I see."

Sharla relaxed a little. Whoever this man was, at least it seemed he could have a sensible conversation. "I have a right to have it back."

"Yes. Tell me about yourself, Meredith. Have you ever been hospitalized before?"

"Hospitalized? Yes, once."

"When was that?"

"I had pneumonia when I was twelve."

"Ever been in a psychiatric hospital?"

"No. Why would I?"

"I don't know. Do you know what day this is?"

"Yes, of course. Wait, let me think. Meredith came on Thursday. I stayed in the closet all night. Then Friday Ramal came and we mixed our blood and drank the potion and slept. We must have slept one night. This must be Saturday."

"Good. And what's the date?"

"The fourth. It's August fourth. A guy at the beach asked me the date. I think he was coming on to me. Are you? Are you coming on to me?"

"No, I just want to talk with you for a while. Do you know where you are?"

"You say it's a hospital. It could be."

"It could be?"

"It could be. Or someplace else."

"Where else?"

"I don't know much about wizards."

"Hm. Tell me something, if you found a letter on the street, and it was sealed and addressed and had a stamp on it, what would you do?"

Sharla looked at him as if he were nuts. "That's a strange question to be asking at a time like this."

The psychiatrist smiled. "Yes. What would you do?"

"I suppose I'd drop it in a mailbox."

"Mm-hm."

The doctor asked Sharla more questions, one after another. She didn't mind answering them. He asked her the meaning of certain proverbs and had her count backwards by threes.

"And have you lived in Chicago long?"

"Yes and no."

"What do you mean?"

"Right now I haven't but after the soul-switch I would have lived here for several years. I came to study film. Columbia College."

"Yes, we noticed you had an ID card from there. But no other ID's. Why is that?"

"I have an identification problem." Sharla smiled, feeling the Meredith in her, then she giggled.

"I see. Do you have a job?"

"No."

"Are you married?"

"No."

149

"How do you support yourself?"

"I write. Filmscripts, mostly."

"Do you live with your family?"

"No."

"Alone?"

"Yes." The sad look was there again.

"You're lonely?"

Sharla looked away. "I need to leave," she said. "I have to find Ramal."

"Where is your family?"

"We have to get on with the soul-switch."

"You wouldn't tell the administrative clerk your address. Will you tell me?"

"No."

"Why not?"

"I don't want you to find Meredith. She has to stay there. I have to find Ramal and go back there."

"Go back where?"

"To the apartment. Oh God, I feel tired."

"Yes, you can sleep soon. You're a troubled woman, Miss Landor. We want to keep you here for a while. You can rest here at the hospital."

"I can't stay."

"It's better that you do. You can understand that, can't you?"

"I'm not sure if you're a doctor or a wizard."

"I'm a doctor. I'd like you to sign into the hospital. I'd like you to sign a paper agreeing to stay here."

"I won't sign."

"So you can rest, and get help."

"Can you find Ramal? That's the help I need."

"We'll talk about that. First, we need you to sign the paper."

"No! I'd like to kill that bastard."

The doctor raised his eyebrows. "Who would you like to kill?"

"That bookstore man."

"The man who called the police?"

"Yes. The bastard. He made this happen. I'll kill him and then I'll go in the back room and find Ramal."

"How would you kill him?"

"I have a gun," Sharla said, smiling coyly. "It's hidden. I bought it at a barbershop. I'll kill him and then Ramal will do the soul-switch."

"You need to be here in the hospital, Ms. Landor," Dr. Eventon said. "Think about signing the paper. I'll ask you again later. If you decide not to sign, then Monday, we'll go talk to the judge and he'll decide if you need to stay here even if you don't sign."

"I can't stay. I have too much to do." Sharla knew she knew what was happening and, at the same time, wouldn't let herself know. "You *are* a wizard."

The doctor left, and the attendant returned. He accompanied her down several long corridors to a locked door that said "Ward 6", then down some more halls to a sleeping room. "This is your bed, Meredith. Your roommates are at activities. You'll be going too, but not today. If you would give us the name of someone to contact, we could get you a toothbrush, pajamas, things like that."

Sharla shook her head. "No, I don't want to do that."

"We can find out, you know, but it would be easier if you just told us. You can go to the dayroom down the hall, if you want. We passed the john on the way here. I'll see you later. By the way, my name is Bill Riley."

Bill Riley left Sharla in the room of four metal beds, some lockers and a window covered with heavy mesh screen. She couldn't tell what she was feeling. Fuzzy, foggy, unreal, but real too and clear. A mental hospital, state-run. She knew that and yet she couldn't get it out of her mind that Ramal's enemies had brought her here. Wizards.

She went back out to the corridor. No one seemed to be around. *I need Ramal.* The thought echoed in her head. He can fix it. I need him. Be calm, Sharla told herself. Call him on the phone. Maybe he's there now and his lying friend is gone. The friend could be a wizard, Sharla thought. I need to call Ramal. She didn't know where her knapsack was. She tried to remember. Yes, they'd taken it from her in that office when she first came. Why had they taken it? She needed a quarter. Sharla walked along the corridor in the direction she had come, past the lines of offices and sleeping rooms. She was looking for the metal entrance door. Around the corner, she came upon an old woman, almost bumped into her. The woman, who was wearing two or three skirts and several blouses, mumbled something to Sharla as they passed. It sounded like "...eat my mother's pussy". Sharla hurried to find the door. It was metal with a small window, she remembered. There it was. She had seen a phone outside the

151

door, by the elevators. The door was locked. Sharla knocked loudly.

"Where you think you goin', honey?" The speaker, a short round black woman, maybe 30 years old, had come up behind Sharla.

"I need to make a phone call. Can I borrow a quarter from you?"

"You need a pass to get outta here."

"A pass? Well, do you have one I could use?"

The woman laughed. "I'm not God. God, I'm not God. I'm not God." She raised her arms high above her head, then lowered them. "You have to see a nurse about passes. Don't make passes at the nurse."

"Well, where's a nurse, then?" Sharla asked. "Can you tell me that?"

"Only God can make a nurse." The woman giggled.

"Do you know where a nurse is?" Sharla persisted.

"God makes passes at nurses' asses."

"Come on, for Christ's sake, where's a nurse?" She felt the Meredith in her.

"Where is Jesus Christ, for Christ's sake?"

"I think he took a pass," Sharla said. She turned and walked away, retraced her steps and continuing along the corridor until she came to the dayroom. A half dozen people sat in front of the TV. The picture flickered but they seemed not to care. Their faces looked blank, removed. Two people were playing cards at a table. Sharla approached them. "Do you know where a nurse is?"

"Who are you?"

"Where's a nurse?"

"You a psychologist or what?"

"No, she's a patient."

"She is? Well, I'll be damned. She looks like a psychologist to me. I believe Miss Harley is back there in the Nurse's Station." She gestured to a room off to the side.

Sharla went there and was told by Miss Harley that she could not make a phone call yet, that there would be a staffing on Monday and after that they'd decide if she could make phone calls.

"But I have to make one now."

"You'll have to wait."

"I don't want to wait."

"Sorry."

"No you're not."

"Go out to the dayroom now."

"I don't belong here."

"Mm."

"I'm not crazy, you know," Sharla said calmly. "This is all a mistake. I'm tremendously sane, can't you see that?" Her voice rose slightly. "I'm coherent, right? I'm in control of my faculties. Well-balanced. I'm absolutely perfectly psychologically sound." This last was said quite vehemently.

The nurse laughed. "I wish I was all of that. I can't talk to you right now. I have work to do."

Sharla left the Nurse's Station and wandered around the ward, exploring it. There was the dayroom, sleeping rooms, two washrooms, offices, a large empty room with a circle of chairs, a cafeteria. There was the door she came in and another door, the fire exit, both locked.

I'm a prisoner, she thought. Like Meredith. Both of us are. I can't even make a phone call. I'm locked in. It's a jail. Not fair. It isn't fair. *I need Ramal.* The panicky feeling was returning. Each time she thought of Meredith, the feeling came and her head felt foggy again.

Patients began returning to the ward. Sharla wanted nothing to do with them. She was not like them and they made her nervous. One of her roommates tried to have a conversation with her. Despite Sharla's attempts to tune her out, she soon found herself engaged. The woman was young and friendly. Her name was Sandra. Only occasionally did she seem any more strange than the people Sharla had met all her life. She showed Sharla a picture she had drawn.

"I'm working out my hostilities." It was drawn thickly in black crayon. A man lying on a hill with ten or twelve knives protruding from various parts of his body.

"That's a lot of hostility," Sharla said.

"I play it up. The art therapist likes it when I make drawings like this."

"Where do you go for art therapy?"

"The Annex. You'll get to go. You can draw whatever you want, but you'll have to talk about it afterwards. You gotta smoke?"

"No, sorry."

Sandra turned to the other woman in the room. She was sitting on the bed, her back to them. "Hey, shitface, gimme a cigarette." The woman ignored Sandra. "I'm always giving you cigarettes when you run out so give me one."

The woman ignored her.

"Is there anywhere you can buy cigarettes?" Sharla asked.

"That bitch won't part with anything. She's selfish. That's what her problem is. I told her that at the ward meeting yesterday. You know what she did when I said it."

"What?"

"Spit."

"She spit?"

"Yep, not at me, I'd have belted her. She spit on the floor. The nurse made her clean it up. Hey, shitface, gimme a goddam cigarette."

The woman leaned forward and spit on the windowsill, her back still turned to Sharla and Sandra.

"Ah, the hell with her. Get in before the streetlights go on," Sandra said and abruptly left the room.

Sharla went to the Nurse's Station again. "When can I leave?" she asked.

"I don't know. Why don't you go meet some of the other patients. See that woman in the corner. Her name is Anna. She's a nice lady. Go talk to her."

"I don't want to talk to her. Listen, I know I have rights. I have the right to a legal hearing before you can keep me here."

"Are you a non-voluntary?"

"What?"

"Did you sign yourself in here, or not?"

"I won't sign anything. I don't want to be in here."

"You'll be staffed on Monday morning. You really ought to just sign in; it makes it easier."

"For whom?"

The nurse looked at Sharla. She looked old, but Sharla had the feeling she really was younger than she appeared. "Go talk to Anna."

"I want to talk to a doctor."

"On Monday."

"I can't wait until Monday."

"You must."

This place is insane, Sharla thought. If I stay, she'll die and I'll never get her soul. If she dies, I'm a murderer. Killing my own sister. Oh, Sharla, no, you would never do that. You're not that bad. I'm not that bad, am I, mommy. "Listen, nurse, please listen." Sharla spoke rapidly, her eyes burning. "I left someone in my apartment, my doppleganger. She's chained there. If I don't get out, she'll die. She has no food and just a little water."

"Your dopple...what?"

"My twin."

"Oh."

"She'll die."

"Why is she chained?"

"Because I can't trust her. She'll try to get away."

"Get away from what?"

"From me. She doesn't want to switch souls. I can't blame her, I wouldn't either if I had the good one. It's my turn to have it."

"Why don't you go watch TV."

"Meredith will die."

"You're not making sense. If you want to talk with me you have to talk sensibly."

"I want to see a doctor."

"On Monday."

"Now."

The nurse turned her back on Sharla.

Sharla went to the opposite end of the dayroom and sat in an easy chair. She thought of Ramal. There must be a way to get out of here. He's probably home now. If I could just talk to him, I know he could fix everything.

Sharla ate at a long table with a room full of other patients. No one spoke much. The meal was macaroni and cheese and dry ground meat patties. She barely ate. Sandra found her and gave her a cigarette.

"I found these. On a table in the dayroom. Good luck, huh?"

Sharla smoked silently, then went to the metal entrance door, hoping it would open and she could slip out. It opened several times, attendants with keys coming and going, but they would not let her go. They let other patients go, but not her.

Sharla slept fitfully. Someone screamed in the night, waking her, and she heard pacing in the hallways. She dreamed of riding a bicycle in the woods with Meredith. They stopped at a stream and went swimming naked. They were both bleeding. They sat next to each other on a large smooth stone bleeding and their menstrual blood mixed and whirled together on the smooth rock and then Meredith disappeared and the sun broke through the trees.

Sunday dragged by painfully. Most of the patients were allowed to leave the ward and go to the canteen or the gym at the Annex, but Sharla was told she could not go. The ones who stayed seemed the craziest. Some were almost stuporous; some paced and gesticulated and talked incoherently. Several times a day, they all lined up for little paper cups of pills. Sharla did not, and wasn't asked to.

She tried to read. She tried to sleep. She tried to play cards or talk, but just grew more and more restless. People rarely approached her, except for Sandra. Sandra would talk warmly, be very friendly, then suddenly leave.

One of the aides talked with her. Elena was her name. Sharla tried to explain the situation to Elena and the aide listened, but shook her head. She must not have wanted to hear about soul-switching and chained doubles. It seemed she just wanted to talk about jobs Sharla had or things she liked to do because whenever Sharla mentioned her double, Elena turned her head away or changed the subject.

Sharla ached with boredom and frustration as the hours dragged endlessly. On Monday morning, Bill Riley, one of the aides, accompanied her to the Staffing Room. Four people were there. One was a psychiatrist, Dr. Greenberg, and there was a nurse and two other people, a man and a women. Later, Sharla found out the woman was a psychologist, her psychologist, the person she was supposed to meet with twice a week for talks. The other man, a social worker, began the "staffing".

"Admitted August 4. Brought in by the police. Making a public disturbance. Delusional. Refused to give much of a history. No address available. Wouldn't give names of any collaterals. Provisional diagnosis by Dr. Eventon is schizophreniform disorder; to rule out acute paranoid disorder."

"Do you know where you are, Miss Landor?" the psychiatrist asked.

The questions were much the same as those asked by Dr. Eventon. Again Sharla was told that she had the right not to answer and that the information she gave might be used in court for possible involuntary commitment. It seemed to Sharla that it was best to explain her situation so they could grasp the importance of releasing her. It occurred to her that they may not believe her, but she thought it best to try.

"I can solve my own problem if you just let me out of here. I'll find Ramal and everything will be OK."

"What's his last name?"

"Just Ramal. He's a wizard."

"What would you do if you found him?"

"Take him back to Meredith. He'd use the dolls and do the soul-switch."

"What you're saying isn't making sense, Miss Landor. If you tell us the name of a family member or someone else who knows you, maybe they can help us understand your story."

"I can't do that."

"What about the man at the bookstore?"

"That bastard."

"Why are you angry at him?"

"He wouldn't let me see Ramal. Don't you understand, I *have* to find Ramal."

"Do you want to harm the bookstore owner?"

"I want him the hell out of my way," Sharla said angrily.

"The things you're telling us lead us to conclude that you're mentally ill, Miss Landor. You threaten to kill people..."

"I just want to get out of here."

"It appears that you present a potential danger to others, Miss Landor...."

"*She's* the danger. Soul thief. She stole my soul from me. You should lock her in here, not me."

"We'd like to contact your family."

Sharla did not reply.

"Will you tell us how to reach them?"

Sharla did not reply.

"I'll call Columbia College," the social worker said. "We ought to be able to get some information from them."

"Fine. She won't sign in so we'll have to take her before the judge. Miss Landor, there will be a hearing this morning." Dr. Greenberg looked at his watch. "In fact, the judge is probably here now." He turned to the psychologist. "We shouldn't have any trouble getting the commitment. You want to take the case?"

The psychologist nodded and spoke to Sharla. "We'll be working together, Meredith. We'll talk about all these feelings you have, and about your double and Ramal and about your past. How does that sound?"

"Sorry," Sharla said. "I just can't stay. No, that doesn't sound so good."

157

The social worker, Dr. Greenberg, and an aide accompanied Sharla to a room in the Annex where a robed judge sat at a long table. Dr. Eventon was there, too. They all concurred that Sharla was suffering from a psychotic condition which rendered her a danger to others. Dr. Eventon diagnosed it as schizophreniform disorder but did not argue with Dr. Greenberg's preference for paranoid disorder.

The proceedings went quickly and left Sharla confused but aware that she had been involuntarily committed to Regan Zone Center. They told her the case would be reviewed in six weeks unless she decided to sign a voluntary admission before then. The psychologist, Dr. Granser, arranged to meet with Sharla after lunch, and then Bill Riley took her back to the ward.

Sharla sat numbly on her bed, one overpowering image filling her mind. The moment she had grasped that they would not let her go, the image came and it would not leave. It had edged in among the others, pushing them aside, until it was all that remained. The image was of Meredith Landor, the real Meredith, lying weakly on the bed, chained and dying, without food, without water. Ramal faded; Sharla's anger at Meredith faded; the hope to switch their souls faded. What remained was the image of Meredith Landor chained and dying.

Sharla's fingers clutched the thin white bedspread. "I can't let her die," she said aloud. Her breath was coming in gasps. I can't kill my sister, my flesh and blood. Her eyes were closed tightly, her fists clenched.

She stole your soul.

No.

Yes.

No.

Then you must die.

Maybe so.

Let her die.

No! She's my sister. She's a human being.

Soul-snatcher.

No. Good person.

Took it from you.

No. I like her so much.

You can be her. Let her die.

No, I must save her. She never hurt me.

Took your soul.

158

No. There's no such thing!

Sharla eyes shot open. She was alone in the sleeping room. She rose from the bed and went to the window, staring unseeing through the mesh covering. "There's no such thing," she said aloud. She let the thought play in her mind. *Was* there such a thing? *Did* she take my soul from me? She did, didn't she? Isn't it her fault? Sharla felt unsteady on her feet; she needed to sit again. Oh, God, I don't know. She sunk down onto the bed; her brain was spinning. Dropping her aching head into her hands, she sat then bent over on the edge of her bed. Doesn't she deserve to die? Wasn't it meant to be?

Yes.

No!

Soul-snatcher.

No such thing. Oh, help me, oh, God, oh, God, what's real? Sharla was moaning, now, her eyes closed again, her face buried in her hands.

"Oh, oh, you're having trouble, girl," the gentle voice said. "Anything I can do?"

Sharla looked up. A motherly-looking aide stood in the doorway. Sharla had seen her once or twice before. She didn't know her name.

"What is it, girl? What's wrong?" The older woman took a few steps into the room.

Sharla stared at her through red-rimmed eyes. "I don't know what to do," she said.

"You don't know what to do?"

Sharla shook her head. "I can't decide whether to kill my sister or not," she said flatly.

The aide pursed her lips. "Oh, my," she said. "Yeah, that's a big one." She came a little closer to Sharla. "Well, you want my opinion?" Sharla, pouting now, nodded her head.

"Well, the way I see it," the woman said, taking a seat next to Sharla on the bed, "sisters are hard to come by. Even if you got a slew of 'em, there's never too many."

Sharla remained silent.

"Now, how many sisters you got?"

"One," Sharla replied softly.

"Ooh, just one, huh? Hm-m. Well, personally, I don't think you oughta kill her." The kindly woman put her hand atop of Sharla's. "If she's givin' you grief, then maybe you just gotta side step her, move on out of her way. You're a big grown up and you got legs.

If you can't take care of a thing by trying then I say move on along on your own way."

Sharla smiled, not removing her hand from under the older woman's warm wrinkled one. "You make it sound easy."

"Ain't nothin' easy, I found."

"She's my identical twin."

The aide looked at Sharla, hesitating for a moment. "Well now, if that's the case, I'd suppose that makes it even harder. Identical twin, huh? Trying to figure out where she ends and you begin and who's who." She laughed robustly. "That's hard."

"Sometimes I think she stole my...my identity."

"I bet. Only mostly you know that really ain't so, don't you?"

Sharla nodded slowly. "Yeah, mostly."

The woman stood then. "Good," she said. She moved to the door, then turned back. "How about a game of rummy?" she asked.

Sharla didn't answer right away. Her thoughts were elsewhere. "I've got...I...I have to talk with someone," she mumbled. "Someone who can..." She looked up the matronly figure. "I have to see the psychologist. Thanks, um...thank you, but I've got to go find Dr. Granser."

Sharla tried to meet right then with Dr. Granser but was reminded by a nurse that her appointment time was for 1:00 and told she would have to wait until then.

Let her die, that's what you really want.

No, I'm not like that.

Yes, you are.

No, I'm not. Am I?

Yes.

No!

By the time 1:00 came, Sharla was frantic and agitated.

"My name is really Sharla Jergens," she blurted the moment she was seated across from the gray-haired psychologist. "I'm from Portland, Oregon. I found out I have a twin sister named Meredith Landor and I'm...I'm envious of her. I wanted to *be* her. That can't be. It's wrong. It's dumb, and...and, I think, impossible. You see, souls can't really be stolen or switched. I'm pretty sure..." Sharla wavered for just a moment. "Yes, I'm sure of it. What I have to do is move on. I have to move on, but I hurt her. I chained her. The address is 286 West Fullerton. Please go there. Send someone."

"OK, slow down a bit, Meredith. Now, let me see if I'm understanding you."

But the psychologist did not understand. She concluded that Meredith Landor's delusion was evolving in a new direction. She did say she'd have the social worker call the number Sharla gave in Portland and talk to the woman Sharla said was her mother. She also said they'd check out the apartment on Fullerton. Sharla gave Dr. Granser other names and numbers and the psychologist wrote them down, but Sharla was convinced nothing would happen, or at least, not soon enough.

Dr. Granser asked Sharla questions about herself, but Sharla did not reply. Meredith will die, she was thinking. Maybe she's already dead. Oh, God. I find my sister and I kill her. Oh no! She tried to calm herself. I have to get out. I have to save Meredith myself. Meredith, I love you. I'm not like that. Maybe somehow you could forgive me. Be calm, she told herself. If you're calm you can think of a way to get out. She responded to the psychologist's questions, talking about her life in Portland, about her parents, her sadness.

"I really find it boring here," she told the psychologist, near the end of their interview. "There's nothing to do."

"There's an Occupational Therapy group today. Would you like to go?"

"Yes."

"That could be arranged."

"Thank you. You'll send someone to Fullerton?"

"We'll check into it. I'll see you on Thursday. Same time, 1:00. Don't forget."

On the way to the Occupational Therapy room in the Annex, and at the group itself, Sharla was friendly and cooperative and consummately appropriate. She made a collage and assisted other patients and forced herself to be cheerful and pleasant. She played the role, acted as she knew Meredith would. When Bill Riley came to escort her and several other restricted patients back to the ward, he saw no reason to be particularly concerned about Sharla.

It was not hard for her to slip away. First she made sure she was at the rear of the group. Then, as they passed a john door in the corridor of the Annex, she slipped in. She counted to sixty then left the john and walked the opposite direction from the others, through the building until she was outside. She was on the grounds, behind the Annex, away from the main hospital building. She walked calmly, not too quickly, along the sidewalk toward the open gate, and out to the street.

161

CHAPTER 23

Moments after Sharla left the apartment on Saturday morning in search of Ramal, Meredith implemented her plan. She wrote a note, fastened it with rubber bands to the wooden box, smashed the bedroom window with a chair, and threw the box out. Then she waited, confident that soon someone would come and she'd be freed.

But hours passed and no one came, nor did Sharla return. Meredith remained alone with her thoughts all day, the silence cut only by the occasional ring of the phone. If she went as close to the bedroom door as possible, she could hear the messages. With two exceptions, they were all from Terri; they had plans for a very special reunion evening tonight. Terri will come, Meredith thought, trying to relax.

As evening fell, there were many calls without messages and then Terri did come. At least, Meredith assumed it was Terri when the doorbell rang; it rang insistently for a time and finally it stopped. Meredith yelled and banged on the floor and screamed for Terri to come around the back, knowing, of course, that she could not possibly be heard by anyone in the lobby. After the doorbell stopped, there was silence again.

Meredith grew increasingly disturbed, her anxiety mounting with

162

each hour that passed. Where the hell is Sharla? Does she intend just to leave me here? Doesn't she realize what will happen? Is that what she wants? Why hasn't anyone found the note? Meredith felt totally powerless, a feeling she hated more than any other. She tried to calm herself, but images of her bloated dehydrated starved body tormented her, stirring panic. She struggled to keep the images away. She yelled out the broken window; she attempted to pick the handcuff lock with her nail file, with a hairpin; and she cried some. Almost constantly, she thought about Sharla, angrily usually, sadly sometimes, sometimes with pity, but mostly she felt anger and rage and disgust and hate.

At 9:30 p.m. on Saturday, Terri came again to 286 West Fullerton. She rang the doorbell, pacing nervously in the foyer. Still there was no answer. She grew angrier and more puzzled. Everything had seemed all right when they were together Thursday night, more than all right. And Friday morning, too. Why would Meredith stand her up? Where was she all day yesterday and today? It didn't make sense. Terri wondered if Meredith was angry about the Alliance meeting last night? Was this her way of getting even? No, that's not like Meredith, not her style at all. Besides, she'd said she understood and even joked about being a "meeting widow". Something must be wrong. Maybe something happened to her. Maybe it has to do with that dream and that twin sister business, her sister, the witch. That whole bizarre episode last month continued to disturb Terri. She hadn't brought up the topic with Meredith but intended to soon, despite Meredith's request. Terri shook her head. Maybe she's flipping out, she thought.

She went around the back and tapped on the door a number of times, and looked into the dark kitchen. Nothing. Obviously she's not home, Terri thought. She's probably out somewhere having a good time. Bitch. Terri started to leave, then stopped suddenly. She thought she'd heard something from inside. Someone calling. She listened, cocking her head, her mouth slightly open. Nothing. My imagination, she thought, and stomped down the stairs.

Meredith was sure she had heard someone at the back door. The bedroom was the furthest room from the kitchen. She wished she had used the study for a bedroom. She had considered it. If only she were in the study now, then the person on the back porch would hear her call. She called out again. Nothing. Maybe no one was there. My imagination, she thought.

She slept fitfully that night. Her throat was dry, hunger pangs gorged her stomach. She awoke before the sun, her mouth feeling sandy, her head light. Panic was churning in her again.

At 8:00 a.m. the phone rang. It rang periodically all day Sunday. Pam called, and Emma and Paula, but most of the calls were without messages.

Meredith couldn't believe no one had found the note. She began throwing things out the window. Surely someone would see. She threw nearly everything the chain allowed her to reach, attaching notes to each object until she ran out of paper. She even threw a chair.

Three stories down, directly below Meredith's bedroom was a patch of weedy grass, garbage cans, and the alley. The grass and garbage area was now cluttered with things Meredith had thrown. They lay haphazardly in the tall weeds, hidden and ignored.

Against her will, the death thoughts came more and more. She tried to fight them but the thoughts kept coming, and, with them, a retrospective of her life, and what she had yet to do but would not. She thought of the people she loved and who loved her. Tears came. Wiping her face, she caught one salty teardrop on her fingertip and stared at it. Without water, she would die. How long does it take, she wondered? She had rationed the pitcher of water that Sharla left, but it was gone now. She thought of her parents. She thought of the ocean and of her friends, of the laughs and struggles and triumphs of her life. She thought of the things that had given her joy and of the sad parts, the disappointments, the losses. She thought of Robin, and missed her. She thought about women, of their ways, *our* ways, our struggle. She thought of Terri and of her sister, Jean, and her brother, Philip. She thought of all the things that gave her life meaning, of the thrill of seeing the first rough cuts of a new film, of crab legs dipped in butter, of trips she'd taken, of making love, of music, of her mother, of Terri. It had been a life she liked. She felt lucky for that, but there was so much more living she had still wanted to do. She thought of all the things she'd never do again, and cried softly, mourning her own death, staring at the tear on her finger getting smaller and smaller until it evaporated completely. After that, Meredith grew strangely calm. She lay back and closed her eyes.

Except for occasional ringings of the phone the next day, it was deathly quiet in apartment 303.

CHAPTER 24

Sharla walked east on Bryn Mawr, then decided she'd be safer taking side streets. She made her way steadily east and south until she was at Halsted and Belmont. She went south on Halsted to Wellington, east to Clark, south to Fullerton.

Under the flower pot, between it and the saucer, Sharla found the key. She had made an extra one and placed it there weeks ago, an old habit learned from her mother.

She was afraid of what she might find when she went inside. If Meredith were dead, Sharla knew her own life was inexorably over. It was not a plan exactly, but somehow she knew what she would do. She would unlock the chain from her sister's wrist and lay her gently on the bed and cover her, but not her face. It always bothered her when they covered the faces. And then she'd get the pills from the dresser drawer. As she waited for the drug to take her worthless life, she'd write a note: *Dear Mrs. Landor...* It would be a sad, guilt-laden confession and futile apology. She would praise Meredith, and praise Mrs. Landor for raising such a wonderful daughter. She would castigate herself and apologize again, explaining everything, knowing no explanation or apology could diminish Mrs. Landor's pain nor alter her own culpability.

The letter done, she would place a chair next to where Meredith lay and look at the lifeless face so like her own and see herself dead and know she was dying.

Sharla's hand shook as she turned the key in the lock.

It was chillingly quiet inside the apartment. Lifeless. She made her way, tiptoeing, through the still kitchen, past the empty living room and john. She went along the hall toward the bedroom but stopped several feet from the doorway, unable to go further.

"Meredith," she called weakly.

She cocked her ear and heard only the silence.

Pushing herself forward, one heavy step after another, she proceeded until she was at the doorway. She made herself turn the knob and forced her eyes to look inside.

The room was empty, very empty. The dresser top was bare, even one of the pillows was gone and the chair. The window had been broken, splintered glass glittered on the floor.

Sharla stared, her mouth wide, her body trembling. The chain was still locked to the radiator, but it had been sawed through and part of it was missing, the part with the other handcuff, the part with Meredith attached.

Sharla, shaking all over, slumped onto the floor in the doorway. *Oh God, it happened! I killed her! I killed my sister.* She bit the knuckles of her trembling hand; her eyes were red and wet. *She died right on the bed and they had to saw the chain to remove her corpse.* Sharla felt a wave of hot nausea. She ran to the john and vomited. Lying weakly on the floor next to the toilet, unable to move, the ugly image of the empty bedroom filled her mind. Gone, she's gone. Dead.

Gone, but maybe not dead, Sharla thought, suddenly, hopefully. Maybe she escaped. Maybe someone rescued her. She was perspiring, her lip quivering. What to do? Should I call hospitals? The morgue? Call Terri? Look around the apartment for clues?

Sharla pulled herself up heavily from the bathroom floor and began to investigate the apartment.

In the kitchen she found the rest of the chain, the handcuff, and the handcuff key, and also some dirty dishes she had not left. She *is* alive! She must be. I told her where the key was. Yes, surely, she's alive. Please be alive.

Sharla collapsed onto a kitchen chair. God, she must hate me. She shook her head. God, what have I done? What I put her through.

She isn't a soul-snatcher, is she? Sharla began to feel dizzy again. She stared at the horrible ugly chain, wishing wishes could take away what was. Taking the chain gingerly in her sweaty hands, she held it away at arm's length. I brought this into her life. Disgusting! She picked up the key, ran to the bedroom and undid the other handcuff, then took the handcuffs and the chain, the tangible reminders of her insane cruelty, and placed them in a paper bag. She found an old beat-up briefcase in the closet and put the few items that were hers, the pills, her wallet, the brass seal, some toiletries and some envelopes into it. The briefcase in one hand, the paper bag in the other, Sharla Jergens went out the back door and down the stairs.

CHAPTER 25

It wasn't until early that morning that Meredith had realized it. Her throat was parched raw, hope nearly gone. She was lying on her back on the bare bed, her eyes blank and dry when she finally thought of it. She remembered that in her backpack, in the bedroom closet, in the little side pocket, there was a saw, a camper's saw. Despite her weakness, she suddenly felt a tremendous surge of energy. It took her six hours. As Sharla was planning her own escape, from the Annex at Regan Zone Center, Meredith, sweating, her hands blistered and sore, sawed through the final sliver of metal on the silver link of chain and was free.

She had been without food for three days and without water for over twenty hours. In the john, she made herself drink slowly. The water was nectar. She allowed herself one glass, then stood leaning over the sink looking at herself. She did not look as bad as she felt, somewhat haggard, but not as different as she expected.

She made her shaky way to the kitchen and prepared a slice of toast. Only then did she allow herself more water. She ate and drank slowly and already could feel some strength returning. The key was in the silverware drawer as Sharla had said. Meredith unlocked the handcuff from her wrist, then phoned Terri.

"You won't believe it," she began; it felt odd hearing her own voice, "...what's been happening since you left Friday morning."

"Did you leave town?"

"Oh no." Meredith almost chuckled. "No, I was here." She rubbed her wrist. It was red, but the skin was not broken.

"I was worried."

"I'll bet. I want to tell you all about it, Terri. It's...it's quite a story. Are you free after work?"

"Yeah. Yes, sure. What happened, Meredith?"

Meredith's head was aching. "Not now," she said. "I'll tell you when we get together. It's a long story. I really need to tell it."

"I need to hear it. Should I come to your place?"

"I'll come downtown and meet you after work. I need to get out. How about Miller's Pub."

"All right. 5:15?"

"See you then."

"Meredith, are you OK?"

"Yes," Just weak, she thought. "I'm fine. I'll see you at quarter after five."

Meredith wanted to make some more calls, let her friends know she was back, see how they were; but she needed to lie down. She was feeling dizzy. She rested for an hour, mostly thinking about Sharla, wondering where she was and why she was as she was, despising her but also hoping she was all right, hoping they could...what? become friends, be sisters? The anger was powerful, and yet Meredith could not let herself believe Sharla had left her there to die. She's mentally disturbed, but not evil. Is she?

As Meredith was showering, Sharla was walking out the exit gate at Regan Zone Center and heading east on Bryn Mawr. Meredith drank some fruit juice, had a boiled egg and more toast and rested some more. Sharla continued walking. It was 4:10. Meredith tried calling Paula. No answer. She tried Nikki. Nikki was tied up at a meeting.

Again Meredith struggled with the questions about Sharla. Had she intended to come back but something interfered? Or had she actually left me here to die? Had she decided that if she couldn't have my soul neither could I? How disturbed is she? Will she be all right? The anger and sadness and concern kept competing. Maybe that Ramal character got ahold of her and drugged her or something. He's probably responsible for the whole soul-switch fanstasy, taking this vulnerable, gullible woman and latching onto her, feeding her crazy thoughts. Would he harm her? Meredith considered calling the police but decided instead to call that bookstore, the Astro Occult Bookstore. Maybe they could tell her how to find Ramal and then maybe she'd find out what happened to Sharla.

Meredith got the number and called. The line was busy. She kept trying, finally deciding she'd stop by on her way to meet Terri. She got the address and drove to the bookstore, still feeling somewhat weak but no longer fearing she might pass out. When she walked into the Astro Occult Bookstore, the proprietor's face whitened.

Obviously, he's met Sharla, Meredith thought, and obviously he's upset.

"I'm looking for Ramal."

"I'll call him and tell him you're here."

"Thanks."

That's strange, Meredith thought, watching him as he walked to the back room. She browsed around the store wondering what she'd do if and when Ramal came.

"He's on his way."

Meredith nodded and continued looking at the books, not seeing them. There were several customers in the store. Meredith wondered if she were being foolish. Was Ramal dangerous? Had he taken Sharla somewhere, harmed her, and now would see Meredith as a threat? Meredith shook her head. I'm getting paranoid. If Ramal wanted me, he knew where I was. Besides, he didn't seem violent, just bizarre, crazy maybe. Did he know Sharla left me there like that?

Three or four minutes later, two uniformed policemen entered the shop. They looked at the proprietor who gestured toward Meredith. The officers approached her.

"Miss Landor, we're going to have to take you back."

Meredith stared at them. "I beg your pardon."

"Let's go."

"What are you talking about? Take me back where?"

"To the hospital. Come along."

"Wait, what do you mean?" Her temples were pounding.

They reached for her and Meredith pulled back.

"Don't give us any trouble, lady."

"Tell me what's going on," Meredith insisted.

The officer looked at his companion, who rolled his eyes. "You belong in the hospital," he said. "You weren't ready to leave. Maybe you don't remember. The doctors will tell you all about it." He took Meredith's arm.

She did not resist, understanding now where Sharla had been. She could mention to the cops that she had a twin, that they were making a mistake. She laughed to herself. They'd really buy that. I'll have to wait until I get to the hospital to explain.

"I'm supposed to meet a friend soon," she said. "Could I make a phone call before we go?"

"You talk that over with the doctors," the officer responded. "Make your phone calls from the hospital."

They took her to Regan Zone Center. Meredith knew of this place. It was supposed to be vile, although she'd also heard it had improved some in the past few years.

"Well, well, look who's back," Bill Riley said.

Meredith looked at him blankly.

"I'm mad at you," he continued. "You got me in big trouble, lady, cutting out like that."

"Can I see the doctor?"

They had taken her straight to the ward. Bill Riley, apparently, had been waiting for her. "You have your appointment with Dr. Granser Thursday."

"I'd like to talk to a doctor right away. It's important."

"Oh, yeah? What's so important. Tell *me*."

Meredith looked down the corridor. It seemed fairly clean. There were several people in street clothes, probably patients, and a nurse. "Nurse," Meredith called.

"Meredith, how nice of you to come back to us."

"Can I talk to you?"

"Not now, dear, I'm preparing meds."

"Just for a minute."

"Now, Meredith, don't start making trouble already."

"Come on, I'll walk you to your room," Bill Riley said.

Meredith followed him.

"So, what did you do while you were gone? You obviously didn't get very far. You were gone...oh, let's see..." He looked at his watch. "About an hour."

"I've never been here before."

"Oh, really."

"The woman you're mistaking me for is Sharla Jergens."

"Mm-hm. She's got your soul, right?"

"Sharla is my twin. She's a very troubled woman. Apparently she left here recently and the police thought I was her."

"Oh, those police, always fucking up."

"I really do need to talk to a psychiatrist."

"I agree."

"How can I arrange it?"

"You could try writing your congressman."

"You're a pain."

"Oh, oh. Watch it, you, no acting-out allowed. Don't give me an excuse to get even with you."

Meredith turned her back to him. "Which is my bed?"

"How quickly they forget," Bill Riley said and left the room.

Meredith looked at the four metal beds and screened window and array of objects and then left the room herself.

In the dayroom, Sandra came up to her. "I thought you split."

Meredith felt uncomfortable. "I'm here," she said.

Sandra laughed. "Right, so how about a game of rummy?"

"I need to talk to a doctor. How can I do it?"

"Waste of time."

"Do you know how?"

"Ask Harley."

"Who's that?"

"Who's that? You goose! Go stick Aunt Rhodie's fat head in the fuckin' mill stream." Sandra walked away.

Meredith didn't get to see a doctor that evening, nor complete more than two minutes of conversation with a nurse. Only the night aide was willing to talk with her. Meredith liked her and also needed to have a normal conversation with someone.

"Have you been working here long?"

"Three years."

"Do you like it?"

"It's a job. The pay sucks."

"I'll bet." Meredith cocked her head. "Do I seem crazy to you?" she asked.

The aide laughed. She was a cheerful, round-faced black woman. "I don't know," she said. "What's crazy, anyway?"

"I don't know. A lot of the patients here seem crazy. Some don't."

"They all have their moments."

"Have I had my moments since I've been here?"

The cheerful aide laughed again. "Oh, you might say that."

"What did I do?"

"You don't know?"

"No."

"I don't know."

"Yes you do."

"Well, why talk about that? It'll just upset you."

"What did I do?"

"Nothing really."

"Nothing?"

"Just that soul-sister talk."

"Hm-m."

"You really believe someone stole your soul?"

"No."

"I didn't think so. Why do you say that stuff?"

"Just kidding."

The attendant laughed and they talked of other things. The next day Meredith asked Miss Harley if she could see a doctor.

"What do you want to see a doctor for?"

"I have to discuss something."

"What?"

"It's private."

The nurse turned her back and started to leave.

"Wait."

She turned.

"It's about that soul-switching business."

"I thought so." The nurse started to leave again.

"Wait. I want to explain why I used to believe that stuff, and why I don't anymore."

"Why?"

"Can I see a doctor?"

"You have an appointment with the psychologist on Thursday. It'll wait."

"I can't wait."

"Oh, yes you can. You've got to learn to be more patient, Meredith. Now, go on. Can't you find something to do?"

"No."

"Well, why not?"

"Why not? Look around. This place is a pit. There *is* nothing to do."

"You have to learn to occupy yourself," the nurse said. She walked away.

Meredith passed her time talking with patients in the dayroom. She was not allowed to leave the ward all day Tuesday. She was not allowed to use the phone. She saw no doctors, no psychologists, no social workers. The only staff was nurses and aides and the janitor, all of whom pretty much ignored her, except for an occasional remark by an aide. The patients fascinated Meredith. She listened to their fears and their delusional stories and quickly adjusted to expecting almost anything. The ones that were like zombies she found the most disturbing, and the ones that screamed.

By Tuesday evening, Meredith began to feel as if she *were* mentally disturbed. It was Kafkaesque. No one would listen, or if they did, they would not take seriously what she said. She felt invisible, at times, and totally ineffectual, as if the stage were set, the play written and her role unalterable. She was seen as mentally disturbed. She behaved as any stable, well-adjusted person in her situation would, and she was seen inexorably as mentally disturbed. After all, she was a patient in a mental hospital.

Wednesday passed much like Tuesday. Most of the patients were psychologically out of reach though there were some with whom Meredith occasionally connected. The nurses were condescending, the aides either rude or gruff or pleasantly friendly, but not at all helpful. Except for Sandra, Meredith's roommates spoke very little. There were moments when Sandra seemed quite real and present and reachable and then she would suddenly say something bizarre and leave.

The ward meeting was the worst. Meredith was told to go. She had nothing else to do anyway, but she was ordered to attend in a way strongly suggesting her preferences did not matter.

The meeting was chaired by Miss Harley. Most of the patients sat silently in the circle, some answered their voices, some complained about their money being stolen or piss on the floor of the john. Passes were discussed. Meredith requested one.

"You're not eligible," Miss Harley retorted sharply. "Anyone else?"

"Why am I not eligible?"

The question was ignored.

"I don't want to go to O.T. no more," a pale, red-headed woman said.

"Why not?" an aide asked. "It's supposed to be good for you."

"I don't like it."

"We're trying to help you," a nurse said.

"I ain't goin' back."

"Amity, you don't know what's in your best interest. I think you should continue going."

Amity got up and tried to leave the circle.

"Come back!"

She hesitated, then walked away. An aide went after her. There was cursing and scuffling.

"I think her Thorazine dosage needs adjustment," Harley whispered to the nurse on her right.

"I want to consult with an attorney," Meredith said.

Miss Harley looked at her coldly. "You, too, Meredith. Attorney's aren't what you people need."

"I insist. I have the right."

"Oh, really."

"It's my legal right."

Harley rolled her eyes. "This rights crap makes our work so tedious."

"I insist." Meredith stood.

"Sit down."

"I insist on seeing my attorney."

"Sit her down."

An aide approached Meredith.

Meredith looked him in the eye. "Don't touch," she said.

"Sit down!"

"Gestapo."

"Sit!" He came closer to her.

Meredith weighed it. Odds were bad. She sat.

The discussion turned to toilet paper.

Thursday at 1:00, Meredith was taken for her appointment with Dr. Granser. Finally, she thought; she hoped.

"I'd like to explain my situation."

"All right."

"I'm adopted. I was left at a hospital door. No knowledge of my parents was available. A week ago I returned from San Francisco where I'd been for three months. A woman came to my apartment. She looked exactly like me, amazingly so. Her name is Sharla Jergens, at least that's what she told me. My inference is that we're identical twins separated at age two months or so. She was raised in

174

Portland. She happened to come to Chicago and people mistook her for me. She's troubled, has had an unhappy life. She began to pose as me. People accepted it and she didn't want to stop when I returned. She came to believe that I had stolen her soul, and she thought we could switch souls through some weird ceremonies conducted by a man named Ramal. She handcuffed me to a radiator in my bedroom. When the soul-switching nonsense didn't work, she panicked. She was trying to get ahold of Ramal and left me chained in my bedroom last Saturday. I finally freed myself on Monday afternoon. I went to where I thought I might find Sharla, an occult bookstore, and the police came and brought me here. Obviously, Sharla had been a patient here and escaped. She's still out there somewhere. I clearly don't belong here."

The psychologist nodded as she listened to Meredith's story. "I see," she said, when Meredith stopped. "Sometimes you're Sharla and sometimes you're Meredith, is that it?"

Meredith looked at Dr. Granser with disbelief. "No, that's not it at all. What I said is true. I know it sounds bizarre, but..."

"It sounds like there are different parts of you, Meredith, that sometimes the Sharla part takes over and..."

"No, no, I see what you're getting at, but that's not it. There really is another separate person. It would be easy to check. Contact her parents in Portland."

"Last time you said they were *your* parents."

"There wasn't a last time, doctor. I really am a different person than you met before."

"Yes, you're behaving differently. You're calmer now, more reasonable. How do you see Sharla, what's she like?"

Meredith sighed. "Troubled," she said, "depressed, insecure, kind of crazy, but needy, hurting, vulnerable, scared, dangerous. I'd like to help her if I could. I think it's possible, but I don't know where she is. I'm worried. This Ramal may have..."

"And Meredith, what's she like?"

"Me?" Meredith was feeling impatient. "I was luckier than Sharla. I'm in pretty good shape. Healthy, basically happy. I'm...wait, are you believing me? Do you accept that there really is another person?"

Dr. Granser nodded. "Yes, metaphorically..."

"Damn!"

"That upsets you?"

"Listen, just for a moment, suspend your assumptions. Imagine that what I'm saying is true. It would mean, for one thing, that I'm being held illegally, right? And it would make a fascinating case for you to discuss with your colleagues, much more interesting than...than..."

"Multiple personalities."

"Multiple per...is that what you think?"

The psychologist didn't answer.

"You have a phone there."

Dr. Granser nodded.

"On the off chance that I might be telling the truth, would you, right now, either make a call for me or let me make one?"

Dr. Granser pushed the phone toward Meredith.

Meredith dialed. "It's making a weird sound."

"Dial 9 first."

Meredith did. "Terri...Yes, I know I did it again. I'm sorry, I couldn't help it. I'm in a mental hospital. Can you believe that? Regan Zone. The whole thing is unbelievable...mistaken identity...yes...it seems I have a twin wandering around the city...What?...What do you mean? I never mentioned her before. I never knew about her...I'm not pulling your leg...Feeble, lamebrained excuse for standing you up? No, really, it's true, I'm at a hospital. I can't get anybody to believe anything anymore. I'm beginning to wonder what *is* true...Damn it, Terri, you gotta come and vouch for me and bail me out of here. They think I'm nuts..."

The psychologist was leaning back in her chair listening.

"Would you come here, please...I am not bullshitting. Here, there's a psychologist right here. She'll tell you what I say is true."

Meredith handed the phone to Dr. Granser.

"Hello, this is Dr. Granser of Regan...No, it's quite true...I'm afraid I can't reveal that...I'm afraid I can't say. Confidentiality doesn't permit...Yes...yes you may."

She handed the phone back to Meredith.

"Good...yes, as soon as possible. Ward 6. Come right away, please, Terri, this is a real bummer. I've got to get out of here...Yeah...I know...I can't either...OK, hurry. See you soon."

Meredith hung up. "She's coming."

"She's a friend of yours?"

"Yes."

"And Sharla's too?"

176

"No, Sharla's never met her."

"I see. You have separate friends."

"Of course. We never knew of each other until...You don't believe a word of this, do you."

"I believe you and I have a lot of work to do."

CHAPTER 26

Terri hung the phone up and sat immobile at her desk. She was shaken from the conversation, unsure what to make of it. Frowning the way she always did when something was on her mind, she picked up a pencil and began to doodle. With Meredith, she expected surprises; that had been part of the attraction from the beginning. But a mental patient! It must be a mistake. Or could it be a joke? She shaded the left edge of the cube she had drawn. No, it wasn't a joke, Terri thought, re-running the conversation through her mind. Meredith had sounded scared, or, at the very least, distraught, and Meredith certainly isn't the hysterical type.

Terri knew she should get going, that Meredith needed her, but something was holding her back. The pensive frown grew even deeper. She realized she was feeling frightened herself, reluctant to go there and find Meredith....what? Find that she's crazy? Impossible. But, what's she doing in a nut house? Terri was drawing a row of question marks now, each one slightly larger than the one before. The memory of last July came again, of the weird conversation with Meredith at the zoo. *Twin sister... freaking me out...wizards...don't ever mention it.*

That conversation had been distressing Terri since it occurred, distressing her greatly, but especially since last Saturday when Meredith disappeared. And that strange dream. Twin sister, Terri thought, as her hand drew pairs of identical intersecting circles. Is it true? Is there a twin, or...? God, a mental hospital. She seemed so normal when she came back, her normal self. No, it couldn't be. Meredith is one of the most together women I know.

Terri recalled how they had met. It was about two years ago at the Lesbian Socialist Alliance. Terri had been the coordinator at that time and had conducted the meeting. Meredith was the only new person there. She seemed to tune in immediately to what was going on, made a number of comments and even one suggestion that the group ended up adopting. Terri had felt instantly drawn to her and, after the meeting, during the social hour, had sought her out.

"I'm glad you came tonight," she said. "You really had some good things to say." And your lips are beautiful. "How did you hear about us?"

"I saw you on TV," Meredith answered.

"Oh, on the panel discussion last week, the battered women's thing."

"Mm-hm. You mentioned this group."

"Are you thinking of joining?" Terri tried not to sound too eager.

"I came to get a closer look." Meredith looked at her closely, the edges of her mouth curling into a very slight smile.

"At me?" Terri thought she might have blushed.

"That's right."

"I'm flattered, but..."

"You're photogenic."

"Oh, then you're a photographer?"

"Filmmaker. I'm working on a film about non-mainstream leftist politicos. You might as well admit that you're one of 'em."

Terri laughed. "I admit it."

"When you mentioned this group on TV, I decided I'd check it out, see about including you in the film."

Terri nodded. "I'd like to hear more about it," she said. "Maybe you'll end up joining us."

Meredith laughed. "I seriously doubt it. I lost my patience with committes long ago." She smiled warmly. "But who knows what will come out of this."

Meredith never did join the Alliance. She did make the film though, and she and Terri got to know each other. It was clear that there was a mutual attraction but, since Meredith was heavily involved with Karin at the time, nothing had developed romantically. After the filming, they saw each other around occasionally. It was not until last winter that more began to happen. Terri had hoped all along that some day they would get together. She found Meredith one of the most interesting and exciting women she'd ever met.

At first, Meredith teased her about her being too busy for romance. "You're in love with the movement," she said. "Aren't you? That's your one and only commitment."

Terri laughed. "To what movement are you referring?"

"You know damn well. That feminist-dyke-pinko one."

"Oh, that one."

"Married to meetings."

"It's not that bad."

"Prove it by going out with me Saturday night."

Terri did, and that was the beginning. It wasn't hard to make room for Meredith in her life. They were growing closer and closer and then Meredith left for San Francisco. The separation increased rather than diminished Terri's feelings for her, and Meredith said she felt the same. The only thing that cast a shadow on it, and it really was weird, Terri had to admit, was that business earlier in the summer, the twin sister stuff.

Terri walked into the next office. "I have to leave early today, Marge. Something important came up."

Forty-five minutes later, Terri was escorted to the drab, cavernous dayroom where Meredith was waiting. She got a strange, sinking feeling to see Meredith there. A patient. Confined. Living behind locked doors. They hugged each other and there were tears.

"God, I'm glad to see you."

"Yeah, me too. What's it all about, Meredith? What happened?"

They sat at a corner table and Meredith told the story, starting with how she woke up to find herself shackled in her bed and confronted by the mind-boggling presence of another version of herself. She told the story slowly giving all the details about Sharla and her own reactions and ended with her visit to the bookstore and her incarceration. Terri asked a few questions here and there, but mostly listened.

"No one believes me," Meredith said at the end. "They think I'm Sharla. They think Sharla and I are one person. It's freaky."

"It is freaky," Terri concurred. "It's really unbelievable how it happened. It's kind of like your dream, isn't it?"

Meredith frowned. "What dream?"

"The one...you know, the recurrent dream...about the two of you bicycling through the forest."

"What are you talking about?"

"Meredith, cut it out. Surely you can talk about it *now*, after all this."

"I don't know what you're talking about." Meredith looked distressed.

So did Terri. "You don't remember our conversation at the zoo?"

"What conversation? When?"

"Last month, a few days after Jodie's party."

"Terri, what are you trying to do? Don't play with my head? It isn't funny."

"I'm not playing."

"You know I wasn't in Chicago last month. You know that. Why are you saying this stuff?"

"You don't remember?"

Meredith's breath was coming in gasps. She looked agitated, then she suddenly calmed and smiled. "Of course. Obviously." She leaned forward resting her arms on the card table. "It was Sharla! Don't you see? That's it, of course. She said she was going around pretending to be me. It was Sharla."

"Sharla?"

"Yes. God, Terri, it had to be. Tell me exactly what happened."

Terri told her.

"That was not me. It was Sharla. Couldn't you tell? Didn't you notice the difference?"

"You seemed strange."

"See! Only don't say 'you', it wasn't me."

"All right, Meredith."

Meredith looked at Terri, looked very intensely at her, directly into her eyes. "Terri, you do believe me, don't you?"

Terri hesitated. "I guess so, Meredith. I don't know. It's so weird. Where's Sharla now?"

Meredith shook her head. "If I knew that, I could get out of here. I have no idea where she is. Maybe she's with Ramal. Maybe she killed herself. Maybe she went back to Portland. Maybe she's at my apartment right now. I have no idea."

Terri nodded without saying anything.

180

"Terri, I've got to get out of here. They don't believe me. They think I'm psychotic. Multiple personality. They're not going to let me go. You've got to help me."

"OK, Meredith. How? What should I do?"

"Tell them. Tell them the truth. I'm me, not her. Convince them."

"OK, I'll try. What do you think I...how can I convince them?"

Meredith thought, looking around the room as she did. The Virgin Mary was in front of the TV crossing herself and mumbling. Sally was pacing back and forth between the center posts. A patient was asleep in the corner, her dress up, exposing the pitted flesh of her abundant thighs. Two aides were playing checkers.

"The best way, of course, would be to find Sharla, but who knows how long that will take. I guess proving that Sharla was running around Chicago last month posing as me while I was in San Francisco." She picked up a candy wrapper and began squeezing it in her hand. "I know! Get that shrink, Granser, to call Cora in San Francisco. Cora will verify that I was there at the same time you saw Sharla here, that I was in San Francisco all that time."

As soon as she finished the sentence, Meredith frowned and a little moan escaped her throat.

"What's the matter?"

Meredith's hand had formed a fist. She was tapping it on the initial-carved table. "I took some trips. I wasn't in San Francisco the whole time. When was that talk with Sharla at the zoo, when, exactly, what date?"

"I'm not sure exactly," Terri said. She unconsciously moved back a few inches. "Let me think. The party was in early July, I think, or was it the end of June."

"I can't remember for sure, either, when I left the city, San Francisco. I left several times. Once to visit my parents and then...I mentioned Chris, didn't I, the pilot?"

"Yes." Terri didn't look pleased.

"I took a couple of trips with her. In her plane."

"Oh."

"I just hope we weren't gone when..."

"Where'd you go?"

Meredith looked at Terri. She was so beautiful and so lovable. God, I've missed her. "It was nothing, Terri, really. Don't be jealous, OK? There's no reason."

Terri nodded and shrugged.

181

"There must be other people, people who saw Sharla in Chicago while I was in San Francisco. All we have to do is prove it. Coordinate it. Compare the stories."

"You never had that dream?"

Meredith glared at Terri. "That wasn't me, dammit! You don't believe it, do you?"

Terri's eyes filled with tears.

Meredith was crying now, too. "You think I'm crazy."

Terri did try to convince Dr. Granser. They met together for over an hour. When Terri left, she felt very sad. She had tried to sound convinced and convincing but it didn't take much time for the two of them to be discussing Meredith's pathological condition, the possible reasons for it, and the treatment Dr. Granser would attempt. Nonetheless, Terri did insist that they try to call this Mrs. Jergens in Portland, and she also decided to go to Meredith's apartment to see if there were any chains. Meredith had insisted she do these two things as well as ask around to determine if any of the women they knew had seen Sharla in Chicago while Meredith was in San Francisco.

Together Dr. Granser and Terri got a list of phone numbers for people named Jergens in Portland. They called a few of them from Dr. Granser's office. None of the people they reached knew a Sharla Jergens. Terri said she'd continue the calls on her own. She promised to visit Meredith again the next evening and to bring some clothes and other things for her. She got Meredith's apartment key and left Regan Zone Center feeling very upset and concerned about the woman she loved and wanted to be her old self.

Terri was not surprised that there were no chains attached to the bedroom radiator and no handcuffs in the kitchen. The apartment looked as it always had. Except for the bedroom. It had been stripped almost bare. Poor Meredith, Terri thought.

CHAPTER 27

The phone rang just as Terri was going to listen to the messages on the answering machine. Meredith had said there might be a message from Sharla.

"Hello."

"Hello, is this Meredith?"

"Who's calling?"

"Allison."

"Oh, Allison, hi, this is Terri. Meredith isn't here."

"Terri Bannister. Oh good, I've been trying to call you, too. Do you know where Meredith is? Have you seen her lately?"

"Yeah, I sure have. You sound kind of...why do you ask?"

"Well, the strangest thing happened. I'm just trying to...I'm real confused and I'm trying to figure out what's going on. I ran into Marla today. She said the weirdest thing. It's got me going in circles. Meredith's out of town, right, at her mother's, isn't she? How come you're at her place?"

"I don't know what your talking about, Allison." Terri sounded irritated. "Why shouldn't I be at her place?"

"Well, she's not there, you said."

"That's right."

"Marla told me this weird story about you picking up Meredith from the airport a week or so ago..."

"Yeah? So?"

"You did then? She's back from Eureka?"

Terri was growing increasingly impatient and annoyed. "What's this all about, Allison?"

"Terri, you know Meredith and I have been seeing each other, don't you? That we're...together. We've been together most of the summer."

"You're nuts! What the hell are you talking about?"

"I'm talking about Meredith, my lover, that's what I'm talking about." Now Allison was sounding as irritated as Terri. "I know you two had a brief fling a while back. She and I have been together since she got back from San Francisco in June, Terri. I can't believe she didn't tell you. Did you think...?"

"*Your* lover?" Terri almost shouted it. "*Brief fling.*" She started to slam down the phone, then suddenly stopped. "Wait a minute," she said. "Allison, tell me more. When did you last hear from Meredith?"

"About two weeks ago. She called from Eureka, California, from her mother's. Her mother was in the hospital and..."

"No, Allison..."

"What do you mean?"

"Oh, wow!" Terri's heart was pounding. "Allison, we've got to talk. Are you busy now? Can we get together? Oh, wow."

They arranged to meet that evening. When they hung up, Terri sat at Meredith's cluttered desk in the study, agitated, for nearly ten minutes digesting the possibilities. Finally she backed up the tape on the answering machine.

Hi, Meredith. Nikki again. Where are you? Call me.

There were several others like that and quite a few with no messages. Terri knew most of those were her own. She kept listening, expecting now that there might actually be one from Sharla. After six in a row with no message, there came a voice.

Meredith, this is Sharla.

Terri got goosebumps. It sounded like Meredith.

I hope you're all right, the message continued. *I'm so worried about you. I have so much I want to say. You'll probably never forgive me. I wouldn't blame you. I'm not sure what I'm going to do. I'm very confused. I just need to think. There's no way to say how sorry*

I am. There was a pause, then what sounded like sobbing. *I wish...* More sobs, followed by a click. Beep, buzz.

Terri stared at the answering machine. She couldn't be sure. Was there a Sharla? Or was the call from Meredith in her Sharla personality? Had she been living two lives, flying back and forth from San Francisco? She was anxiously eager for her meeting with Allison. In the meantime, she decided to try some more calls to Portland. She dialed the next Jergens on her list.

"Hello."

"Hello, is this Ms. Jergens?"

"This is *Mrs.* Jergens."

"Do you know a Sharla Jergens?"

"Who is this? Is Sharla all right?"

"Ms. Jergens, my name is Terri Bannister. I'm calling from Chicago..."

"Is Sharla OK? She's OK, isn't she? Tell me, she's not..."

"She's OK. As far as I know, she's OK. Are you her mother?"

"Yes I am. What...?"

"I'm...this is difficult..."

"What is it? What's wrong with Sharla?"

"I'm afraid I can't give you a lot of information about Sharla. There's something very confusing going on here. I need to ask you some questions."

"What questions? What are you...?"

"Sharla. How old...when was she born, Ms. Jergens?"

"Why are you asking that? What's going on?"

"Please. I'll explain as much as I can in a minute, but please answer."

"She was born in 1955, May 28."

"Did...by any chance, was there a twin?"

"A twin?"

"Yes."

"No."

"No twin."

"I don't know."

"You don't know if..."

"We adopted Sharla."

"Oh, I see. And her biological parents, what do you know...?"

"Nothing. She was left at a hospital. There was no information. Why? Why are you asking this?"

185

"She's not there now?"

"No, she's there, isn't she? In Chicago. You know her, don't you? You're a friend of hers?"

"I met her," Terri said. She was believing now that she had. "She came to Chicago, right?"

"Yes, last April. I've hardly heard from her. I'm worried sick."

"Did she say anything about a twin?"

"No, is there...?"

"She never...?"

"She asked if she was adopted. She asked that recently, but she never said anything about a twin."

"What does she look like?"

Gloria Jergens described her daughter. Terri saw Meredith's form emerging with the description.

"Could you send me a picture of her?"

"Would you please tell me what this is about," Gloria Jergens insisted. Her voice was close to hysterical.

Terri took a deep breath. How to begin? "I have a friend named Meredith," she began. "Meredith told me that she just discovered she has a twin sister named Sharla Jergens. It's very confusing, Ms. Jergens, but what probably happened is that Sharla had some trouble, some emotional trouble, and ended up in a hospital..."

"Oh, no. What hospital? Tell me. I'm coming."

"Let me finish. She left the hospital...you know, without permission. She just ran off. Then, because apparently they're identical in appearance, the police..."

"The police!"

"They found Meredith and thought she was Sharla and brought her to the hospital."

"Where is Sharla?"

"I don't know. Could you send the picture, maybe lots of pictures, dated things, graduation pictures, stuff like that. You see, we have to prove that Meredith isn't Sharla. They've got her locked in a hospital."

"But where's Sharla, where's my baby?"

"She called. Not long ago. She didn't say where she was, but she called. She'll probably call again. As soon as we hear, we'll let you know, all right?"

"I'm coming there."

"Here?"

"Yes. Your name is what? Terri, you said. Terri what?"

"Bannister."

"Sharla mentioned a 'Terry', but...no. And your address? I need your address and your phone number."

Terri told her. She also gave her Meredith's last name and her phone number and the location of the hospital.

"I'll come immediately."

"You'll bring the pictures?"

"Yes. Yes, I will."

They hung up and Terri went to the couch and collapsed. Her head was whirling.

CHAPTER 28

The meeting took place in a conference room at the Regan Zone Center. Gloria Jergens was there and Marian Landor, who Terri had called and who had flown in from Eureka. There was Terri and Meredith and Dr. Eventon and Dr. Granser and Allison.

Meredith sat between her mother and Terri. She felt anxious even though she knew this meeting would end her incarceration and the nightmare of having her sanity and identity denied. She wanted to be far away from this place.

At first Gloria Jergens would not believe Meredith was not her daughter. She called her Sharla and told her to stop this foolishness, but as she looked at the photos Marian Landor had brought, and listened to Meredith's story, she had no choice but to accept the bizarre truth. Both mothers had brought a stack of photographs of their daughters, baby pictures, childhood pictures, recent ones. Each talked about her daughter's life. The doctors' initial skepticism, like Gloria Jergen's, gave way inexorably to amazement.

"Meredith was left at a hospital," Marian Landor said. "They found her early in the morning, in a cardboard box. It was in Miranda, California. That's about forty miles from where we lived, my husband and I, in Eureka. It was in 1955. She was left there July

20. We adopted her a week later."

"Sharla was left at a hospital, too," Gloria Jergens said. "In Portland. July 3, 1955. We never found out anything about the parents." Gloria's bony fingers gripped her purse. "I was so glad to have her."

"We were also." Marian gave Meredith's hand a squeeze. "Joel and I weren't able to have children of our own. We adopted three. Meredith was the middle one. She's the one we knew so little about. There was a note in the box with her, and that's all. They gave me a copy of it."

"There was no note with Sharla," Gloria said. "Nothing at all. We wondered about it, about her background, about how anyone could give her up. She was healthy and...she was so beautiful."

"Oh, yes, weren't they? All that hair." Marian smiled warmly at Sharla's mother.

Gloria seemed near tears.

"What did the note say?" Dr. Granser asked.

Meredith smiled. She knew her mother knew it by heart. Years ago, her mother had shown her the note and it had set off a string of fantasies about her biological parents.

Marian chuckled. "I remember it verbatim." She tilted her head back as she recited. "*Please find a good home for her. I cannot be a mother now. She is a good baby. She was born on June 1, 1955. She is healthy and is just...*"

"June first?" Gloria looked upset. "No, it was May 28. Sharla was born May 28. That's what the doctors said." She looked at Dr. Eventon and then at Marian Landor. "I guess they couldn't tell exactly. They said she was five weeks old. They put down May 28. We thought her birthday was May 28."

"That must have been hard," Marian said, "having no information at all."

Gloria stared at the floor. "I'm sorry," she said. "I interrupted you. You were telling us about the note."

"Yes. It said that she was born June 1, 1955, and that *she is healthy and is just beginning to eat cereal and pureed carrots.*"

"Oh, how sweet." Gloria's eyes glistened. "Sharla loved the Gerber carrots. Carrots and plums, those were her favorites."

Meredith felt terribly sad for Sharla's mother. So did the others in the room.

"*I am 19 years old,*" Marian continued. "*I am a college student. I am Irish, Hungarian, German, and French. The only diseases I know about in my family are my uncle who died of cancer of the throat and an aunt who has cataracts. The baby's father is part Italian and I'm not sure what else. We tried to be parents but it didn't work. We just couldn't do it. Someday I hope to have more children. I'm going to return to college. Please find a good home for my baby. I'm sorry."*

Both mothers were crying. Meredith was also. The others waited quietly.

"I thought there might have been some Italian blood," Gloria said at last. "Oh God, oh, my Sharla. I love her so."

Marian reached over and placed her hand over Gloria's. Everyone in the room was clearly moved.

"It seems very obvious," Dr. Granser said after a long pause, "that they are, indeed, identical twins."

"I wonder why there was no note with Sharla," Gloria said to no one in particular.

"I've never heard anything like this," Dr. Eventon said. "It's like television, isn't it?" He seemed almost amused.

The twins' mothers continued comparing memories and photographs, while the others listened silently. Allison was shaken, overwhelmed by what she was learning, and having a very difficult time trying to integrate it. She was in love with a woman who wasn't the woman she was in love with. Confusion and fear had been tormenting her ever since her long talk with Terri two days earlier.

Every so often, Gloria Jergens would stare at Meredith, scrutinize her, then shake her head. "If only we could find Sharla," she said at one point, looking beseechingly at Dr. Eventon. "What could be wrong with her, doctor? Is she sick?"

"Yes, I'm afraid she is," Dr. Eventon said. His tone was low and cool. "She's experiencing a form of mental illness, Mrs. Jergens, serious mental illness, but if she continues in treatment..."

"Actually," Dr. Granser interrupted, "in light of what we're hearing today, Mrs. Jergens, I believe that, while your daughter did experience a psychotic break, she was no longer actively psychotic when I spoke to her on Monday."

Gloria Jergens stared intently at the psychologist, nodding her head, trying to understand.

"When she first came to the hospital," Dr. Granser continued, "she was clearly delusional. Unfortunately..." The psychologist shrugged her shoulders, "...but understandably, we thought that more of what she told us was delusional than it actually was. Nonetheless, much of what she said, even now that we know the truth, was not reality-based — the business about her soul being stolen and so forth."

The psychologist directed her next statements to Dr. Eventon. "With the hindsight afforded by this meeting, *our* 'reality-testing', so to speak, I now see Sharla's behavior with me on Monday as very appropriate and insightful, quite different from how she was earlier. She talked about the soul-switching obsession as a function of her envy of Meredith and realized it was not a real possibility. Of course, when she told me this I didn't know there really was a twin. In light of this new information, it now seems to me that Sharla was not psychotic when I last spoke to her, as she clearly was earlier. And I think it was her fear that Meredith would die that jarred her out of it. That's a positive note, a strength that augers well for her."

"Can it just go away?" Allison asked.

Everyone looked at Allison. This was the first time since the initial introductions that she had spoken.

"People can have stress-related brief psychotic episodes, yes," Dr. Granser replied. "At this point, that's what I think happened to Sharla."

"Oh, I hope she's all right." Sharla's mother was crying. Before Sharla's move to Chicago, Gloria Jergens never cried in front of others. She looked at Dr. Granser hopefully.

"Let's hope she contacts someone soon."

"Well, if she's not psychotic, doctor, then does that mean she's all right? I mean, she is going to be all right, isn't she?" Gloria Jergens pleaded.

Dr. Granser's brow formed a deep frown. "I wish I could say 'relax'," she replied. "Your daughter is a troubled woman, Mrs. Jergens. The soul-switch delusion, I believe, was her defense against a very deep depression. It may have been a choice between being psychotic and...well, and extreme hopelessness. She..."

"Oh dear," Gloria Jergens moaned. "Sharla...several times she...she cut her wrists. I could never understand it, why she would..."

"Hopefully she'll get in touch with us," Dr. Granser said.

After the meeting, out in the long yellow corridor, Marian Landor spoke for several minutes with Gloria Jergens. They exchanged numbers and agreed to keep in contact. Allison drove Gloria Jergens to her hotel, then went to the beach and sat staring numbly at the waves, her vision tear-blurred.

Meredith and Terri and Meredith's mother left the hospital together and went to Meredith's apartment. Terri was unusually quiet. She hoped Sharla had disappeared for good. Marian Landor worried about Sharla's mother. Meredith worried about Sharla. Would she turn up suddenly, crazy again, perhaps? Dangerous? Or could she have recovered sufficiently to have gone away to start anew? Would there be no word for years, maybe ever? Would they learn some day of her suicide? Would she develop some other delusion? Meredith wished desparately that Sharla would contact her. She knew she would not feel at ease until she could satisfy the magnetic pull she felt, to know Sharla, be with her, talk as sisters with this unhappy, complex, lost woman who was genetically identical to herself. The prospect of such contact frightened her as well.

The next day, Saturday, Marian Landor returned to Eureka. What was going on was fascinating, she and Meredith had agreed, as well as disturbing. They had shared at length their feelings about Meredith having a twin and about what had happened and about Sharla's condition. They felt even closer than they had before and parted warmly with Marian Landor's uncustomary admonition for Meredith to be careful.

Sharla had not called.

Meredith and Terri talked endlessly. It seemed that Terri was even more disturbed than Meredith about what had happened and the implications. She dwelled on it incessantly, apparently threatened somehow. Their reunion was marred by it.

"I just can't adjust to there being a person out there who looks just like you and acts like you and can fool people who know you, even me. She fooled me, Meredith," Terri said for fifth or sixth time.

"I know," Meredith said patiently, feeling her patience waning. "I wish she'd call though."

"I don't."

Gloria Jergens stayed in town for several days. She talked to the police. They said they were searching. She talked to Dr. Granser again and to Dr. Eventon. They said the prognosis seemed good if Sharla could get some help but they worried about the depression. She wanted to talk with Meredith, but could not bring herself to do it. Later, she thought. She talked with Allison. Allison wished she could tell Ms. Jergens how deeply her attachment went, that she and Sharla were far more than friends, but she knew she could not.

191

Allison fluctuated between depression and anger and confusion. Had she fallen in love with Sharla because she thought she was Meredith to whom she'd been attracted in the past and had never gotten over? Did she still love her now that she knew she wasn't who she'd thought she was? Or was it the real Meredith she loved? It had been very painful for Allison seeing Meredith, knowing that she was not the Meredith she had come to love, having trouble accepting it, feeling jealous of Terri. She decided she needed to talk with Meredith. When she called her, Meredith was more than willing for them to meet. They got together the next day.

"I can imagine what it's doing to you," Meredith said. "Such a weird who's-who trip, my head's still reeling from it."

"I thought she was you."

"I know, of course you did. She really worked at it."

"I mean, I fell in love with her, and it was all fake. She wasn't..."

"I don't think so, Allison, I mean, that it was fake. How could it be? Yes, I know in a way it was, imitating me and all, but there had to be something inside her that let her do it, I mean, do it so well that she fooled even Terri and you." Meredith paused. "You and I know each other pretty well, you know," she said fondly. "She couldn't have faked..."

"We do, don't we...know each other well. I never really got over it, you know, I mean, my feelings for you, and then when you...when Sharla started coming on to me and then we got together and it was so good...God...I..."

"Yeah."

"If I didn't know better, I'd swear you are..." She shook her head. "I feel right now like...about you, being with you...I feel the same right now, being with you, as I have for the past month...I..."

Meredith put her hand on Allison's shoulder. They were sitting in the grass near the Lincoln Park Lagoon. Allison felt a shiver of pleasure at the touch.

"I don't know who I'm in love with."

Allison held onto Meredith and Meredith embraced her also, warmly, caringly. Meredith felt some of the old feelings for Allison stirring her again. She wondered how it would have been had she not been afraid of them before. The two stayed in the park, talking, for a long time.

The day after Gloria Jergens flew back to Portland, Sharla called Meredith. When she heard the voice, Meredith immediately felt her heart rate shoot up. "Sharla?"

"It's really you, Meredith!"

"Yes."

"Then you're all right. Thank God!"

"I'm all right."

"I couldn't have stood it if something had happened to you."

"I'm fine, Sharla, yes. I've been hoping you'd call. I've been worried, too. About you."

"Worried? You have? You've been worried about me? Don't you hate me?"

"No."

"What I did...I can't believe I did it." The sounds caught in her throat. "I'm so ashamed. You must be furious, disgusted."

"I'm angry."

"I'm sorry. I *am* sorry, very sorry."

"I believe you are."

"I wish it could have been different."

"Yeah, well...maybe it still can, Sharla."

"I can't erase what I did to you. My God, I..."

"No, that's right, you can't erase it. It was pretty bad what you did. Very bad. But, you weren't...you were compelled by... Sharla, it's over now, right? You're not like that... You..."

Sharla was close to tears. "I was afraid you'd die of dehydration."

"So was I."

"How did you...?"

"I sawed through the chain."

"I'm so sorry, Meredith."

"I know. You're sounding better, less...upset. Where are you? What have you been doing?"

"I'm hiding. Retreating, thinking. Mostly about you, about what I did, and about my life, and about how it was when I pretended I was you."

"When you let yourself feel valuable and likable, you mean."

"Yes."

"It was good then."

"It was great."

"So you know the secret."

"What?"

"Feeling that way about yourself, valuable, worthwhile."

"That's not easy. I could do it when I pretended I was you, when people treated me like someone who was someone."

"You are, Sharla. It was you. Can't you see that? You *are* someone and that's why they treated you that way. That was you."

"I can't believe you're being so kind to me."

Meredith was gripping the phone tightly. "Well..." She couldn't find the words. Finally one came out. "Sister," she said. She was crying.

Sharla didn't respond. She was crying, too. When she spoke, her voice cracked. "You know, I told you I've been thinking about my life, my real life I mean, my Sharla life."

"Yes?"

"It was different this time. Not always, but some of the time. I haven't been feeling quite as...as hopeless, and now that I know you're OK, well, maybe...I don't know, I..."

"I think a lot can happen, now, Sharla, if you let it. You can change things, you can..."

"Meredith." Sharla needed to shift the focus. For some reason it disturbed her that Meredith was being so caring, that she seemed to want to help her. Was she being patronizing? Did she pity her?

"Yeah?"

"About our being twins...do you...? I've been thinking a lot about it and, you know, wondering how it came about and...Are you curious about...?"

"Our parents?"

"Yeah."

"Yes, sure I am. I know a few things. I'd be happy to share them with you. Yes, I'm curious about our parents, but I'm more interested in you."

"You are?" People aren't interested in me.

"I'd like to get to know you."

"You would? I'm...I'm surprised, especially after..."

"That soul-stealing business. Do you still...?"

"No. I can't tell you how strange it's been, I mean, to know I was...I know it was crazy, Meredith. I know what I thought, what I believed, was absurd, absolutely ridiculous, thinking that you stole my soul, and, in a way, I knew it then, too, that it was ridiculous, but still, at the same time, I...I don't know...I was so desparate."

Meredith was sure Sharla was being sincere, yet felt a need to test it more. Terri had gotten to her. "Well, I don't know," she said. "Maybe it did happen that way, maybe I did take something from you that..."

"Hey, don't you start, now." Sharla laughed. "You're not serious, are you?."

"Not really. What if I were?"

"I'd worry about you. That's crazy thinking, Meredith."

"You're sure?"

"You're testing me."

Meredith was silent for a time. "Yeah. You were pretty out of control."

"OK, well...yeah, I understand. I just called to make sure you're not dead, so you're not, and don't worry, I'll never bother you again. Just try to forget I ever..."

"Sharla!" Meredith said loudly.

"What?"

"Stop, OK? I just...So, tell me what your plans are. What will you do now?"

"I don't know." Sharla sounded gloomy.

"Why don't you come here so we can talk, come to my place. Are you nearby?"

"No."

"Where are you?"

"I took a bus."

"Why don't you come back? I really want to...to be with you, talk with you. I think we have a lot to talk about. We're sisters, we..."

"They'll arrest me."

"No they won't. I mean, you could go to the hospital and clear things up there, but that won't be any big deal. Dr. Granser says you're much better."

"You know her? You know about that, about the hospital?"

"Oh, yes, I know."

"Aren't they looking for me?"

"Yes, but not to lock you up, I don't think. Once you talk to them, it will be clear that you don't need to be in a hospital. They can't make you stay if you're not crazy."

"I talked pretty crazy then."

"You aren't talking crazy now."

"I was so afraid you were going to die, that I was going to be responsible for your death."

"And you didn't want that. You tried to..."

"I did before, you know. That was one option I considered, tak-

195

ing over your identity after you were…isn't that disgusting?"

"Yes. But you didn't do it."

"No, I didn't. That Ramal. He played into my stupid ideas. He ripped me off, you know, the bastard."

"He's not important."

"No." There was a moment of silence. "Well, really, I just called to make sure you were all right, Meredith. And I wanted to let you know how sorry I am."

"Yes, I'm glad…"

"So, I…I don't know. Maybe I'll talk to you sometime."

"How can I reach you, Sharla?"

"Oh, I don't think…"

"Can't we meet somewhere?"

"You really want to, don't you? I mean you really do?"

"Very much."

"You really do."

"Yes."

"It's not just to get me to come back so they can lock me up again?"

"No."

"I believe you. I know you very well, you know, how you think and…" Sharla sort of chuckled. "Well, maybe we *could* meet. It makes me nervous, though, scared to…"

"It's scarey for me, too."

"We can't meet there; I don't want to go there, Meredith."

"All right. We'll meet somewhere else. Name the place."

"Don't tell anyone."

"All right."

Sharla was quiet for several seconds. "It's pretty far."

"Where?"

"Where I am."

"Where's that?"

"A place called Silver Lake. It's in Michigan."

"Michigan's not that far. Do you have somewhere to stay there?"

"Yes."

"Are you alone?"

"Yes. You won't bring anyone else, will you?"

"No. I want to come soon. Tomorrow, maybe. Would that be OK?"

"I should contact my mother. I know she must be worried."

"She is."

"You talked to her?"

"She was here."

Sharla was silent for a while again. "I'll call her. Maybe I'll call her today. Do you think I should?"

"I think she'd be relieved to hear from you."

"I've worried her enough. Even she doesn't deserve that."

"No. She'll be very glad to hear from you. Shall I come tomorrow, Sharla?"

"Yes, tomorrow. Will you drive?"

"Yes."

"You found your car OK, by the conservatory?"

"Yes."

"I came by bus."

"I'll drive. Where should I go?"

"Are you coming tomorrow?"

"Yes."

"It's about a five hour trip, I think, by car."

"All right. I can be there in the afternoon. Where should I go?"

Sharla told her where Silver Lake was located. "There's a restaurant in the town of Shelby. It's called Dunesbury's. It's easy to find. I'll meet you there."

"Let's make it 3:00. Is that all right?"

"Yes, 3:00. I'll be there."

"We have a lot to talk about."

"I'm so glad you're like you are."

"I think things can be OK. I'll be there at three."

"Goodbye, Meredith."

"Goodbye, Sharla."

Terri objected strongly, vehemently. "How do you know you can trust her? She might be nuts again. It's not safe to go, certainly not by yourself."

"I think it's safe."

They argued angrily. Meredith was determined and Terri knew it. Things did not feel so good between them. They spent the night together but were not loving and did not make love. The next morning, Terri went to work feeling very uneasy. At 9:30, Meredith began the drive toward Michigan.

197

CHAPTER 29

There was plenty of time to think, more than five hours. Meredith was unsure what to expect from Sharla, but sure of what she wanted—to get to know her, for Sharla to be open to it. Why this was so important, she didn't know, and yet felt it as her primary need right now, what was driving her to what Terri had called an "ill-fated rendezvous". It overrode her anger and her fear. Beyond question, Sharla's behavior had been despicable—entering her home, taking over her possessions, her life, chaining her, almost causing her death. Had it been anyone else on earth besides this one woman, Meredith would have found the heinous acts absolutely unforgivable.

Driving down the highway, she tried to imagine how it would go, what would happen in Michigan. Doubts nagged at her, refusing to be dismissed. Would seeing me set it off again? Could Terri be right? Dr. Granser was optimistic, though Eventon was more skeptical. It could be just a temporary remission, he had said. The outcome is unpredictable. Meredith turned the steering wheel sharply, just missing a skunk. Unpredictable, she thought. So true. I probably should have insisted that she come to Chicago. Meredith tried to slough off the nervous tension. No, she thought, this feels right, to meet some-

198

where on neutral turf. She thought again about what Sharla had told her of her life, the pain and loneliness. She thought of the contrast. It *was* unfair. Who could deny that?

The aging but faithful Volvo crossed the border from Indiana into Michigan. Meredith had heard of Silver Lake. It was a resort area near Lake Michigan, a small lake surrounded by sand dunes. Very beautiful, she'd been told. I wonder how Sharla ended up there. I wonder what she'll be like.

Meredith found the Dunesbury Restaurant without any trouble. When she walked in, the waitress stared at her, rather wide-eyed, then looked toward the back booth. Sharla was there. She smiled nervously at Meredith.

"Hello," Meredith said warmly, though somewhat tentatively, as she slipped into the booth.

"Hi. You made it OK." Sharla did not meet Meredith's eyes.

"Yes, I...uh, yeah, no problem finding it. Your directions were good."

"Thank you." Sharla still did not look directly at her sister. "Are you hungry? Shall we eat or...or what?"

"I could eat. How about you?"

Sharla nodded.

Meredith felt uncomfortable with Sharla's shyness. She seemed so harmless, so totally unthreatening now. "This is a beautiful area," she said, groping for some way to ease the tension.

"Yes."

"Did you just come here by chance, or..."

"By chance, yes."

"This is hard, isn't it?" Meredith said empathically.

Sharla nodded, looking at Meredith now. "Yes...I...it is. I feel terribly...um, I don't know..."

"All the way up here, I was wondering what it would be like."

"Am I making it difficult?"   —

"No, no, I..."

"I've been told I'm hard to talk to."

The waitress came then. "I have a hunch you like corned beef, Sharla. Am I right?" Meredith asked.

"Yes, I love corned beef." Sharla seemed pleased.

"I thought so. Me too."

They both ordered corned beef sandwiches and made small talk which was beginning to come easier now. Meredith talked about the trip from Chicago, the deer she had seen on the road and Sharla talked some about the town of Silver Lake.

"How was it for you, Sharla?" Meredith asked after a while. "When you first realized it...about us, I mean?"

"About having a twin?"

"Yes."

"It was shocking at first, but exciting, too, fascinating." Sharla's eyes shone bright. "Right away, when I saw the first photograph of you, I became obsessed with finding out everything I could about you." She looked down at her hands. "I went through all your things, Meredith. I...I'm sorry. I felt like I couldn't help it. I couldn't stop myself. I looked at all your films, too."

"Oh, yeah?" Meredith already knew this. Sharla had mentioned it, bragged of it, actually, in the bedroom when she had Meredith captive. Her attitude was certainly different now. "What did you think of the films?"

"And your journal."

"Hm-mm."

Sharla could not look at Meredith as she spoke, but she felt compelled to continue her confession. "I read your letters to Robin."

Meredith nodded. Had it been anyone else, she knew these violations would have enraged her. "It was more than mere curiosity, wasn't it?"

"Oh God, yes." Sharla raised her head. "I've never snooped into another's...I've always had a great respect for people's privacy, Meredith. My mother used to go through my things and I just hated it. It felt like..." Sharla stopped, looking very pained.

"Like a personal violation? Almost like rape?"

"Yes! Oh, damn, Meredith. I feel awful...I just..."

"So, you went through everything and learned all about me. How did you react, Sharla? I mean, what kind of...?"

"I went through stages. At first, I was like a detective, fascinated by each new thing I discovered about you."

"And then?"

"Well, when I found out you were a lesbian, I was disgusted." Meredith smiled. "That was hard to handle, huh?"

"But not for long. I got fascinated by it, then. I don't know why. I read your books."

Meredith raised her eyebrows. "Good," she said. "You learned some things."

"I think I was real ready. But after a while, I got so into you and into your life that I began to lose myself. I got scared. Really, more angry than scared. I wanted to lose myself. I wanted to be you. But I couldn't fool myself. I wasn't that nuts. I knew I was stuck with being my disgusting self."

Meredith reached for Sharla's hand but Sharla would not accept the gesture. She pulled away.

"I hated you. God, how I hated you. I was so fucking envious. I went into a terrible depression. I'm not sure how long it lasted, but then it lifted." Sharla raised her head. There was a hint of a smile in her tearful eyes."

"How..?"

"I decided to kill myself."

Meredith nodded sadly.

"I felt tremendous relief. Really, it was great. I felt exhilarated. I finally fully accepted that it was futile...that I could never attain a fraction of what you had. And with that acceptance came a wonderful feeling of peace." Sharla smiled. "It really felt good. I felt free. I didn't have to struggle. I could die and it would all be over."

Meredith wanted to take this woman into her arms and hold her and hold her. Instead, she waited for Sharla to go on.

"But for some reason...I'm not sure now just how it came about, but for some reason...Maybe I was just afraid of dying, I don't know, but anyway, I decided to pretend I was you for awhile and then, after I'd experienced some of the joy of being...of...well, then I'd be ready to go."

"Yes, I see," Meredith said, nodding. "What happened then?"

Sharla told her, step by step, told her how she prepared for the role, then of each venture into the world as Meredith Landor. She explained again and again how exciting and gratifying it had been to be accepted and respected and valued and sought after. Her face glowed as she spoke, especially when she talked of Allison.

Meredith listened, fascinated, imagining people she knew relating to Sharla as if she were herself. "And no one suspected you weren't really me?"

Sharla shook her head. "How could they? I mean, look at us."

"Yeah."

"Like I said, I even got my hair cut like yours, and wore your clothes."

Meredith took a drink of her 7-up. "Didn't people talk about things that you didn't understand, make allusions to things...?"

"Oh, yeah. There were some uncomfortable moments. Especially when Terri showed up at that party."

"That was rough on her."

Sharla's face grew somber. "I hope I didn't mess things up for you two. How are things...?"

"Oh, OK, I guess. I don't know, a little strained maybe. Well, actually, things aren't that great, but it's not because of you, not directly. I don't know, she seems different to me somehow. She didn't believe me in the hospital." Meredith told Sharla the story. "Possibly, we'll work things out," she said at the end. "Who knows what will happen?"

"I'm really sorry about the hospital thing," Sharla said. Her lower lip was quivering. "About everything, Meredith. I'm sorry about..."

"I know. I know you are. We'll just go on from here. You got some mustard on your cheek.

Sharla wiped it off.

"You know," Meredith said, "it's interesting that you and Allison..." She had a strange expression on her face. "For a while, she and I were really close. Did you know that? Yes, I suppose you did. I think I was in love with her. I think, at the time, though, I couldn't deal with the kind of closeness she wanted. I still think about her sometimes. She and I talked the other day. It was...I don't know. Anyway, well, she's having a hard time, you know. Will you call her?"

Sharla looked out the restaurant window. "I guess," she said. "I'm still hanging, Meredith. I don't know what I'm going to do."

"Yeah. It's a lot to integrate, that's for sure."

They left the restaurant and Sharla directed Meredith to the cabin she had rented. Meredith realized she was hoping it wasn't in an isolated place, that the possibility of this sweet, shy woman being potentially dangerous still pricked at her.

"The cabin is tiny but cute," Sharla warned.

It was both, and it was surrounded by other cabins. They sat on lawn chairs in front of the little wooden structure, looking toward the lake. "Do you have freckles on your back?" Sharla asked.

Meredith laughed. "What?"

"Do you? I do."

"Yes, as a matter of fact, I do." She laughed again. She knew exactly what Sharla was experiencing, the curiousity about the little details of the person genetically exactly like herself. She had had the same questions. "How are your teeth?" she asked, still chuckling, feeling almost silly. "Have you had trouble with them?"

"Yes. Lotsa fillings. A couple root canals."

"Me too."

They laughed.

"You got any scars or anything? Did you ever have surgery or break any bones?"

"No. You?"

"No." Sharla rubbed her left wrist. "I did have some scars," she said softly, "but they faded."

Meredith nodded. "How old were you when you got your period?" she asked lightly.

Once they started on this track, they couldn't seem to stop. Neither of them wanted to. They talked for a couple of hours, making their comparisons while gingerly avoiding areas that would be painful for Sharla, both enjoying it very much, ralaxing with each other. Each hour that passed, Meredith felt more and more sure that it had been right to come, that Sharla was quite rational and not the least dangerous, and that her need to get to know her sister was going to be satisfied. Just before sunset, they went for a swim. They both realized they were scrutinizing each other's bodies, very similar, athletic bodies, though Meredith's was more in shape.

Back at the cabin, they talked some more. "We're so alike and yet so different," Sharla observed. "Such different personalities."

"Yes, in a lot of ways. Nature-nurture, I guess."

"It's fascinating. Why do you think it turned out that way? I mean, you developed into such a...I don't know, a self-confident person, I guess, and I..."

"I don't know. I would imagine our childhoods had a lot to do with it."

"Yeah. I turned out to be the frog. You're the prince."

"You learned to think of yourself that way."

"Hm."

"I'm rather arrogant sometimes," Meredith said.

"I know. It's better than being self-effacing like I am."

"You're probably more sensitive than I, though...more responsive to other's feelings."

"I can certainly empathize with what it feels like to be rejected and put down."

"I guess I've been more on the rejecting, put-down side, at times."

"Oh, I don't believe that."

"It's true, Sharla. Sometimes I'm not real patient with people and I can be pretty sarcastic and critical."

"Oh, I do that, too. But usually not to people's faces. You're bolder."

"Fools rush in."

"No, you're assertive."

"Yeah, usually. Sometimes a bit selfish, I suspect."

"Comes from having a strong sense of self."

"Too strong, sometimes, I've been told."

"I wonder why you became a lesbian and I didn't."

They were sitting on old rocking chairs in the rustic cabin kitchen. Meredith began rocking slightly. "I don't know," she said. "Did you ever feel attracted to women?"

Sharla didn't answer right away. "There's Allison," she said at last.

Meredith's face darkened for an instant. "Before that?" she said.

"Maybe."

Meredith smiled. "Tell me about it."

Sharla talked of Greta, beginning hesitantly, then losing her self-consciousness, and speaking freely. She cried as she did.

Meredith felt tremendous empathy. "God, I wish I'd met you sooner."

"Me, too."

"Wouldn't it have been fun if we'd been raised together?"

Sharla's face lit up briefly, then she frowned. "Not by *my* parents, though."

"It might have been different if there were two of us. We could have stuck up for each other, supported each other."

"I suppose."

"We still can."

"You don't need my support."

Meredith rocked in her chair, not answering.

"You hate it when I say things like that."

"It's not that I hate it, I just..."

"I wish I were different."

"I think you're changing."

"I wish I were you."

Meredith stopped rocking. Her heart began to pound. She looked at her twin. "You're not going to start that again, are you?" It was dark out now, and quiet.

"I really flipped out, didn't I?"

"I guess."

"I lost it. I lost touch with reality. I was nuts."

Meredith didn't answer.

"I really believed it."

Meredith remained silent, feeling increasingly uncomfortable. She found herself planning strategies if Sharla tried anything.

"But that's over."

Meredith let her breath out. I'm being paranoid, she thought. "I hear you write," she said, eager to change the subject.

"Who told you that?"

"You. You talked about it some...back at my apartment. But, Emma told me, too. She said you're working on a script for her."

"I was."

"Will you continue?"

Sharla looked out the little, gingham-framed window. "I don't know," she said, shaking her head.

They went out for dinner at a Pizza Hut, and later they walked along the shore and talked some more. Meredith phoned Terri to let her know that things were going very well. Unreassured, Terri urged her not to spend the night, which irritated Meredith. The conversation ended abruptly.

"Are you religious?" Sharla asked on their walk by the lake.

"No. Are you?"

"I used to be. Are you a Democrat or Republican?" Clearly, Sharla had not yet gotten her fill of comparisons, even though she already knew much of the information.

"Socialist."

"Really?" Sharla said, then added, "You mentioned it in your journal, but I like to..."

"Sure. How about you? Not a Commie, I wouldn't imagine."

"I used to be a Republican."

Meredith laughed.

"My father's influence."

"Mr. Business."

"Right."

"How about now?"

"I don't know. I don't know what I am." Sharla looked away. "I don't know *who* I am."

"You'll find yourself, sister," Meredith said gently, sounding more sure and relaxed than she felt.

They slept in twin beds, side by side. Meredith had a little trouble falling asleep because of those damn flashes she couldn't totally stop, Terri-inspired images of Sharla trying to tie her up or knife her as she slept. She talked to herself reassuringly, and pretty soon, was able to let go and find comfort in her pleasant dreams.

She dreamed of two identical women on identical horses riding through the hills together, spurring each other on, faster, more joyfully, until they rode so fast the horses feet no longer touched the ground. They rose higher and higher. The horses, Pegasuses now, took them through the sky, around the globe, touching down to earth whenever the riders wanted to rest, or, side by side, to explore new worlds.

Sharla dreamed of a doll. It was a very pretty doll with creamy soft skin and vibrant auburn hair. But inside, the doll was ooze — black, murky, soggy, gloppy ooze. The doll sprung a leak, at its left eye, and the black slime squeezed out through the eye socket dripping down the doll's soft rosy cheek, covering the peachy skin with steamy tarry slop. And then the gook started coming from the nostrils and the sweet little mouth. Ooze poured out of the ears then and the vagina and anus, covering the pretty doll, burying her, drowning her in pitch black smelly slime.

The next morning they went on a dune buggy ride. Meredith loved it, flying through the amber hills and Sharla, too, enjoyed herself. They swam and talked and bought some groceries to cook on the two-burner stove in the cabin. That evening Merdith suggested they go bowling.

"I've never bowled," Sharla said.

"Try it."

"All right."

"Do you want to drive?" Meredith asked as they walked to the car.

Sharla looked at her sister. "I've always been scared of it," she said. "I have my license, though, and I keep renewing it. I took lessons, but I can't remember when I last drove, several years ago, I think. I get safety citations every year."

Meredith laughed. "Well, there's not much traffic here. You want to try?"

Sharla hesitated.

Meredith watched her.

"Yes," Sharla said. "I want to."

She drove adequately, slowly, but she had the basic skills, just needed practice. She drove them to the bowling alley.

Sharla caught onto the game quickly and they had good laughs together. In the middle of the second game, two men approached them.

"Hi, girls, how do you know which of you is which? Do you ever fool each other?"

Sharla felt the immediate grip of squirmy self-consciousness.

Meredith looked at the men cooly.

"Mind if we join you?" one of them said.

"Yes, we mind. We'd rather you didn't," Meredith replied.

"We've been watching you two," he said, ignoring Meredith's response. "You're twins, huh?"

"We don't want you to join us," Meredith reiterated.

Sharla felt increasingly uncomfortable. She knew if it were a few weeks ago in Chicago, she'd be handling this just as Meredith was.

"Now, don't be so crabby," the man said to Meredith. "Is your sister always this unfriendly?" he asked Sharla.

"OK, boys," Meredith said sharply. "That's enough. I want you to leave now."

"How about you, honey?" The man reached for Sharla's cheek. "You're the sweet one, aren't you? I bet you let this one push you around."

"Get lost!" Sharla said.

"Hey, wow. Tough girl." The man chuckled. "OK, OK," he said. "We'll leave you two alone. They probably do it with each other," he said to his friend. They left.

"Creeps," Meredith said.

Sharla laughed. "Yeah," she replied. "Your basic pig mentality. I know there are a lot of guys around like that but I think I've been fairly lucky with the men I've known. Most of them were pretty decent people. Go ahead, Meredith, you got a spare to pick up."

That night, Meredith had no trouble sleeping. She was feeling closer and closer to her sister, just as she had hoped. She had called Terri again and, although the conversation was more pleasant this time, it still left Meredith with a disquieted feeling. The next day the twins drove to Lake Michigan and swam there and then played a game of miniature golf. They had a leisurely sea food dinner at one of the area's classier restaurants. Sharla worried about their casual attire. Meredith told her it wasn't important.

Sharla did most of the driving that day. She was getting more confident, but continued to grip the wheel tightly and lean forward as she drove. Meredith praised and encouraged her and Sharla continued to improve. After dinner, they stopped at a roadside bar about ten miles away from Silver Lake.

"Did you ever go fishing?" Sharla asked.

"A few times."

"I love it. I have the best fantasies while I'm sitting there waiting for a tug on the line."

"Ahh. Tell me about your fantasies," Meredith purred, stroking her smooth chin as if it were bearded.

Sharla laughed. They were sitting at a corner table in the nearly empty bar. Sharla took a swallow of her beer. "That's why I go fishing. For the fantasies."

"So tell me." Meredith smiled. "Or are they too private?"

"Not from you." Sharla smiled warmly. "They usually start out with me falling in love."

"Good beginning."

"I meet this guy..." Sharla chuckled. "If I went fishing now, it would probably be a woman I'd meet."

Meredith nodded, still smiling. She was liking this woman.

"So, I meet this wonderful person. He or she is very sensitive, nonjudgmental. I feel comfortable immediately. Not shy at all. We talk for hours and then we go to a cabin somewhere, somewhere in the woods nearby. There's a fireplace and..."

"And you make great warm passionate—popcorn. Ha! Ha! You make love there in front of the fire."

"How did you know?"

"I'm psychic."

"It goes on from there. We do things together, I mean, besides making love, all kinds of things, travel, share things. She's very good to me and I to her and I don't feel nervous at all. That feeling, you know, that heavy feeling I told you about, the feeling that's always there, in my chest and stomach..."

"Mm-hm."

"It goes away. I start to feel happy, really happy. And she genuinely likes me. We get to know each other and she continues to be warm and...respectful."

"Respectful?"

"Yeah. Not in the...you know, not in a distant way, the authority way, but, just...she values me. Respects who I am. My ways. My ideas. My feelings."

"Sounds great. Then what?"

"I think I'm gonna make a phone call."

Meredith nodded. "To Allison?"

"How did you know?"

Meredith smiled. She played Pac-Man while her sister was on the phone but could not concentrate. Her thoughts were on Sharla and Allison. It felt like jealousy, but she pushed the feeling away. "How did it go?" she asked when Sharla returned.

"Allison's having a hard time with it, like you said, but...I think it went well. She wants to get together. She's scared, though. So am I. She says she's real confused about her feelings."

Meredith nodded. She felt confused herself. "Allison's a very special person," she said, not meeting Sharla's eyes. "I think I'll give Terri another call."

Terri was getting impatient. "So, she's still behaving herself, OK, great, but how far are you going to push it? Why don't you come back now? The woman's not well. You can't be sure..."

"She's fine, Terri. She's like a different person from...from what she was. She's been through a lot but she's coming along. I think she'll make it. And I like her, I really do. I want to help and I think my being with her is good for her."

"How long do you plan to stay?"

"I don't know. I'm playing it by ear. I want Sharla to come back, too. I'm not sure she's ready yet."

"I feel like I'm losing you, Meredith. Things seem different with us."

Meredith didn't answer right away. "Well, we've been through shit," she said at last. "I feel it too, you know. This whole business is...I think we're both under a tremendous strain, Terri. We've got to give it time."

"Yeah, right. So, what have you two been doing?"

"Talking mostly. We're at a local podunk boonie bar now, you know, real folk."

Terri laughed. "She's not going to stay in Chicago, is she?"

Meredith did not answer. She was aware of a painful angry feeling.

"Meredith..."

"Yeah."

"I'm having a lot of trouble with it. I don't want there to be two of you."

"Shit, Terri. What are you talking about? We're two separate people. Very different people."

"She fooled me."

Meredith was quiet again. She wished Terri would get over that. "She was acting," she said at last. "We're really very different."

"Maybe she'll want to go back to Portland."

"Terri, I'm having trouble with how you're dealing with this."

"I'm not being very sensitive, am I?"

"No. Can you be cool? Let it happen. See what it's like. You're pre-judging, I think."

"It's so eerie realizing I had a long conversation with somebody I thought was the woman I love and wasn't."

"I know, I know." They had been over this a dozen times. "I'm still freaked by the whole thing. Partly I feel sorry for her. But, it's more than that. I feel this...this bond. It's like an irresistible attraction."

"What kind of attraction?"

"Don't be a creep, Terri."

"You know what they say—vice is nice, but incest is best."

"I'm not liking this conversation."

"Sorry...I'm being awful."

"You've been better."

"I'm working on it. I just wish..."

"I know. But, we've got to cope with it."

They talked a few minutes longer, then Meredith promised to call the following night and they hung up.

The sisters stayed another half hour in the bar. They each had one more beer, then left. Sharla still had the car keys. She drove.

It was a dark night, overcast sky, not much illumination from the stars. Sharla was thinking of what had transpired the past few days, of how much she liked and admired Meredith. And envied her, that too. What would the future hold, she wondered. Meredith will go back to her comfortable, interesting, fulfilling life and I will...what? Live in Chicago in her shadow? Shit. Be the loser half of the Bobbsy twins.

Meredith was sleepy. The beers and the rhythmic movement of the car were lulling her.

I could go somewhere else, Sharla thought. Start another new life.

Her foot rested heavily on the accelerator, her mind fully occupied with her thoughts.

Maybe Allison will still want to be with me.

They were going 65 now. Meredith nodded, her eyes almost closed.

I could kill myself.

The car raced along at 70 m.p.h.

Maybe Meredith's right. Maybe I am changing. Maybe the way I was when I pretended I was her is really part of me.

They flew down the highway at over 75 m.p.h.

If only she hadn't come back. If only she would disappear. Oh, ick, what ugly thoughts. I should die.

Suddenly there was a curve. Sharla had not seen the warning sign. They were going 80 m.p.h. She slammed on the brakes. The car screeched and swerved. Meredith jerked alert, heart pounding, a scream on her lips. And then came the deafening thud and blinding crash and the clamor of smashed, jangled metal and broken glass and broken bodies and then blackness and silence.

CHAPTER 30

They were both in critical condition; neither had regained consciousness.

Marian Landor paced in the waiting room while her husband, Joel, watched her nervously. The coffee in the paper cups was cold. The call had come to them in Eureka just before midnight. There were two women injured, twins apparently, the caller said, but only one set of identification cards. Marian Landor had called Gloria Jergens immediately and then she and Joel sped to the airport.

"We'll inform you the moment there's any change," the nurse had said, directing them to the waiting room. Marian Landor couldn't sit still, though the pacing didn't help at all. Both parents turned expectantly when the waiting room door opened. It was another couple, around their own ages who entered the room. Marian Landor went to the woman and put her arms around her. They cried together. The men shook hands and introduced themselves.

"Did you see them?"

"Yes."

"It's so ironic, isn't it?" Marian Landor said. Tears wet her cheeks. "Our daughters...and we don't even know which is which." She wiped her eyes with the big checkered handkerchief she kept in the pocket of her khaki pants. "We can't tell, can you, Gloria?"

Gloria Jergens shook her head. She looked very thin and pale. "My own daughter and I'm not even sure..."

"We were talking about sending for Meredith's dental records if..."

"Do they know which one was driving?" Bud Jergens asked.

Joel Landor shook his head. "They were both thrown from the car. There was no way to tell."

"Sharla never liked driving," Gloria Jergens said.

No one spoke for a while. They were seated in a semi-circle on plastic chairs.

"It's the head injuries I'm worried about," Joel Landor said.

"Oh, poor Sharla." Gloria Jergens was crying pitifully. She took Marian Landor's hand. "Poor Meredith. Oh, God help them."

"The doctor said the punctured spleen shouldn't be a problem. It will heal fine."

"And the broken leg that...that the other one has."

"It's their heads."

"Do you think there'll be brain damage?"

Marian Landor shook her head. "No one knows."

The day dragged on. From time to time, one of the forlorn parents spoke to another, or offered a gesture of support. Mostly they were silent.

At 4:30 in the afternoon, a doctor entered the waiting room.

All eight eyes looked hopefully, fearfully, into the young physician's face.

"I'm sorry to say...," he began.

There was a groan from someone.

"...we lost one of them. I'm sorry. Cerebral hemorrhage. There was nothing we could do."

Two women cried and one of the men, Joel Landor. His lip quivered as he spoke. "And the other?"

"She's doing better. All her vital signs are good. There's a very good chance she'll make it."

They felt the confusing hope and despair.

"This is very unusual," the doctor said. He stood uncomfortably in front of the group, his fingers playing with the rubber cord of his stethescope. "We don't know which one..."

"Yes, we know," Joel Landor said.

"Would you like to come and see the...the one we lost?" The doctor spoke to all four of them and all four numbly rose and followed him down the hall.

She lay still and white. The parents did not know what to do. They looked at the young woman who lay lifelessly gone. She might be the child they'd raised and loved. She might be a stranger, sadly dead now.

At three in the morning, Bud Jergens dozed fitfully on the plastic sofa, Marian Landor rested her head on her husband's shoulder, Gloria Jergens sat stiffly, chewing on her lip, her eyes blank. "Perhaps we should go to a motel," Joel Landor had suggested over an hour ago. There were nods but no one moved.

Marian Landor needed to pace some more. As she moved to rise, a nurse walked in. "Mr. and Mrs. Landor and Jergens, she's regained consciousness."

Everyone stood at once.

"She's able to have a visit, just a short one. I'm afraid not all of you."

"The mothers," Joel Landor said. "You two go."

From a hanging bottle something dripped into the patient's vein. Her rumpled auburn-tinged hair lay spread softly on the white pillow. Gloria Jergens and Marian Landor approached slowly, both afraid, both painfully eager. The patient's forehead was bandaged. Her eyes looked clear as they skimmed quickly over the hopeful face of Gloria Jergens, then met the eyes of Marian Landor.

"Mom."

"Oh, Meredith!"

Gloria Jergen's stifled moan raised goosebumps along the nurse's spine. She walked with her from the room.

"They told me about Sharla. I feel so bad, mom."

"Yes, a terrible thing. Oh, darling girl, it's you! I love you. I was so afraid." She held her daughter's hand gently, sending an ocean of mother love. "How do you feel, dear?"

"My head is pounding. I feel awful about Sharla. I can't believe this happened."

Her mother stroked the soft pale cheek. "You're going to be OK, I just know you are."

The visit was kept short. In the days that followed, Meredith progressed rapidly. By the second day, she was eating normally, reading, playing card games with her mother and having phone conversations with friends from home, long and emotional ones with Terri and with Allison. She discouraged Terri and other friends from visiting, since she would be discharged within three or four more days and her mother would drive her home.

Allison felt the grief deeply. She also continued to feel confused. She told Meredith repeatedly how important their phone conversations were and Meredith said she felt the same.

Terri alternated between relief and joy, and anger and suspicion. "How do I know you're really Meredith?" she said at one point, laughing weakly.

"Oh God!"

"I'm just kidding."

"I don't think you are. I think at this point your thoughts and feelings about me are so messed up that things can never..."

"Meredith, stop. It's just that...shit! Hey, remember that time, about a week or so after we first got together? What movie was it we finally decided...?"

"Goddam it, Terri, I won't be put through this. I won't have you testing me. You make me feel like I did in that goddam mental hospital. I won't go through it again. I mean it."

"I'm sorry. OK, I just..."

"So how are things at work?" Meredith asked, and Terri allowed the change of topic.

The next time they spoke, though, she started again. "I really feel bad for you about the head injury," Terri said, "about the memory lapses the doctors said would happen."

"Yeah, well, I can live with that. I mean, God, it's a small price to pay considering..."

"Of course, it *is* real convenient."

"What?" The anger in Meredith's voice bristled through the phone wire.

Terri backed off immediately. "Any news about your discharge date? Will it still be Tuesday?"

"Yes, I think so. Terri, I'm feeling tired," Meredith said, heavily, and the conversation soon ended.

On Monday, the doctors told Meredith her spleen was continuing to heal nicely and she could leave the following day.

Terri came to Meredith's apartment on Tuesday evening as soon as Meredith called. She was surprised when Meredith answered the door herself. She looked around. "You're alone?"

"Yes, my mom just left for the airport. I'm really feeling pretty good."

They hugged each other.

"God, it's good to see you." Terri scrutinized her. "You look...you look good, just like I remembered. Here, I brought you something." She handed Meredith a bouquet of feather flowers. "I thought the place might have gotten dusty."

"Ha! I love it. Thanks, Ter."

They spent the evening talking. Meredith seemed more able than she had been at the hospital to talk about the accident and about Sharla and about her pain at losing the sister she had so recently found. Terri listened caringly and tried to help her heal, having many thoughts and feelings toward Meredith, but mostly loving ones.

"The doctors said there should be no after-effects from the spleen injury."

"Great."

"The memory loss is kind of annoying, though. I've noticed a few lapses already. Just little things. Mom noticed, too."

"Hm-m," Terri said.

"But I seem to be able to think OK. Same old perverted mind. I think I've got a tough brain. Actually, I feel very good, not like running a marathon yet, but good. And happy, Terri, happy to be alive. I came so close to dying."

Terri stroked her hand, her own eyes wet. "You have to take it easy for a while, sweet. Damn, I sure wish I had known your mother would be leaving so soon. I would have tried to get the day off work tomorrow."

"That's OK, Terri," Meredith reassured.

"You shouldn't be alone."

"It's OK, really. Well, actually, I'm not going to be alone. Uh...someone's coming over tomorrow. Not that I really need it, but..."

"Well, that's good." Terri looked at her, her head slightly tilted. "Who's coming, Meredith?"

Hesitating, Meredith looked away, then turned back to Terri. She smiled a rather strange smile and then she answered.

"Allison," she said, "Allison is going to spend the day." She was looking out the window at Lincoln Park, at the trees and the beach beyond. She was feeling very happy, indeed, happy to be alive, happy to be who she was.

A few of the publications of
THE NAIAD PRESS, INC.
P.O. Box 10543 ● Tallahassee, Florida 32302
Phone (904) 539-9322
Mail orders welcome. Please include 15% postage.

CHERISHED LOVE by Evelyn Kennedy. 224 pp. Erotic
Lesbian love story. ISBN 0-941483-08-8 $8.95

LAST SEPTEMBER by Helen R. Hull. 208 pp. Six stories & a
glorious novella. ISBN 0-941483-09-6   8.95

THE SECRET IN THE BIRD by Camarin Grae. 312 pp. Striking,
psychological suspense novel. ISBN 0-941483-05-3   8.95

TO THE LIGHTNING by Catherine Ennis. 208 pp. Romantic
Lesbian 'Robinson Crusoe' adventure. ISBN 0-941483-06-1   8.95

THE OTHER SIDE OF VENUS by Shirley Verel. 224 pp.
Luminous, romantic love story. ISBN 0-941483-07-X   8.95

MEMORY BOARD by Jane Rule. 336 pp. Memorable novel
about an aging Lesbian couple. ISBN 0-941483-02-9   8.95

THE ALWAYS ANONYMOUS BEAST by Lauren Wright
Douglas. 224 pp. A Caitlin Reese mystery. First in a series.
ISBN 0-941483-04-5   8.95

SEARCHING FOR SPRING by Patricia A. Murphy. 224 pp.
Novel about the recovery of love. ISBN 0-941483-00-2   8.95

DUSTY'S QUEEN OF HEARTS DINER by Lee Lynch. 240 pp.
Romantic blue-collar novel. ISBN 0-941483-01-0   8.95

PARENTS MATTER by Ann Muller. 240 pp. Parents'
relationships with Lesbian daughters and gay sons.
ISBN 0-930044-91-6   9.95

THE PEARLS by Shelley Smith. 176 pp. Passion and fun in
the Caribbean sun. ISBN 0-930044-93-2   7.95

MAGDALENA by Sarah Aldridge. 352 pp. Epic Lesbian novel
set on three continents. ISBN 0-930044-99-1   8.95

THE BLACK AND WHITE OF IT by Ann Allen Shockley.
144 pp. Short stories. ISBN 0-930044-96-7   7.95

SAY JESUS AND COME TO ME by Ann Allen Shockley. 288
pp. Contemporary romance. ISBN 0-930044-98-3   8.95

LOVING HER by Ann Allen Shockley. 192 pp. Romantic love
story. ISBN 0-930044-97-5   7.95

MURDER AT THE NIGHTWOOD BAR by Katherine V.
Forrest. 240 pp. A Kate Delafield mystery. Second in a series.
ISBN 0-930044-92-4   8.95

ZOE'S BOOK by Gail Pass. 224 pp. Passionate, obsessive love story. ISBN 0-930044-95-9   7.95

WINGED DANCER by Camarin Grae. 228 pp. Erotic Lesbian adventure story. ISBN 0-930044-88-6   8.95

PAZ by Camarin Grae. 336 pp. Romantic Lesbian adventurer with the power to change the world. ISBN 0-930044-89-4   8.95

SOUL SNATCHER by Camarin Grae. 224 pp. A puzzle, an adventure, a mystery — Lesbian romance. ISBN 0-930044-90-8   8.95

THE LOVE OF GOOD WOMEN by Isabel Miller. 224 pp. Long-awaited new novel by the author of the beloved *Patience and Sarah.* ISBN 0-930044-81-9   8.95

THE HOUSE AT PELHAM FALLS by Brenda Weathers. 240 pp. Suspenseful Lesbian ghost story. ISBN 0-930044-79-7   7.95

HOME IN YOUR HANDS by Lee Lynch. 240 pp. More stories from the author of *Old Dyke Tales.* ISBN 0-930044-80-0   7.95

EACH HAND A MAP by Anita Skeen. 112 pp. Real-life poems that touch us all. ISBN 0-930044-82-7   6.95

SURPLUS by Sylvia Stevenson. 342 pp. A classic early Lesbian novel. ISBN 0-930044-78-9   6.95

PEMBROKE PARK by Michelle Martin. 256 pp. Derring-do and daring romance in Regency England. ISBN 0-930044-77-0   7.95

THE LONG TRAIL by Penny Hayes. 248 pp. Vivid adventures of two women in love in the old west. ISBN 0-930044-76-2   8.95

HORIZON OF THE HEART by Shelley Smith. 192 pp. Hot romance in summertime New England. ISBN 0-930044-75-4   7.95

AN EMERGENCE OF GREEN by Katherine V. Forrest. 288 pp. Powerful novel of sexual discovery. ISBN 0-930044-69-X   8.95

THE LESBIAN PERIODICALS INDEX edited by Claire Potter. 432 pp. Author & subject index. ISBN 0-930044-74-6   29.95

DESERT OF THE HEART by Jane Rule. 224 pp. A classic; basis for the movie *Desert Hearts.* ISBN 0-930044-73-8   7.95

SPRING FORWARD/FALL BACK by Sheila Ortiz Taylor. 288 pp. Literary novel of timeless love. ISBN 0-930044-70-3   7.95

FOR KEEPS by Elisabeth Nonas. 144 pp. Contemporary novel about losing and finding love. ISBN 0-930044-71-1   7.95

TORCHLIGHT TO VALHALLA by Gale Wilhelm. 128 pp. Classic novel by a great Lesbian writer. ISBN 0-930044-68-1   7.95

LESBIAN NUNS: BREAKING SILENCE edited by Rosemary Curb and Nancy Manahan. 432 pp. Unprecedented autobiographies of religious life. ISBN 0-930044-62-2   9.95

THE SWASHBUCKLER by Lee Lynch. 288 pp. Colorful novel set in Greenwich Village in the sixties. ISBN 0-930044-66-5   7.95

MISFORTUNE'S FRIEND by Sarah Aldridge. 320 pp. Historical Lesbian novel set on two continents.   ISBN 0-930044-67-3   7.95

A STUDIO OF ONE'S OWN by Ann Stokes. Edited by
Dolores Klaich. 128 pp. Autobiography.   ISBN 0-930044-64-9   7.95

SEX VARIANT WOMEN IN LITERATURE by Jeannette
Howard Foster. 448 pp. Literary history.   ISBN 0-930044-65-7   8.95

A HOT-EYED MODERATE by Jane Rule. 252 pp. Hard-hitting
essays on gay life; writing; art.   ISBN 0-930044-57-6   7.95

INLAND PASSAGE AND OTHER STORIES by Jane Rule.
288 pp. Wide-ranging new collection.   ISBN 0-930044-56-8   7.95

WE TOO ARE DRIFTING by Gale Wilhelm. 128 pp. Timeless
Lesbian novel, a masterpiece.   ISBN 0-930044-61-4   6.95

AMATEUR CITY by Katherine V. Forrest. 224 pp. A Kate
Delafield mystery. First in a series.   ISBN 0-930044-55-X   7.95

THE SOPHIE HOROWITZ STORY by Sarah Schulman. 176
pp. Engaging novel of madcap intrigue.   ISBN 0-930044-54-1   7.95

THE BURNTON WIDOWS by Vickie P. McConnell. 272 pp. A
Nyla Wade mystery, second in the series.   ISBN 0-930044-52-5   7.95

OLD DYKE TALES by Lee Lynch. 224 pp. Extraordinary
stories of our diverse Lesbian lives.   ISBN 0-930044-51-7   7.95

DAUGHTERS OF A CORAL DAWN by Katherine V. Forrest.
240 pp. Novel set in a Lesbian new world.   ISBN 0-930044-50-9   7.95

THE PRICE OF SALT by Claire Morgan. 288 pp. A milestone
novel, a beloved classic.   ISBN 0-930044-49-5   8.95

AGAINST THE SEASON by Jane Rule. 224 pp. Luminous,
complex novel of interrelationships.   ISBN 0-930044-48-7   7.95

LOVERS IN THE PRESENT AFTERNOON by Kathleen
Fleming. 288 pp. A novel about recovery and growth.
   ISBN 0-930044-46-0   8.95

TOOTHPICK HOUSE by Lee Lynch. 264 pp. Love between
two Lesbians of different classes.   ISBN 0-930044-45-2   7.95

MADAME AURORA by Sarah Aldridge. 256 pp. Historical
novel featuring a charismatic "seer."   ISBN 0-930044-44-4   7.95

CURIOUS WINE by Katherine V. Forrest. 176 pp. Passionate
Lesbian love story, a best-seller.   ISBN 0-930044-43-6   7.95

BLACK LESBIAN IN WHITE AMERICA by Anita Cornwell.
141 pp. Stories, essays, autobiography.   ISBN 0-930044-41-X   7.50

CONTRACT WITH THE WORLD by Jane Rule. 340 pp.
Powerful, panoramic novel of gay life.   ISBN 0-930044-28-2   7.95

YANTRAS OF WOMANLOVE by Tee A. Corinne. 64 pp.
Photos by noted Lesbian photographer.   ISBN 0-930044-30-4   6.95

MRS. PORTER'S LETTER by Vicki P. McConnell. 224 pp.
The first Nyla Wade mystery. ISBN 0-930044-29-0 7.95

TO THE CLEVELAND STATION by Carol Anne Douglas.
192 pp. Interracial Lesbian love story. ISBN 0-930044-27-4 6.95

THE NESTING PLACE by Sarah Aldridge. 224 pp. A
three-woman triangle—love conquers all! ISBN 0-930044-26-6 7.95

THIS IS NOT FOR YOU by Jane Rule. 284 pp. A letter to a
beloved is also an intricate novel. ISBN 0-930044-25-8 8.95

FAULTLINE by Sheila Ortiz Taylor. 140 pp. Warm, funny,
literate story of a startling family. ISBN 0-930044-24-X 6.95

THE LESBIAN IN LITERATURE by Barbara Grier. 3d ed.
Foreword by Maida Tilchen. 240 pp. Comprehensive bibliography.
Literary ratings; rare photos. ISBN 0-930044-23-1 7.95

ANNA'S COUNTRY by Elizabeth Lang. 208 pp. A woman
finds her Lesbian identity. ISBN 0-930044-19-3 6.95

PRISM by Valerie Taylor. 158 pp. A love affair between two
women in their sixties. ISBN 0-930044-18-5 6.95

BLACK LESBIANS: AN ANNOTATED BIBLIOGRAPHY
compiled by J. R. Roberts. Foreword by Barbara Smith. 112 pp.
Award-winning bibliography. ISBN 0-930044-21-5 5.95

THE MARQUISE AND THE NOVICE by Victoria Ramstetter.
108 pp. A Lesbian Gothic novel. ISBN 0-930044-16-9 4.95

OUTLANDER by Jane Rule. 207 pp. Short stories and essays
by one of our finest writers. ISBN 0-930044-17-7 6.95

SAPPHISTRY: THE BOOK OF LESBIAN SEXUALITY by
Pat Califia. 2d edition, revised. 195 pp. ISBN 0-9330044-47-9 7.95

ALL TRUE LOVERS by Sarah Aldridge. 292 pp. Romantic
novel set in the 1930s and 1940s. ISBN 0-930044-10-X 7.95

A WOMAN APPEARED TO ME by Renee Vivien. 65 pp. A
classic; translated by Jeannette H. Foster. ISBN 0-930044-06-1 5.00

CYTHEREA'S BREATH by Sarah Aldridge. 240 pp. Romantic
novel about women's entrance into medicine.
ISBN 0-930044-02-9 6.95

TOTTIE by Sarah Aldridge. 181 pp. Lesbian romance in the
turmoil of the sixties. ISBN 0-930044-01-0 6.95

These are just a few of the many Naiad Press titles — we are the oldest and
largest lesbian/feminist publishing company in the world. Please request a
complete catalog. We offer personal service; we encourage and welcome
direct mail orders from individuals who have limited access to bookstores
carrying our publications.